# DISAVOW

## OTHER TITLES BY KARINA HALLE

### Contemporary Romances

*Love, in English*
*Love, in Spanish*
*Where Sea Meets Sky*
*Racing the Sun*
*The Pact*
*The Offer*
*The Play*
*Winter Wishes*
*The Lie*
*The Debt*
*Smut*
*Heat Wave*
*Before I Ever Met You*
*After All*
*Rocked Up*
*Wild Card*
*Maverick*
*Hot Shot*
*Bad at Love*
*The Swedish Prince*
*The Wild Heir*
*A Nordic King*
*Nothing Personal*
*My Life in Shambles*

# Romantic Suspense Novels

*Discretion* (The Dumonts #1)

*Disarm* (The Dumonts #2)

*Sins and Needles* (The Artists Trilogy #1)

*On Every Street* (An Artists Trilogy Novella #0.5)

*Shooting Scars* (The Artists Trilogy #2)

*Bold Tricks* (The Artists Trilogy #3)

*Dirty Angels* (Dirty Angels #1)

*Dirty Deeds* (Dirty Angels #2)

*Dirty Promises* (Dirty Angels #3)

*Black Hearts* (Sins Duet #1)

*Dirty Souls* (Sins Duet #2)


# Horror Romance

*Darkhouse* (EIT #1)

*Red Fox* (EIT #2)

*The Benson* (EIT #2.5)

*Dead Sky Morning* (EIT #3)

*Lying Season* (EIT #4)

*On Demon Wings* (EIT #5)

*Old Blood* (EIT #5.5)

*The Dex-Files* (EIT #5.7)

*Into the Hollow* (EIT #6)

*And With Madness Comes the Light* (EIT #6.5)

*Come Alive* (EIT #7)

*Ashes to Ashes* (EIT #8)

*Dust to Dust* (EIT #9)

*The Devil's Duology*

*Donners of the Dead*

*Veiled*

# DISAVOW

## KARINA HALLE

 Montlake

Published by Montlake, Seattle

www.apub.com

Amazon, the Amazon logo, and Montlake are trademarks of Amazon.com, Inc., or its affiliates.

ISBN-13: 9781542010245
ISBN-10: 1542010241

Cover design by Hang Le

Cover photography © 2019 Thiago Martini

Printed in the United States of America

# DISAVOW

# PROLOGUE

## Gabrielle

"You have no reason to be afraid of me," he says.

I stiffen, my back to him. I thought I was safe in the kitchen, out in the open where anyone could see us, but of course that's not true.

Nowhere is safe in this house.

Especially not at night.

"Gabrielle." He says my name. This time his voice is softer and therefore more cunning. He's used that voice on me so many times in the last few years. Once upon a time, when I was young and I was off-limits, I was given only a simple smile. I wish I had known then how much malice that simple smile held.

I don't want to turn around, but I have to. I don't want to be caught off guard like I have been before.

I twist my body to look at him over my shoulder. "Can I help you, sir?"

"I would like a bottle of Bordeaux, vintage 1986, in my room. I would like you to sit and have a drink with me."

I know this routine. I've tried to say no before, but it never works. It only makes him angrier. It only makes the suffering worse.

"I'm not sure that your wife would like that," I say, even though I know once the words are out of my mouth, they were a mistake.

There is silence behind me, a stiff kind of silence, like how a forest must go quiet before a volcano explodes, igniting every tree in flames.

I turn around fully to see him paused in the doorway. The light from the hall illuminates his silhouette, hides his face. It doesn't make him any less scary.

"You know better than to mention her," he says, his voice dripping with venom.

My heart beats loudly in my ears, faster, turning into a drumroll, and the pain that I've carried with me these last few days spikes through my core, making me want to hunch over. I fight against it, pressing my fingernails into my palms. I feel nothing but scar tissue from doing this so often.

I'm so fucking afraid.

I can't go through this again.

"I'm sorry," I say quietly, even though I'm not. I'm only sorry that I wasn't quick enough. I should have run to my room when I had the chance, though there is nothing stopping him when he's determined.

He sighs loudly and then straightens up, chin raised. "It doesn't matter. She's not here anyway. No one is. You can't get in trouble, Gabrielle."

"I . . . I'm not feeling well," I tell him, averting my eyes. "You know I was at the doctor's the other day."

"Yes . . . what was that for? Is there something wrong with you?"

I can't tell him the truth. It would either enrage him or make him proud of me, and I'm not sure which one is worse.

"I'm fine," I lie.

I'll never be fine.

Not after what he did.

What I had to do.

Before I can even process what's happening, suddenly he's no longer across the kitchen. He's at me, pressing me back against the counter and wrapping a hand around my throat. He's pushing me back enough that the counter digs into my lower back, causing me to convulse with pain.

"You know what?" he hisses at me, his face just inches from mine. "I think you're lying. I don't even believe that you went to the doctor. You just wanted a day off. You just wanted to be fucking lazy, didn't you?"

I can barely breathe. My hand moves around the counter, searching for something, anything, to defend myself with. He likes to play rough, but I live in fear he might take it too far, further than he already has.

I don't doubt he has it in him to kill without conscience.

His grip on my throat tightens, his fingers digging in, as if to prove my point. I stare up at his eyes, awful eyes that are dark and lit only by the blue electronic clock of the nearby microwave. They glint like fires of ice.

"You think you're better than me, isn't that right?" he asks, voice rough and rising. "You think you're something special, Gabrielle? That I feel something special for you? I don't. You're nothing to me, just something to keep me entertained until I've grown bored of you. And when I grow bored of you, I will dispose of you." He leans in so close, I can smell the booze on his breath. "But only I get to decide that. Not you. And when I tell you to get me a fucking bottle of vintage 1986 Bordeaux, then that's what you're fucking going to do!"

Spittle flies from his mouth onto my face. I try to speak, but I can't. I can't get in any air.

His grip gets tighter and tighter, and the world starts to turn black.

"Trash," he growls at me and lets go, stepping back.

I gasp for air, hunching over and wheezing to get my breath, my throat burning. I can feel wetness in my underwear, probably blood. It reminds me that no matter what happens, I will not go with him to his room.

If he wants to try to rape me here, so be it.

*I'll be ready.*

The thought gives me the last bit of power I have.

I slowly straighten myself up and, out of the corner of my eye, spot the drawer that has the knives. It's close, but I'm not sure I can get to it without making him suspicious.

"Well," he says, gesturing at me, "catch your breath and get the wine."

The wine is in the cellar, a place I normally hate going to, but tonight, dread fills me head to toe. He could get away with anything down there. He could lock me up there for all he wanted. Dead or alive. Beaten or not. Would anyone notice? Would my own mother?

That's my greatest fear. That she wouldn't even notice if I were gone, that she would be so blinded by her duty and devotion, so fucking brainwashed, that she wouldn't even care.

I nod, gathering my thoughts, trying to stall going down there. "I'll just get the corkscrew and the glasses first," I say, heading to the drawer. I pull it open and see the knives, but then he's right behind me, hovering. I grab the corkscrew and slam the drawer shut, trying to sidle out of the way, but he's pulling my hair back over my shoulder and placing his lips at my neck.

It takes all the strength I have left not to shudder, to hide my revulsion.

"You never wear your hair down," he murmurs while my hand tightens over the corkscrew. "Perhaps I should make that a rule."

I don't say anything. My eyes are closed, and I'm just praying for him to step away.

Instead he presses himself against me, and I can feel his erection.

"On second thought, I don't think we need the wine," he says, and then suddenly he grabs my hair, making a fist, yanking my head back. A sharp cry dies on my lips. "I don't think we need to go anywhere at all."

I hear the unzip of his pants and feel his free hand move up my legs, pushing up my skirt while the other hand pulls my head back so hard and far that I'm afraid my back is going to crack in two.

"No," I tell him, as I've told him many times before, my voice ragged and gasping. "Get your fucking hands off me."

That last part is new. I've never said that before.

I'm so afraid now that I'm no longer afraid. Like the fear and the knowledge of what this monster is capable of have morphed into something bigger than my fear.

It wants justice.

It wants revenge.

It won't take this anymore.

Suddenly he lets go of my hair and forces me to spin around before he pulls back and hits me right across the face with a loud *crack*. The world goes fuzzy and spinning, my cheek exploding into sharp shards of pain as I fall to the side, barely hanging on to the counter to keep me up.

But that corkscrew is still in my hand.

He comes at me again, and this time I scream. I scream nonsense, just a high-pitched yell of all my pain and terror, and I take the corkscrew and ram it right into his forearm as he's trying to grab me, driving it in as deep as it will go.

He's screaming now, too, loud and bloodcurdling, and I have just enough time to try to make a run for it while he's occupied.

"You bitch!" he yells and swipes out for me, trying to get me.

But I'm fast enough that I make it all the way to the french doors that lead out into the backyard.

Just as I'm undoing the lock and opening them, I see my mother on the other side in her pajamas, staring at me.

"I heard a scream!" she exclaims as I open the door. She quickly looks me up and down before literally pushing me out of the way and stepping inside, heading toward him. "What happened?"

He's bent over, holding his arm to stop the bleeding, the corkscrew on the floor. "She stabbed me!"

My mother gasps and looks at me. "Gabrielle."

"He's a fucking monster!" I scream at her, my face going hot, my heart wanting to explode out of my chest and run away. "He's hurt me." I pause, trying to breathe, because the next words are so hard for me to say, even to myself. "He . . . he raped me, Mama."

Her eyes widen, and she peers at me closer, as if she has a hard time believing me, as if I didn't just open myself bare, raw and vulnerable, showing her my deepest wounds, the kinds that dig into your soul and never heal.

"She's full of lies," he says, practically snarling as he grabs a dish-cloth and holds it against his arm. "She's done nothing but try to seduce me since the day you brought her here."

"No," I tell her, grabbing her arm so that she'll look at me, really see me, listen to me. We went through this with my father—can't she see that it's happening again? "Please, Mama, please listen to me. Believe me. Can't you see what he's doing to us? He's trying to turn you against me. He's brainwashed you into thinking he's your savior, but he's not. He's going to be the ruin of you. He's already ruined me."

"And if you keep telling your mother these lies, I'm going to have you both fired, and I'll make sure none of you works again," he says. "Is that what you want, Gabrielle? Is that what you want for your mother?"

"You son of a bitch!" I scream at him.

"Contrary to popular belief, my mother was actually nice. At least she was to my brother, Ludovic," he says. "If you're trying to insult me, you better try again." He starts walking toward us, and now from the motion lights in the backyard, I can see his face fully.

How horribly smug he is. Like he knows he's won.

Because he has.

Because no matter what my mother chooses to believe, no matter how she chooses him over me and betrays me, I won't betray her. I won't cost her her job, even if it's a job that may kill her one day.

I know I have no choice but to leave.

I can't stay.

I won't survive it.

"Now, what will it be, Gabrielle?" he asks. "Are you going to continue to treat your poor mother like an idiot and keep lying to her face, or are you going to apologize to me for stabbing me with a fucking corkscrew?"

I stare at him with all I have, and it's like looking right into the abyss. And this time, when the abyss looks back, it gives me purpose.

It gives me conviction and a backbone.

"I'm sorry for stabbing you with a corkscrew," I say, and the words come out so clean and polished, I have to wonder if I've already stepped into another role of pretending.

"Oh, why on earth did you do that, Gabby?" my mother cries out, short of stamping her foot like in a temper tantrum. She always seems to revert back a few years in intellect when she's around him. "Why would you do that to Mr. Dumont when he's been nothing but good to us?"

I try to swallow the brick in my throat but can't. "I guess I'm not myself lately," I tell her.

I look at him one more time, knowing that freedom is around the corner and that I'm no longer afraid to leave.

And I'm never coming back.

# CHAPTER ONE

## PASCAL

*Eight years later*

Everything about the letter screamed *blackmail*. From the envelope with no return address to the cryptic words typed out on paper inside.

*The world will know what you've done.*

I have to chuckle at it, even though there's a glimmer of fear in my heart. Whoever sent this watches too many movies. Whoever sent this just wants to scare me and doesn't know how. There isn't even a threat attached to it. It's just supposed knowledge.

What I've done? I've done a lot of things. None of them good in the true sense of the word—at least none of them good for anyone but me.

But despite the theatrics of the letter, I know I should take it seriously.

Because I know, deep inside, exactly what they're talking about.

What they suspect.

Nearly one year ago, my uncle Ludovic Dumont collapsed at our annual masquerade ball. The doctors ruled it a heart attack, despite the fact that he'd gotten a clean bill of health only a few weeks earlier. Some people, such as my cousin Seraphine and eventually my own brother, Blaise, put the blame on my father. They accused him of murdering Ludovic in cold blood in order to take over the company.

They were taken care of. Blaise and Seraphine dropped the accusations in exchange for a new life in Dubai. If they didn't, well, they knew they would pay with their lives. It's never been a secret that my father is ruthless and has probably committed more crimes than I can even start to imagine. But I never knew he would actually go after family like that. That when it came down to it, he'd have my own cousin murdered rather than let her spread her version of the truth.

I assume Seraphine wouldn't have forgotten that, which is why the letter is confusing. She and Blaise have been in Dubai for about five months now. (I suppose I'm happy for them, though I still find the fact that they're together—even though they aren't blood related—rather distasteful.) Why would she start up again with these accusations when she has so much to lose? And why do it in such a hokey way when she's never had a problem saying this to our faces?

There's only one way to find out.

I get up from my desk and look outside the door. The hall is empty. The house is quiet except for a faint murmur of the television in my mother's room down the other wing.

The *maison* Dumont is a peculiar setup. The sprawling estate is the same house I grew up in. I know a lot of people wonder why I, at thirty-one years old, still live here, even though I own several apartments in Paris and property around the world. But aside from it being the place I feel most comfortable, the house is practically a castle. I live in the east wing, with my own office and bedroom and private entrance at the side of the house, and I have more than enough privacy.

At least I did.

Ever since Blaise left, my father has become increasingly suspicious of me, as if I'm about to accuse him next. I wouldn't be surprised if there was a bug somewhere in my office, which is why I head next door to my bedroom to make the call.

I sit down on the couch and dial, even though it's late here and even later in Dubai. It rings and rings, and I'm prepared to hang up when Blaise finally answers.

"What do you want?" he asks in a tired voice. I must have woken him up.

"Is this how we're greeting each other now?" I ask.

Silence. Then: "What do you want, Pascal?"

Blaise and I were never close. I used to think that maybe we were, if only because of proximity. We're brothers and we're close in age, but that's about the extent of it all. The distance between us only became more apparent in the last year, and ever since he left for Dubai, it's almost irreparable. Not that I care much. I wouldn't have gotten that far in my life had I cared about people like I should.

"I got a letter," I tell him.

More silence.

I go on. "I believe Seraphine sent it."

He clears his throat. "A letter? What does it say?"

"Ask Seraphine if she knows. She's there in bed with you, isn't she?"

"What does it say, Pascal?" he repeats, and I can hear Seraphine in the background saying my name in surprise.

"It says, 'The world will know what you've done.' Did Seraphine send it or not?"

He lets out a sour laugh. "I don't even have to ask her to know she didn't. You think she'd start acting out *I Know What You Did Last Summer*?"

His laugh irks me. "I know the note is theatrical," I tell him stiffly. "Which is why I figured it was her."

"What is going on?" I hear Seraphine say. "Are you talking about me?"

"Nothing for you to worry about," Blaise tells her. "Pascal received a letter, he thought it was from you. Something vaguely threatening.

11

Perhaps someone else out there thinks he had something to do with your father's murder."

"I didn't have anything to do with it," I remind him carefully.

"And yet you're not disputing my choice of words. 'Murder.' How is it living in that house of horrors, knowing full well what our father is capable of? How does that sit with your conscience?"

"You know I don't have one," I tell him, refusing to even let his words sink in.

"Of course you don't."

"So you swear you or Seraphine didn't send it?"

"I'm not swearing anything to you, brother, but it's quite obvious that Seraphine didn't send you a letter. What good would that do?"

"No good, unless it was meant for our father."

"Is it addressed to you?"

"It's addressed to the Dumonts," I tell him, staring at the address on the envelope. It's typed, and the stamp is from France.

"Then it's probably for Father, not you," he says, yawning. "Looks like the truth can't stay buried for long. Good luck with that. If I were you, I'd take those letters as a sign to leave."

"So I can do what you did, take off to another country? Like a coward?"

"Goodbye, Pascal," he says, and before I even get a chance to ask how he is, how the baby is, he hangs up on me.

It's just as well. The less I know about them, the better.

I hang up, even more disturbed than before. I knew it wasn't Seraphine, and yet I'd hoped it was her, just so I could forget about it.

What I need to do is try to find out where the letter came from. When I came home from work, it was on the floor with the rest of the mail, spilled out on the tiles beneath the mail slot. My mother and father were out for dinner at the time, so they hadn't seen it.

I have to wonder if perhaps there had been a letter prior to this one. If so, then either my mother or father would have opened it and yet not said anything to me.

*I should ask Charlotte.* The thought flits across my mind.

But Charlotte, my personal maid, quit two weeks ago in a fiery rage. Something about me being cruel and careless, which is an odd accusation considering she's someone I've rarely given more than a second thought to. She was just a maid.

Unfortunately, she was someone I do need in my life. With Blaise and Seraphine no longer working for the Dumont brand, I've been entrusted with all the new hires, making sure everyone and everything is working smoothly. As much as I hate to admit it, if I'm the backbone of the company, then Blaise and Seraphine were crucial organs the label needed to survive.

As a result, I'm working long hours, and I need someone to tend to my every need when I come home. For the last year, that's exactly what Charlotte did, and though in hindsight I can see she was crazy and emotional, she at least knew how to do her job.

My problem is I'm picky and I'm busy, so there isn't a lot of time for me to find a suitable candidate. It has to be someone discreet and professional, who won't burst into tears if I hurl a few insults her way when she's behaving like an idiot. That's not always easy to find.

Though it's late, I go out into the hall and walk down it toward my mother's room, portraits of Dumonts staring down at me from the walls. Blaise used to say he felt judgment in their following eyes, but I like to think they're just envious.

The door to my mother's room is ajar, and I lightly rap on it.

There's no response, so I push the door open and peer inside.

She's on her couch, eyes closed, head back, an empty bottle of gin beside her, the TV illuminating her in shifting shades of light.

It's not unusual to find her passed out like this, and I'm not about to wake a sleeping beast. I start to close the door when suddenly she sits upright and says, "What is it, Pascal?" while staring right at the TV.

My mother can be motherfucking creepy.

"I didn't want to disturb you," I tell her.

"You're my son. I can feel your presence from a mile away," she says and then finally looks at me. Still creepy. "Come in. What is it?"

I step inside her room. I've never found it odd that my parents have had separate bedrooms for as long as I can remember. Her room is all white walls and gold accents, with gaudy art and even a statue of the Venus de Milo beside the bathroom. She has everything she needs in here, and the best part, to her, is that it doesn't contain my father.

"I'm going to need your help," I tell her, wincing inwardly for muttering those words. My mother is no different from my father, and any admittance of weakness signals their predatory instincts.

She cocks her head at me and sits up straighter, as if she has someone to impress, never mind the fact that she has mascara smudged underneath her eyes. "My help?" she repeats. "Whatever for?"

"I need a new maid. Charlotte quit two weeks ago."

"I'm aware. I had to drive her to the train station, tears running down her face. What did you do to her?"

"I didn't do anything. She just couldn't handle pressure."

She raises her brows.

"It's true," I go on. "And I don't have the time to find anyone suitable. I've been too fucking busy now with Blaise and Seraphine gone. The new hires are of piss-poor quality."

"You hired them."

"And they were the best of the lot. Now I need you to find me someone who I can depend on, who can handle working for me, who can take shit and thrive on it. Someone smarter than your average maid. Someone who can handle more than just wiping piss off my toilet seat and making the bed."

Her upper lip curls in distaste. "Really, Pascal."

I shrug. "At least I'm honest about it."

She frowns, her nostrils widening as she inhales. I'm surprised that part of her face can even move, considering the amount of Botox she has injected in there.

"As it so happens," she says slowly, with a touch of smugness in her eyes, "I do know of someone who would be perfect for you. Perfect for this family."

I give her an expectant look to go on.

"Gabrielle."

Though the name is instantly familiar, I have to rack my brain for the meaning.

"Gabrielle Caron," she goes on, though the last name means nothing to me. "Jolie's daughter."

Jolie. My mother and father's maid, who has been with the family for the last twelve years. I'd almost forgotten that Gabrielle had been living in the servants' quarters with her mother until some years ago, when she suddenly disappeared.

"She's here?" I ask. "How do you know?" I certainly haven't seen her around, but then again, I've been at the office most of the time.

"Jolie told me the other day."

"And is Gabrielle here to get her job back?" I was seventeen by the time Gabrielle came to live with her mother. I'm guessing she was around twelve or thirteen at the time. A gangly-looking girl with big teeth and even bigger eyes. Kept to herself. I rarely saw her much until she was sixteen and started working alongside her mother. I remember liking her, as much as I liked anyone. At the very least, she did what she was told and always had a warm yet professional demeanor about her. She became my father's personal maid for two years. Seemed to handle it well, perhaps because my father always acted rather fond of her. Then one day she left, never to return.

Until now.

"I'm not sure why she's back," my mother says. "But Jolie says she's been studying in New York all this time. Business, I think. She was a smart girl, if I remember."

"I don't remember much of what goes on with the staff," I say, "but I do know that she was working for us full-time when she should have been in school. Her mother was never smart enough to teach her anything, so she's really just a dropout. Business school in New York sounds like a stretch."

My mother yawns and gets to her feet, clutching her silk robe. "You asked me to find you someone, and I just gave you an option. I'll ask Jolie tomorrow."

"I'll ask," I tell her. "And I'll put Gabrielle through a proper interview."

"Suit yourself. I'm going to bed."

Her walk to the bedroom is a mix of drunken staggering and the overcorrection of that, causing her to sway with her head held high. Once she's in her room, I hear the pop of a cork and assume she's having another nightcap.

I shake my head, and for a brief instant, I feel something like pity for my mother. To have everything and find alcohol the only way to enjoy it. To waste a life like that.

But those feelings never stay long for me. I turn to head back to my room, and they dissolve like dust behind me.

I wake up the next day with an erection the size of a skyscraper. I can't remember my dreams, but images flit through my mind, me balls deep inside some leggy blonde up against the wall of my office. It makes sense; I've been so busy lately in the office that I haven't had time to get off.

*I'll fix that tonight,* I tell myself. Scroll through my phone and find a model who knows how to give me a good time. I should do something about my erection, too, but as my mind latches on to all the things I need to do today, it fades in an instant.

There's work, of course, but then there's Gabrielle.

I hate hiring people, and I'm already doubting she'll be good enough.

I take a shower and get dressed, a sharp black Dumont suit with an ice-blue tie that I know brings out my eyes. I might have to be a bit charming today, so it can't hurt.

Then I head downstairs, swinging by the kitchen where Jolie is making the morning espresso for my mother. My father has most likely left for work already. He can't afford to be outdone by me. Always the first one in the office these days, though I'm more than certain he's not particularly doing anything. I've been carrying the entire weight of the company's changes.

"Jolie," I say to her as I adjust my cuff links. She looks up from her duties with surprise. I rarely address her, nor pay her any attention.

I'm sure I would have when she was younger. I suppose she's still an attractive woman, if she wasn't so thin and didn't look so hardened. She's tall, with frizzy blonde hair that never seems tame despite it being tied back, but her eyes always vacillate between eerie blankness and pure anxiety, as if she can't choose which state to live in.

"Yes, Mr. Dumont," she says, standing at attention.

"It's Pascal," I tell her. I hate being called Mr. Dumont.

She just nods curtly and waits for me to go on.

"I heard your daughter was back in Paris," I tell her.

A tight smile comes across her face. "She is."

"Is she here to work? Because I might have a job for her."

Her expression doesn't change. Perhaps she was waiting for someone to ask, or maybe my mother already said something to her.

"I can't speak directly for her, but I think that would be wonderful," she says.

I nod and flip through my phone to check my schedule. "Where is she staying? Would she be able to come by the office at noon?"

"I believe she is in a hotel." She pauses. "She did not think it right to stay in the guesthouse with me. I can text her and let her know. Your office at noon."

"You do that. Thank you."

After that, I get in my Audi and drive to work. Traffic can be hellish, and we live quite a bit outside Paris, but I don't mind the time in the car when it's just me and I can think.

Naturally, my mind goes back to the letter.

It goes to my father.

It goes to what Blaise said last night: *How is it living in that house of horrors, knowing full well what our father is capable of? How does that sit with your conscience?*

The truth is, I don't let myself think about it. That's how I get through it. That's how you can get through anything in life, no matter how horrific, immoral, or appalling. Just don't think about it.

Pretend it doesn't exist.

Pretend that there is no truth.

And yet . . . I can feel something stirring inside me, sinking through my veins like black oil. Maybe it is the truth. Maybe it's the realization that as the days tick on and the closer I work with my father, the more I become my father.

For once in my life, I'm not sure that's who I want to be.

And yet I can't see myself becoming anyone else.

Once at the office, I sink into the strife and hustle. It's been nearly a year since Ludovic's death, and though all the staff is new—save the receptionist—it's taken this long for the company to really hit its stride. In some ways it's true of the world. Ludovic was revered and admired for sticking to his morals and ideals when it came to the Dumont label.

He was against collaborations with artists, against online shopping, against sales. He held true to tradition no matter the cost.

The moment my father and I were able to take over, we changed it all up. We shook every part of this company loose and made it so that it could compete in this century. Ludovic's tenacity and old-fashioned leanings may have been quaint, but we were finally able to bring the brand to the next level.

Sales are up, across the board and in every sector. Sure, I know we take a hit when it comes to our twice-yearly sales, and die-hard fans have complained that the brand is more accessible now, no longer so exclusive. Some have even said we've sold out.

But selling out just brings in money, and in the end, that's all that matters with our family. Money is our legacy. Greed is our strength.

And getting what I want is where I really shine.

Currently what I want is a new fucking maid, so when noon rolls around and Gabrielle hasn't shown up to the office, I get a bit pissy. I text my mother to talk to Jolie, berating myself for not getting Jolie's contact info myself; then once I discover where Gabrielle is staying, I head on out of the office.

Of course there's a chance she could be on her way over to see me and is running late, but texts to Gabrielle's cell aren't going through (maybe because she still has a New York number). I only have her hotel.

Surprisingly, she's staying at a nice one. Not the Dumont brand, of course, owned by my cousin Olivier, but definitely not the hostels or cheap hotels I'd expect to find her in. I figured someone who came back in need of work wouldn't have the extra money to spend.

Even more of a surprise is that I recognize the girl at the front desk.

Her name, however, escapes me, but those plush, dick-sucking lips do not.

"Pascal," she says to me, giving me a beguiling smile and a fluttering of fake lashes. "Long time no see."

I quickly glance at her name tag. "Hello, Aurelie," I tell her. "I have a favor to ask you." I lower my voice and give her the eye, the one that hints at promises I'll never keep.

"A favor?" she asks brightly. She eyes the other front desk crew, who are trying not to pay attention to us or, should I say, to me. Since I'm the face of the Dumont men's cologne, I have quite the recognizable mug. She leans in and whispers, staring up at me through her lashes, "Why should I do you a favor when you never called me back?"

Whoops.

I grin at her. "You can't blame me for being busy."

She straightens up and purses her lips. "Mm-hmm."

Maybe getting a favor out of her will be harder than I thought.

Luckily, I know how to bargain.

"Listen, how about I take you for dinner on Friday night," I tell her. "You get to pick the spot."

Her face lights up, and I go on. "I'm sure you get a great discount at this hotel, too, but where I'll end up fucking you will make this place look like a dump."

Her eyes widen at that, and she bites those juicy lips of hers. My erection springs to life, pressing against the front of my dress pants. Another sign of how badly I need to get laid.

I can hear the murmurs of the staff and guests, who probably over-heard me, but I don't really care. I turn my charming smile to them, too, just to let them know exactly how I bargain.

They look away, blushing, and I eye Aurelie expectantly. "So about that favor?" She swallows hard and nods, and I lean in closer, my breath on her ear. "You have a guest staying here," I whisper. "Gabrielle Caron. I need to know what room she's in."

She stiffens and pulls back enough to give me a look. A jealous one.

"Don't worry, she's an ex-employee. A maid," I clarify. "She's here visiting her mother."

"A maid and she's staying here?" she asks quietly, a wash of disdain on her face.

I shrug. "Perhaps she's cleaning the rooms to pay for it. I don't know. But I did have an appointment with her today, and she never showed up, nor is she answering her phone. So if you could . . ."

Aurelie seems to think about it for a moment and then nods. "Okay. But I could get in trouble for this."

I lean in closer again, grazing her earlobe with my lips. She smells like vanilla, and if I remember correctly, that's exactly the way she likes her sex. Oh well.

"I'll make it worth your while."

She lets out a shaky breath and checks for Gabrielle on her computer.

"Room 512," she says quietly.

"Thank you," I tell her.

"And dinner?" she asks, her tone anxious.

"I'll call you," I say and then head through the spacious lobby toward the elevators. I probably will keep my word, but Friday is days away, and I'm going to need to fuck someone before then.

Naturally, after that exchange, I start thinking about Gabrielle. She would most likely be twenty-five now. When I think back to the way she was back then, I have a hard time seeing her as anything beyond the age of thirteen. Even though she was around eighteen when she left, I can only see her as something blank and disposable.

I get to her floor, find her room, and knock on it.

I wait.

Hear nothing.

Knock on her door again.

Press my ear against it.

For some reason I have this insane image of a room filled with blood, with a body on the floor, blonde hair spilled out and sticking to it.

The door opens an inch, caught by the chain lock.

The biggest, most intensely blue eyes stare back at me. They stare at me with such ferocity that I'm momentarily stunned. I've forgotten why I'm here or even where I am.

"Can I help you?" she says, and it takes a moment to realize that this is not only an actual person—not some nymph or princess from a fantasy, her white-blonde hair spilling around her in waves—but that it's Gabrielle.

It has to be.

"Gabrielle?" I ask.

"Pascal Dumont," she says coolly, eyeing me up and down. "What are you doing here?"

I frown. "Well, we had a meeting at noon, and when you didn't show up at the office and didn't answer your phone, I decided to track you down."

Her eyes narrow just a bit, just enough to break the spell. I swear she was fucking hypnotizing me. "Is stalking something you do for fun? What if I didn't want to be tracked down?"

I blink at her. "Excuse me? We had a meeting."

"No," she says. "You tried to set up a meeting with me through my mother, who of course agreed on my behalf. The truth is, I don't like you and have no desire to work for you or the Dumont name, in any shape or form. Have a good day."

Then she closes the door in my face.

# CHAPTER TWO

## PASCAL

I stare at the door for a few moments. I've had quite a few doors slammed in my face by women, but this one feels different. For one, this should have been business-related but instead feels personal, and two, she wasn't irate. Just cool and calm, like I was beneath her.

Me . . . beneath a maid. How she figured that, I have no idea, but this woman needs to be reminded just where I stand in this world.

I take in a sharp breath through my nose, trying to calm down and soothe my ego, and knock again.

The door opens right away.

Gabrielle stares at me, brows raised.

I don't ever remember her being this . . . alluring. She always had the potential of being pretty, but now it's like she either grew into her features or she amassed a world's worth of confidence. She's gorgeous in the most ethereal, almost supernatural way.

"You back for more?" she asks.

I swear I see a glimmer of something playful in her eyes, but that might be wishful thinking on my part because fucking hell if I'm not turned on just looking at her.

I clear my throat, trying to shake it off and focus on the task at hand.

"I'm just a little confused," I admit carefully.

"I thought the Dumonts never got confused," she says. "That's how you built your empire. With the belief that you're right, no matter what the cost."

*What the hell is her deal?*

"Do you want the job or not?" I blurt out, strangely flustered.

She bites back a smile. "No. I thought that was obvious when I told you that much and then closed the door in your face. I'm about to do it again . . ."

She starts to close the door, but I jam my foot in between so she can't.

"I just want a moment to speak with you," I tell her as I wedge in my shoulder. I know pleading probably won't work with her—nor does it work with me—so I switch tactics. "You should have seen your mother's face this morning when I asked about you. She lit up, so happy just thinking about you working alongside her again."

I'm watching her face closely, noticing even the slightest emotions that show up in her eyes. First she's struck with guilt or shame, but then it turns into something hard and bitter. Not exactly what I was going for.

"This isn't about her," she says, her voice stiff. She raises her chin.

"Then what is it about? Why are you back here? If you don't want to work for me, fine, but you did once live with me; what's so wrong with us catching up?"

She lets out a sharp laugh. "You're kidding me. First of all, I never lived with you, Pascal. I lived with my mother in the servants' quarters."

"It's a guesthouse," I interject, "and a very nice one. And because it's *my* family's guesthouse and you frequented *my* house, that counts as living with me."

"You never even gave me the time of day. You treated me like how you treat all of your servants or really anyone you deem beneath you, which is pretty much everyone."

"I'm insulted," I say mildly.

"Oh, sure you are. You're proud of it."

"That's not part of my reputation."

"And that's another thing you're proud of. Your reputation. You're arrogant, misogynistic, womanizing, vain, greedy, immoral, and slightly off."

"*Slightly* off?" I repeat and try not to roll my eyes. "Don't believe everything you hear."

"If you think I'm gleaning this from the tabloids, you're wrong. I know you. I've seen it firsthand."

"I thought we didn't live together."

"We were close enough. You learn a lot about someone when you have to clean up after them. And that's enough for me to know that I don't want to work for you."

Damn. She's a stubborn-as-hell, feisty little thing. I don't remember her being that way when she was young, but I have to admit, I like it.

"So what's the second thing?" I ask.

"Second thing?"

"You said, first of all, you never lived with me. Which is a lie that you're bending to suit your own truth but whatever, we can overlook it. What's the second of all?"

I think I've caught her off guard because she frowns, thinking. Finally she says, "You're not the type to catch up with anyone."

"No?" I ask, holding out my hand and ticking off my fingers. "I believe you just called me vain, arrogant, womanizing, greedy, immoral, and . . . what was the phrase you used again? A little off?"

"Don't forget misogynistic."

"Wherever would you get that idea?"

"Goes part and parcel with the womanizing thing," she says. "Not to mention the fact that you've forced yourself in my doorway."

"Thank God you have that chain across, right?"

She narrows her eyes. "Are you threatening me?"

I lean in as close as I can, and to her credit, she doesn't move away. "Oh no, my little sprite. I rarely threaten. I just do what needs to be done. Why give warning? Why ruin the element of surprise?" I give her a wolfish smile until she finally looks away. "At any rate, you mentioned I am many types but not the type who wouldn't catch up. So. Shall we?"

"Shall we what?" she asks cautiously.

"Let me take you out for lunch," I tell her. "And we can talk. Dare I say, catch up. I haven't seen you in years."

She scoffs to herself and shakes her head slightly, still avoiding my eyes. "You act as if we have a past. We have nothing. I was a maid, and you were the rich prick son."

"My father had two rich prick sons."

"Yes, well, you were the worst." She pauses, eyes darting to me. "Almost worse than him."

I stiffen, my palms feeling clammy all of a sudden. "Worse than who?"

"Worse than *whom*," she corrects. "And what will happen to me if I don't have lunch with you?"

"I'll keep hounding you."

"You're the head of the company now; I doubt you would have the time."

"I would find the time. I always do for what's important."

"You just enjoy harassing women."

I shrug one shoulder. "Eh. What can I say, I like the chase, and I refuse to believe any woman wouldn't be interested in me."

"If I have lunch with you, will you leave me alone?"

My mouth cracks into a grin. "I promise."

But she probably knows my promises aren't worth shit.

She tilts her head, a piece of blonde hair falling across her face. I'm itching to reach out and push it behind her ear, but I think she might slam the door on my arm and sever it.

"Okay."

"Okay," I tell her. "Do you want me to wait here or in the lobby?"

"You mean now?" she asks, wide-eyed.

"Yes, *now*," I say. "You look decent enough. Grab your purse and let's go."

She sighs as she shuts the door. "Just . . . give me a minute."

I stand back against the hallway wall, wondering if this is her way of faking me out, when I hear the chain slide across, and then the door opens.

Gabrielle steps out.

Now that I can look at her fully, not just a slice of a face in the doorway, she looks nothing like the girl I remember. Her strange eyes now have a captivating beauty; her gangly limbs and awkwardness have turned into sleek arms and legs, moving with grace and purpose in her rust-colored dress with kimono sleeves. Her pale blonde hair is half–tied back, spilling over her shoulders. On her feet, simple slides, and in her hands she carries a black clutch that looks well made, though certainly nothing like the Dumont label.

"Nice dress," I tell her.

She raises a brow and closes the door behind her. "You'll take that back when you know where it's from."

"Where?"

"H and M."

I laugh. "I guess what I'm trying to say is you look nice. And just because fashion is my job doesn't mean I don't appreciate the work that the chain stores do."

"Even though they rip off labels like Dumont on a daily basis?"

I bite my lip and smile. "Imitation is just a form of flattery, my little sprite."

She grumbles. "Can you try and make it through lunch without insulting me?" She starts walking down the hall, and my eyes take a moment to pause on her extremely shapely ass. She must have been doing squats for the last eight years or something.

"How am I insulting you?" I say, catching up with her. I'm six feet tall and have long legs and she's got to be at least six inches shorter than me, but she's awfully quick.

She presses the elevator call button and folds her arms, staring straight ahead at the closed doors. "Your little sprite? Please. How demeaning can you be?"

"Oh, I can be extremely demeaning."

A hint of a smile ghosts her lips.

Her lips.

Not sure I even noticed them until now, all pouting and full and wet, like she's been using them for something she shouldn't.

*Stay focused,* I remind myself. It's a very strange feeling to keep myself in check. Not sure I like it. Usually I let myself do and say what I want without consequences. But I have a feeling that Gabrielle will take any opportunity to call the whole thing off, and for reasons I don't completely understand, I need to have lunch with her. I need to convince her.

I'm not even sure of what.

"You do know what a sprite is, don't you?" I tell her, hoping she'll see it as a compliment.

"A tiny winged creature of the supernatural, closely related to plant life, as imbued with the natural world as possible," she says, like she just riffled through a dictionary in her head.

"And you take that as an insult?"

"I take issue with the words 'my' and 'little,' since I am not little in any way and I'm most certainly not yours." She pauses. "I can deal with being a sprite, especially since they're harmless . . . until they're threatened."

She gives me a warning look as the elevator doors open, revealing an elderly couple dressed to the nines. I give them a polite nod and gesture to Gabrielle to go in first. I may be all those things she mentioned, but I do know my manners when it counts.

Elevators are small in Europe, and this hotel is no exception. I'm nearly pressed right up against Gabrielle's back. Her hair smells like honey, and it's just as alluring. I have to close my eyes and breathe in deep through my nose to keep from reaching out and seeing if her hair is as soft and silky as it looks, but that only makes things worse. The blood in my veins starts to run hot and fast, my cock increasingly stiff.

After what feels like an eternity, the doors open, and we step out into the lobby. It feels like I can breathe again.

We pass by the front desks, where Aurelie is watching us carefully. Now that she sees what Gabrielle looks like, perhaps that accounts for the suspicious expression on her face. Though Gabrielle is walking ahead of me, head high, like she doesn't know me at all.

"Where are we going?" Gabrielle asks me once we're out on the street, her eyes scanning her surroundings like she's unsure of where she is and needs to be on alert.

"Anywhere you'd like," I tell her. "My driver is around the corner."

"I'd rather not get in the car with you."

*Ouch.*

"What do you think is going to happen?" I ask curiously, taking a step closer to her.

She stiffens up and keeps her attention on the road. She nods across the street. "There's a café. That will do."

She's avoiding my question but still I look. It's a total tourist trap, the kind that serves escargots and croque monsieurs to unsuspecting travelers who think that is what real Parisian cuisine is. I wouldn't be caught dead in there.

Which is probably why she picked it. She knows that.

She's staring at me now with a look of challenge in her eyes, which only confirms it.

"No problem," I tell her. I look both ways to cross the street and try to take her arm, but she deftly escapes my grasp and trots ahead of me, her sandals smacking the pavement as she goes.

I guess the bright side of eating in a place like this is that the tourists who frequent it have no idea who I am and therefore can't judge me for being here. They probably just think I'm some ridiculously handsome Frenchman on a date with a lady.

A lady who hates me, but I think in time I'll win her over. The Dumonts are persistent, if nothing else.

We take a booth in the corner, and the waiter tosses some menus at us with disdain.

Gabrielle gives him an unimpressed look in return, takes her menu, and peers at it. "I'd forgotten how the service was in Paris."

"Compared to where?"

"Everywhere else," she says, watching as the waiter does the same to a few other tables, rarely speaking or looking at the customers.

"Is that a bad thing?" I ask. "Why should a waiter spend his time pretending to be your friend? You don't tip here. There's no money involved in it."

"So you think people should only be nice if money is involved."

I give her a look that says, *Oh come on.* "Look who you're dealing with here."

"*Dealing with* is one way to put it," she mutters under her breath.

I flag down the waiter and order myself an espresso in French, which seems to take the waiter by surprise. Doesn't make him any friendlier, though, but I respect that.

After Gabrielle orders a cappuccino, I fold my hands together on the table and say to her, "How about we put the fact that you don't like me, for whatever poorly formed reason, to the side and pretend like we're long-lost friends. Fill me in on what you've been doing."

"I thought you don't pretend if there's no money involved."

I can't help but smirk. "I think I really like you, you know that?"

She rolls her eyes and tucks a wayward strand of hair behind her ear. It's then that I catch a glimpse of her left hand. A ring on her wedding finger.

Normally that doesn't bother me. I was married once, and those vows didn't mean a thing in the end. Maybe not even in the beginning. But there's a hot poker in my stomach at the thought of Gabrielle with someone. She seems too free-spirited for that, though I obviously don't know her at all.

"How about we start with who you're married to," I say, nodding at the ring.

She glances down at it and smiles sheepishly. "Oh. No. This is just for show."

"Just for show?"

"It's just glass, not a diamond," she says, holding out her hand. "It's from a dollar store in the US."

"I see that now. The question is why? Are you married or not?"

"*No,*" she says emphatically, sitting back in the booth and slipping her hand underneath the table. "But it helps keep creeps away."

"I would think the real creeps wouldn't care if you're married or not."

"Every bit helps." Her expression grows hard.

"You have a problem with men hitting on you?"

"I take it that's hard for you to believe," she says mildly, then smiles for the waiter when he comes back with our drinks. Her smile is so bright and beautiful, it's like a gut punch, and when the waiter finally takes the time to look at her, I can tell he's affected in the same way.

"Not at all," I manage to say after he leaves. "You're unusually beautiful. That is to say, beautiful in an unusual way."

She smiles wryly as she picks up her cappuccino and blows on it with those unusually perfect lips. "You could have left it at the first sentence."

"I could have, but it wouldn't have been honest."

"Yes. I'm sure honesty is what runs Pascal Dumont, one of the most ruthless and richest men in France."

"Ruthless?" I repeat, brows raised. "That's new. You should have added that to your list of adjectives."

"I'm sure I'll have more to come. I should be writing these down."

"You should. In the meantime, I know you're not married. Are you seeing anyone?"

She nearly snorts into her drink. "You're awful."

"That has already been established."

"I'm not seeing anyone. If I were, I doubt I would have left New York." But as she says this, something dark clouds her eyes. It's absolutely fascinating, like watching a summer storm come in.

"And so why did you leave New York?"

She shrugs and taps her nails along the cup. "It was time."

"Rather cryptic answer."

"But it's the only answer," she says. "It was time to return."

"Okay. So what did you do in New York? My mother told me you were in business school or something like that?"

She looks at me sharply. "Does that surprise you?" I can tell this is a touchy subject, but I don't think I know how to tread carefully.

"Yes, it does," I tell her. "You dropped out of high school and started working for us when you were sixteen, all the way until you left. Rather abruptly, I might add."

"That doesn't mean I didn't further my education elsewhere."

"Why business?"

"Perhaps I was inspired by living amongst the Dumonts."

I watch her for a moment, seeing an array of emotions on her face and yet unable to pin down any of them. "I don't buy that."

"It's not for you to buy or not."

"So when you left, when you stopped working for us, where did you go? I remember your mother was terribly upset that you disappeared."

Those storm clouds in her eyes get larger, darker. "I didn't disappear. I told her I was done. I was going."

"Well, from the way my parents yelled about it, you didn't tell *them* anything. You know, your employers."

"Who was doing the yelling? Your mother or your father?"

"Does it matter?"

She blinks, as if caught off guard. "No."

"My father. Of course. You were his personal maid, weren't you?"

"I don't think that was my title. I was equal to my mother."

But she wasn't. I remember Gabrielle as being my father's special little pet. Although I've seen what happens to pets in this household. I had a hamster once when I was a child, until my mother flushed it down the toilet. Certainly taught me a valuable lesson about getting too attached to things.

"And so where did you go then? Right to New York?"

She seems to think that over, as if she's not sure. Or she doesn't want to say and is crafting a lie. Why, I have no idea. "I was all over Europe. Then London. Then the US."

"And now you're here with your business degree to do what? Your mother had said you wanted your job back."

"My mother is delusional," she says quietly. "I'm surprised you don't know that."

I frown. "I don't pay your mother much attention."

"Because she's beneath you."

"Because she's the help. That's up to you to decide whether that's beneath me or not. At any rate, I have no reason to believe she's delusional. About what? She works hard and does it with a smile."

"Exactly," she says before busying herself with a sip. Then she puts the mug down and looks me straight in the eye. "I'm going to level with you, Pascal. I'm worried about her."

"Why?"

"I can't explain. It's a gut feeling."

"Gut feelings come from somewhere. Has she said anything?"

I try to think back to my recent interactions with her, but I come up with nothing unusual. Jolie is just always the same. Although maybe that's because I don't see her often, and when I do, she's working. I might have to ask my mother about her.

Gabrielle shakes her head. "No. We didn't talk much while I was away either. There wasn't much to say." She rubs her lips together, and a shy expression comes across her brow. "Listen, now that we're here and we're talking . . . I think I should move in with her for a few months."

This completely catches me off guard. "Now you want to move in? You do realize that's not something either you or your mother has any say in, right? That's not her house. It's mine. I decide who moves in and who doesn't."

Or technically my father does.

Heat flashes through her eyes, turning her pupils into tiny pricks of coal. "I'm aware. I assumed you would let me do it because you like me. You said so yourself."

I let out a loud laugh. "Like you? Well, I suppose I do. And I find you incredibly attractive in ways I can't quite put into words. Maybe because you despise me so. It's so *refreshing.* But that only goes so far, and why should I give you what you want when you haven't given me what I want?"

Her throat bobs as she swallows anxiously. "And what is that?" she asks in a tight voice.

"You know what it is," I tell her, leaning in closer and smiling. "I need a maid."

"I'm sure you can find one."

"I want you. I want someone I can trust."

She stares at me for a moment before she says, "And what makes you think you can trust me?"

"Because you're being honest with your feelings toward me. That's always a good step. I can't tell you how many people, women especially but men, too, kiss my fucking ass and hail me as their king when they secretly hate me. They do it because they want something, and they think I'm too vain and arrogant, as you have said, to catch on. But I know. I always do. And when you find someone who is the opposite of all that, well, you better make sure you hang on to them."

"But I am better than a maid," she argues.

"Would your mother like to hear you say that?"

She sighs. "What I mean is, I can do more than that. I've learned so much. Use me."

My brow shoots up. Use her? "I like the sound of that." I suddenly have an image of me using her in a very naked, very sweaty, very wild way.

"Use me for something more," she clarifies.

For the first time since I've been in Gabrielle's company, I've remembered the true reason why I need someone I can trust. The letter. I need someone who can look into this for me, someone smart who I can rely on. She's right. I would need her for something more.

"Okay," I tell her, displaying my palms on the table. "How about this? You're my personal assistant who occasionally cleans my toilet."

Her nose crinkles as she gives me a look of utter disgust. "You have a way with words, don't you?"

"If you want to live with your mother, on our property, you have to pull your weight. And no, you can't just pay rent. That's not how this works."

"I thought you liked money," she says, folding her arms and sitting back.

"I do. And I have a fuckload of it, more than I know what to do with. But sometimes, even a Dumont has to admit that money isn't everything. Sometimes we all need a little help."

She seems to mull that over, staring down at her fingernails. A few seconds pass like hours until she finally looks at me. "Fine."

"Fine what?"

"I'll be whatever it is you want me to be."

I give her a crooked smile. "Be careful, little sprite. You should know better than to leave it open-ended like that. I have a very wicked imagination."

"And like a sprite, I'm harmless until threatened. So take that as a warning."

"How did I get so lucky?" I muse.

"There's no such thing as luck," she says and then waves over the waiter.

"You're going so soon?" I ask as she hands him a few euros, as if I weren't going to pay for her.

"I have to pack up my things," she says, glancing at me. "If I'm going to move in tomorrow, which I assume I am."

So presumptuous.

"You know, I'll probably be at work, if you wanted to stop by the office first," I call after her as she walks away.

She doesn't answer. I watch that ass as she disappears out of the café and across the street. In a few seconds she's completely gone, and I have to pause and wonder if I just had coffee with something supernatural.

I'm also not sure if she blinded me in such a way that I just committed to the worst idea I've ever had.

# CHAPTER THREE

## GABRIELLE

*You've made a huge mistake.*

*What were you thinking?*

*How did you even think you would survive this?*

Those thoughts and countless more run through my head as the taxi takes me up the long, tree-lined driveway to the Dumont estate. With each second that ticks on, each stately, flourishing tree that passes by, I feel the knot of dread in my stomach tightening and tightening until I don't even think I can breathe.

The driver stops out front, and I breathe out a sigh of relief to see no cars in the driveway and no sign of anyone at home. I figured both Gautier and Pascal would be at work, which will make this so much easier. If Camille is out, even better. I would only have to deal with my mother.

"We're here," the driver says to me in broken French. I get out of the car, and as he hands me my suitcases from the trunk, he says something to me about being lucky.

This has nothing to do with luck.

I chose to do this.

I chose to return here.

For eight years I have done my best to try to right the wrongs that were done to me, to no avail. The fact that I'm here is probably a sign that I should have stayed in therapy instead of bailing after one session, but it doesn't matter in the end. This was a choice, and I have to see it through.

Once I make up my mind about something, I don't back down.

Even if I should.

Even if my mind might be questionable at times.

Besides, my mother deserves to be liberated. I'm not sure many would agree with me on that front, especially after what happened. She chose her employer over her own daughter.

But blood is a funny thing. She's really all I have left in this world, and she's just a victim when it comes down to it. I can free her, though. I can help her discover how wrong she was to stay. At the very least, I can try.

And when I leave here, I'll know I did all I could.

The driver drops my suitcases off at the front door and then tells me, "Good luck," as if he knows I'll need it. He doesn't drive away, though; instead he waits. He wants to make sure I go inside, either for my own protection or to ensure that he's not just dropped off a crazy person at the Dumonts', though the latter would not be a stretch.

I ring the doorbell, and the moment I hear the familiar chime, I immediately want to be sick.

*Hold it together,* I scold myself, swallowing down bile. *You won't last long here if you don't.*

It feels like forever before the door opens and I'm face-to-face with my mother.

My first reaction is one of shock.

She is so much older, it nearly shatters my heart on the spot. It's as if fifty years have passed by, not eight.

"Mama," I cry out softly, shocked at my own reaction. I wanted to remain levelheaded and calm and impersonal, at least at first, at least until I knew what I was up against. But the moment I see her with thick bags under her eyes, the lines between her brows, the hollowness of her cheeks, I know that being here has ravaged her more than I imagined.

And even if it hadn't taken a toll on her skin, even if Camille had sprung for some surgeon's skilled hands to do their magic on my mother, you could never hide the emptiness in her eyes.

"Gabrielle," she says and gives me a shaky smile. "It's really you."

For a moment we stand there, staring at each other in shock and awe until we finally snap out of it at the same time, coming forward in an embrace. It's light at first, but then she holds me tight and I have to breathe deep through my nose, all the way to the back of my lungs, to keep the tears at bay. I've refused to cry about what happened to me, and I'll be damned if I lose it now.

I'm not sure how long we hug for, but it's enough so that the driver pulls away and disappears down the driveway, and then I know, then I really feel it, that I'm here.

But it's not home. It has never been a home.

"Oh, my darling," she says to me, kissing me on both cheeks and holding me at arm's length. At least her hands are stronger than they look. "I didn't think you'd show up."

"Well, I'm here," I tell her. I'm about to crouch down to pick up the suitcases when I hear the clack of heels on the tile floor and see Camille appearing behind my mother. She's wearing a flowing white caftan, her hair perfectly done, her face stretched beyond recognition. Her arms are out, and she practically shoves my mother aside to kiss me on the cheeks.

"My goodness, Gabrielle," she says, and I nearly choke on her Dumont perfume. She looks me up and down. "Look at you. You've changed. You're so beautiful now, a real young lady." She gives my mother a wink. "Looks like I'll have to try and hide her from Gautier."

That wave of nausea rolls through me again. Camille said it as a joke. It has to be. There's no way she would let me in this house if she really knew what Gautier did to me back then.

My mother nods and smiles at Camille, but her eyes are curiously blank. They feel nothing, maybe even see nothing as far as this subject is concerned.

*Just like before,* I think. And then I remember why I'm here, and I quickly paste on a smile for Camille's sake. "Thank you for your kind words. You look as stunning as always."

"Oh, come now," she says with false humility. "Can you handle the suitcases? I'm afraid I just had my nails done and none of the men are at home."

"I've got them," I say, and when my mother tries to take them from me, I shoo her away.

I walk through the house, following Camille as she sashays. We go through the foyer, past the grand study and the dining room, and through the kitchen. My heart picks up speed with each step I take until the suitcases feel like lead and I start to feel dizzy.

This place.

This kitchen.

That scene that's embedded in my head, the fear so real.

Somehow I make it through by forcing myself to listen to Camille blather on about this and that, probably all the upgrades the house has gotten since I left, though it all looks the same to me.

I breathe a sigh of relief when I step through the french doors out into the yard, expansive, green, and well manicured as always, following the stone path that leads to the servants' quarters that are buried back among chestnut trees. I can still hear the thud of the chestnuts that fall on the roof every autumn.

At least this house looks a little different now. It's a miniature version of the main house, old as hell and made of stone with a gray tile roof, but even though it still seems to be the same size—two bedrooms, a kitchen, a living room, and bathroom—there's an outdoor patio that's half-covered with a bistro table and chairs set up, and there are lilies growing from earthen pots. It looks a lot homier. As it should, I suppose. At this point it's my mother's home more than anywhere else has been.

"So," Camille says to me after I put my suitcases outside my room. I'm not sure I want to step in there yet. Not while she's here. "Feel free to ask me anything. Gautier is away on business until the weekend." At those words, the relief flowing through me is as palpable as a landslide. "Pascal is at work and isn't expected to be back until late. I'm not sure what Pascal has planned for you, but you can always start by helping your mother around the house, just to get back in the swing of things."

"Is it just Pascal living here?" I ask, not wanting to say Gautier's name. "Where is Blaise?"

Camille purses her lips like she just ate something sour. "Blaise is in Dubai. He moved."

The way she says it is so clipped that I don't need to ask what happened. Something did, and it pissed her off.

*Way to go, Blaise,* I think to myself. I never liked Blaise that much, but he was better than the rest of them. An outlier of sorts. It makes sense if he moved far away and distanced himself.

Come to think of it, I think I remember their cousin Seraphine doing the same. After Ludovic died, everything in the company completely changed, in Gautier and Pascal's favor, no surprise. Now Blaise and Seraphine are both in Dubai. I'm guessing that's not a coincidence.

*I'll have to ask Pascal about that later.*

Then the thought makes a knot form in my stomach again.

Pascal.

I can't believe I'm working for him.

I can't believe this is where eight years away has gotten me, working for the devil's son, in the devil's house.

"I'll leave you two to get reacquainted," Camille says as she begins to leave. She pauses in the doorway. "Just don't take too long or it will come out of your paycheck."

Then she leaves, and I know she wasn't kidding.

"Well, where shall we start?" my mother says a little too brightly. "Oh, we should get you into uniform."

"Uniform?" I ask. When I was younger, I never had to wear one.

"Yes," she says. She disappears into her room and comes out with a black dress with a scoop neck in one hand and black ballet slippers in the other. "I have extra but figured you had probably gained some weight and wouldn't fit. I was right. So Camille went and ordered this in. I hope it works. We can get another if not."

I take the dress from her and the shoes and while I'm inspecting the material, finding a Dumont tag, she goes back to her room and grabs a frilly apron, shoving it into my hands.

Really? A frilly apron? Are we stereotypical French maids now? Might as well change my name to Fifi.

"Go on," my mother says, ushering me toward my bedroom.

Well, it's time to face this place and get it over with.

I step inside, and she shuts the door behind me.

It looks exactly like it did, down to the gray pillow with faded yellow flowers and the pastel pink bed cover, the same one where Gautier pinned me down, one hand over my mouth, the other wrapped around my wrists above my head. I can almost hear him in my ear: "Don't breathe, don't scream, don't make a sound."

I shut my eyes, filling my lungs with air. When I open them, I realize I've been holding on to the uniform so hard that it hurts my hands to release it.

*You can do this,* I tell myself. *You've survived the worst. You'll survive this. And remember—this is your choice.*

*You don't have to be here.*

I square my shoulders as if posturing against an invisible opponent and face my room again.

It's just furniture. A single bed, a desk, a small bookshelf that is still stocked with the same books. Most in French, some in English when I wanted to teach myself. The window looks out—well, unfortunately it looks right out at the house and, in particular, Pascal's bedroom window.

I draw the airy curtains shut to block him out, and before I can change my mind about any of this, I get dressed in the uniform, finishing by pulling my hair back into a bun. I didn't think I would be put to work right away, but I should have known better.

When I step out of the room, my mother appraises me with a shaky smile. "Why, don't you look perfect? Now come on and help me clean the dining room. There was a dinner party last night for some of Mrs. Dumont's friends, and things are still in a bit of disarray."

We set off to the house with my mother's trusty cleaning organizer, and I do my best to listen to what she's saying and not get swept up in the memories.

They weren't all bad memories here. At first, this place seemed like paradise. We were dirt-poor, living with my father, who used to beat my mother on a regular basis and who berated me with emotional abuse. How we got here was kind of a fairy tale, and the first few months of living in the guest quarters and attending a new school felt like we were both starting over.

I used to feel safe here.

Until I learned I wasn't.

The conversation between my mother and me seems so forced. There isn't a moment of silence—my mother would never let it lapse into that—so she goes on and on about trivial things about the Dumonts, as if I'd find it fascinating. The more I talk to her, the more it becomes apparent that she doesn't have anyone else and that this family is her whole life, and that convincing her to leave is going to be even harder than I thought.

While she starts working upstairs, I start dusting the study downstairs. I'm peering at some of the books on the shelf behind the desk, noticing something peculiar just as I hear the crunch of gravel and a car door slam.

I freeze, duster in my hand.

It can't be him.

He can't be home yet.

I'm not ready to face him.

I'm especially not ready to face him alone.

I hear the front door open, and I close my eyes, offering up a silent prayer.

"Well, well, well." Pascal's voice echoes across the foyer.

I exhale loudly in relief and turn around. Pascal is standing outside the archway between the study and the foyer, placing his car keys in a bowl on a side table. He's dressed in a black suit, maroon tie, and as usual he has a wicked grin on his face.

That's one thing about Pascal; he's rarely serious. That's a good thing. If I remember correctly, if he is serious, he's rather terrifying.

But today, right now, his pale eyes are dancing with amusement, his smile crooked. If he wasn't a Dumont, I'd probably think he's as strangely handsome as everyone else seems to, but I have a hard time being objective.

*Nor should you be objective about that,* I remind myself.

"What on earth are you wearing?" he asks, looking me up and down and running his hand over his distinctive chin. "Not that I'm complaining, but it does look like you raided a costume place."

I give him a steady look. "It was my mother and your mother's idea, apparently. Guess I should be relieved to hear it wasn't yours."

"Yes," he says, striding into the study, "but now that I've seen you in this, I don't think you should ever take it off." His eyes linger on my ass, and I have to remind myself to try to play nice with him.

"Let me ask you something," I say as I ignore that comment and wag my finger for him to come forward.

He does so, and I can feel the heat of his body at my back, the smell of his cologne, which I don't think is the one he wears in the ad campaigns at all. He smells like the ocean, something sweet, and a bit of cigarette smoke.

I wave my duster at a book with a splintering hole through the spine. "Are my eyes deceiving me, or is this a *bullet* hole?"

"Ah, yes," he says, and I glance at him over my shoulder.

"Really? What happened?" Who was shooting guns in the study?

He bites his lip and raises his arched brows for a moment. "I'm going to need you to sign your contract first."

"I thought you trusted me?" I ask, though I know he shouldn't trust me at all.

"I do," he says, stepping away from me. He pauses by the desk and picks up a cane that was resting against it and raps it into his palm a few times. "But I'm not an idiot. If you're going to work for me, you're going to learn a lot of things. Some of them aren't pretty. If I know that you're locked in with an NDA, then I'll sleep better at night."

"You don't seem like the type that has anything keeping him up," I tell him.

"Well, I have been told I lack a conscience," he muses thoughtfully. He puts the cane back and then gestures with his head. "Here. Come with me to my office. This is your mother's area anyway. Your job is to tend entirely to me."

As much as I hate that idea, I hate the idea of being among Gautier's stuff even more, so I follow him as he exits the study and heads up the spiral staircase to the second floor, the crystal chandelier glittering above us.

"Why are you home so early?" I ask as we reach the second floor and go down the east wing of the house, past the rows of portraits in gilded frames that hang on the wall, their eyes following our every move.

"Everyone is a fucking moron," he says, glancing at me quickly over his shoulder. "I don't have patience for idiots."

"I assume these are the new hires since Seraphine and Blaise left?"

He stops and gives me a look I can't read. "I'd like to hear what you know about Blaise and Seraphine. But that can wait for later." He pushes the door open to his office, and I follow him inside. "Besides, I guess the real reason I came home early is because I wanted to see if you really were here."

"You didn't think I'd show?"

He gives me that crooked grin again while his glacier-blue eyes spear me. He's got quite an unusual way of looking at you, always has. Like he can see right through you, but it's also more than that. Like he knows all your secrets, and plans on using them against you later. "After you left the café, I spent the evening convincing myself that our conversation actually happened. You're very bewitching, you know that? Anyway, I couldn't be sure that you actually meant what you said. You were so adamant against working for me, and then you suddenly changed your mind. I get that you needed a favor, but still . . ." He sits down at his desk and stares up at me. "I wasn't counting on you."

I give him a quick smile and stand on the other side of the desk. I knew I shouldn't have been so standoffish with him at the beginning. I also knew that he was the type who loved the chase, and if I had shown up at his office like I was originally supposed to, I doubt I would have held any power with him.

"You can count on me now," I assure him.

He raises a brow and opens up his laptop. "We'll see, my little sprite."

My cheeks go hot at that. God, that infuriates me so much. This is where I've learned that it's best to just ignore whatever Pascal says or does, especially if he's doing it to get a rise out of you. The more you fuss, the more he'll do it, like the boy who used to pull my hair in grade school.

He's watching me closely, that sly smile on his lips. I raise my chin in response, hoping to look nonplussed.

"Here we go," he says after clicking a few keys, and the printer on the bookshelf behind him starts printing.

"Don't we need a lawyer to get involved?" I ask him as he goes to the printer and removes a few sheets of paper.

Another crooked smile. "These NDAs are airtight. If you're not convinced, you should just try and break it and see what happens to you." He signs with a fancy-looking pen and then holds it out for me. "Your turn."

I come over to his side of the desk with caution and stand beside him as he hands me the pen. Our shoulders are touching, and again my nose fills with his scent, something that's becoming more alluring in a way I wish it wouldn't.

Taking the pen from him, I stare at it for a moment and then give him a glance. He's so close to me that I can see how clear his eyes are. There are barely any lines of color or serrations in his irises; they're just blue, like the kind a child would draw with a single crayon, coloring over and over until it's completely saturated and ringing the outside with a thick, dark line.

"Having second thoughts?" he asks, his voice on a lower register and gravelly, those eyes of his skimming over my face, focusing on my lips.

I blink and look back at the document. The truth is, I *am* having second thoughts. I wasn't exactly looking for a job when I planned to come back here. I had made it an option, a last resort. Now that the opportunity has opened up, though, I know it's the best way to do what I need to do.

But there's a chance that I'll have to break his NDA.

*There's a chance of a lot worse than that,* I remind myself.

I clear my throat and pick up the pages. "I should probably look it over."

"Take your time," he says, turning around so that he's leaning back against the desk, feet casually crossed at the ankle. I feel his eyes burning through me, watching my every move, especially my face, as I try to concentrate on the contract.

I won't admit this to him, but I don't really have much experience looking over contracts. The only one I had to sign was my lease of the last place I lived in New York, and that was a whole other ball game. So far there doesn't seem to be anything strange or damaging in the contract, basically just says that I won't tell a soul of what happens here at the Dumont house.

*Here goes nothing.*

With a nod, I place the papers down on his desk and I sign on the line. My hand wants to shake, but I think I hide it well.

"Perfect," he says, taking the papers from me when I'm done. He opens his desk drawer and slips them inside, quickly closing it. If my eyes weren't deceiving me, I think I saw a handgun in there.

The corner of his mouth ticks up as he notices my focus. "One can never be too careful," he says, putting weight in his words.

"Are you the one who shot the book in the study?" I ask. I wave the pen at him. "I signed the contract; you can tell me everything now."

"Mm, how about we start with you telling *me* everything," he says smoothly, and for a moment I think he must know. But his eyes are merely curious as they study me.

"Tell you what?" I ask, putting on my most innocent look.

"Everything," he says. "We're now in a contractually secure working environment. The NDA goes both ways—didn't you read that?"

"What do you want to know?" I ask, because I should have read that contract a little better.

"I want to know who I'm working with. Who is working for me. I want to know what you want out of life, I want to know what makes you tick. I'm starting to think I do. I think I infuriate you a lot. Which begs the question, why would you work for a man you so despise?"

We're still standing close to each other, and now it's starting to feel suffocating. I make a move to inch back, but he quickly reaches out and grabs me by the wrist, and his grip is tight.

It's enough to make me raise my arm in defense, to set off alarms throughout my body, to remember that this is the son of the devil, and the apple never falls far from the tree.

"Easy now," he says, frowning at my raised arm, and yet he doesn't let go. "You're a little reactive, don't you think?"

"I've had some bad experiences," I say, my voice hard, my head echoing with my heartbeat.

"I can see that," he says, peering at me closely. I stare right back, not willing to give him anything. Finally, he lets go. "I suppose I can relate in some way."

*Not even close,* I think, quickly stepping back so I'm on the other side of the desk again. Out of habit, I rub at my wrist.

He stares, brows raised in surprise. "Did I hurt you? You can't be that fragile . . ." His eyes trail over my body. "Even if you do look like you might dissolve into fairy dust at any given time."

"I'm fine," I tell him quickly. "Being in New York teaches you a lot about boundaries. I've taken self-defense. You can never be too careful, as you say."

"No," he says slowly. "But New York's crime is no different from Paris or London."

I shrug. "Then I guess I can handle myself anywhere now."

"As long as you can handle working for me," he says. "Now, how about we begin by giving you my schedule for the week." He reaches across the desk and hands me a smartphone. "Here. This is yours. This is my link to you. It's your job to keep up with it, to check in on me regularly in case there are appointments made that I forget to tell you about. This includes all appointments, including dates."

I can't help but laugh. "Dates? Do you even go out on dates?"

His eyes narrow just a bit. "You think I don't?"

"I think you're not one for formalities. That whole getting to know each other business."

"How can you say that when all I wanted to do yesterday was catch up? And I still want to know more about you."

"That's different . . ." *You're not trying to fuck me.*

I don't think.

At least I sure as hell hope not.

I start to slip the phone into my apron pocket, but he jerks his chin at it.

"Don't put it away yet; I happen to have a date you need to add," he says. "Tomorrow night with the front-desk clerk at your old hotel."

I roll my eyes. "You made a date while you were there to get me?"

"How do you think I got your room number? I have to have something to trade, and my cock is a *very* hot commodity."

My eyes go to the ceiling again. The ego on this guy.

I bring out my phone, and when I open the calendar app, I can see his schedule already. He's not kidding when he says he's busy. In fact, I can see he has numerous meetings today that he's already missing.

"Now," he goes on, "I don't remember her name, but I have no doubt she'll be texting me to remind me about the date. So put it in for Friday, make reservations at the fanciest place you can think of, and then it's your job to find out her name so I don't look like a complete pig. Got that?"

"I got that," I tell him. "Anything else?"

"Sure," he says, getting up and walking around the desk to the door of the office. "This place is a bit of a mess. Tidy it, will you? I want to see it shine."

Then he's gone, and I'm left staring at his phone, wondering what I've gotten myself into.

# CHAPTER FOUR

## Pascal

*You're not above the law.*

Other than a different catchphrase, the letter is exactly the same as before. Same typed address, same stamp, same envelope. More or less the same threat.

I hadn't gotten a letter in a few days and was starting to think that maybe it was a one-off thing, but here it is in my hands.

"What do you have there?" my mother asks as she comes down the hall to the foyer, where I'm standing.

I quickly slip the letter into my pocket, chiding myself for being so impatient and not waiting to open it until I got to my room.

"Nothing," I tell her, handing her the rest of the mail. "Some fan letter, I'm sure."

"You're home early today," she says. "I thought you'd be working extra-long hours, since your father is out of town."

I glare at her, but she doesn't seem to notice. "I *have been* working extra-long hours all week. Haven't you noticed I'm not around? I came home early because I have a date tonight."

"A date?" My mother gives me a sidelong look. "So how is Gabrielle working out? She's turned into quite the beautiful girl, hasn't she?"

She has this sparkling look in her eye, the kind she gets when she sees something she wants, like the way she tries to set me up with rich millennials on the weekly.

"Don't get any ideas," I warn her.

"Ideas?" she repeats. "About you and Gabrielle? Oh, heavens no, Pascal, don't be an idiot. She's a maid. You're Pascal Dumont. She couldn't be more beneath you if she tried, and you're so much better than that, dear boy." She pauses. "Besides, you don't want to follow in your father's footsteps."

I give her a sharp look. "What is that supposed to mean?"

"Please," she says, lowering her voice and shooting a glance into the kitchen. "If you think your father has kept his hands to himself this whole time, you're even more naive than I thought."

Everything inside me stills. "He . . . With Gabrielle?"

Another roll of her eyes, which brings a spike of relief into my veins. "No. Jesus," she says with disgust. "She was a child, Pascal." But she leaves it at that and turns around, walking back into the kitchen. I catch a glimpse of Jolie in there, wiping down the microwave.

Contrary to what my mother thinks, I'm not naive. I have no doubt my parents' marriage vows are as sacred as the ones I once held, and that goes for both of them. What they do is none of my fucking business. It does surprise me that it seems my mother was hinting at my father and Jolie being . . . together.

But that's also none of my business and nothing I want to let occupy my brain. What I do need to concentrate on is the letter.

Which means it's time to confide in Gabrielle.

The idea still puts me a bit on edge, even though she signed the contract, and I can and would sue the fuck out of her if she ever dared to open her mouth to anyone else.

There's something about her that I don't quite trust, and I'm not sure what it is. She's not been very forthcoming about her past, but granted it's only been a few days since she started working for me, and I really haven't had the time to talk to her.

*Why do you even want to talk to her anyway?* A voice in my head speaks up. *You've never given a shit about any of your maids before, or fuck, even your Dumont staff.*

I don't have an answer for that.

And it bothers me.

Movement catches the corner of my eye, and I glance upstairs to see Gabrielle standing at the top of the staircase, about to walk down it toward me.

"Stay there," I yell at her and then go up the stairs two at a time.

I want to grab her arm and pull her with me, but the last time I touched her like that, she flinched like I was going to hurt her. Another reason why I want to know more about her, why she is the way she is and what made her that way.

So I walk down the hall toward my office and wave at her for her to follow.

I enter the room and sit down at my desk, telling her to close the door and sit down in the seat across from me.

She does so, sitting primly with her hands in her lap, still wearing her uniform, which I have no complaints about, not with the way it shows off her ass and plays into a million fantasies I've had, fantasies I've even acted out before. Women will wear anything you tell them to when your cock is big enough and you have enough money.

I take a moment to study her, the way her light hair is pulled back, showcasing a long, delicate neck. She's got the kind of soft throat that makes me understand vampirism.

"Is everything all right?" she asks. The more curious she is about something, the larger her eyes get. Now they look at me like two polished gemstones.

"Not quite," I tell her grimly. "I've been, well, *dealing* with something that I don't want to. Perhaps it's best to ignore it, but it's the kind of thing that could blow up in my face at the same time." She's still watching me intently, so I reach into my pocket and pull out the envelope, handing it to her.

"What's this?" she asks, and I reach into the drawer and pull out the first letter, placing it on the desk.

"I don't know what this is. I was hoping you could tell me."

Her eyes widen. "Me?"

"Maybe you can make sense of it," I tell her. I lean back, my leather chair squeaking as I do so, and steeple my fingers together, watching her.

She looks over both letters and envelopes for a bit and then finally shakes her head before looking up at me. "I don't understand. You must know what these are about."

I press my lips together a moment and nod. "I have an idea, yes."

"So? What is it? What did you do?"

"I didn't do anything," I say quickly, though the more I say that, the more I wonder if I did in some way.

I never wanted my uncle to die, and yet . . .

Gabrielle squints at me, and I remember to slip on my mask, even though I'm about to tell her everything.

Or almost everything.

"I think the person who sent these letters thinks that my father murdered Ludovic."

Her brows shoot up. "Your father murdered his own brother?"

*Careful,* I tell myself. *Be very careful right here.*

"No." I pause, composing my thoughts. "This is just what someone thinks."

"And what makes you so sure of that? Why jump to that conclusion? Surely you've done many horrible things that would make someone want to blackmail you."

It shouldn't bother me that she said that, because it's completely true, but it does anyway. "Don't be so sure."

"I'm more than sure," she says, and for a moment I wonder if she's talking about my cousin Olivier and the fact that I had a hand in blackmailing him for ten years. "You don't get to the top without crushing people on the way up. Everyone knows that."

I don't know what to say to that. I can't argue with her.

"Look," she says, placing her delicate hands on the papers. "I can help you, but you have to help me. And you're holding a lot back, which makes me think that NDA was worthless. So why don't you tell me the truth?"

"Why don't you tell me the truth?"

She shakes her head, a strand of hair falling across her eyes that she quickly brushes back. "I'm not hiding anything. And this isn't about me, not even a little. Tell me the truth, Pascal. Why do you think this is about your uncle? Has anyone told you they have this theory?"

I sigh and run my hand down my face, feeling exhausted all of a sudden. "Yes," I say after a moment, my gaze absently sliding over the bookshelf. "My cousin Seraphine. She was convinced that my father murdered her father, that it wasn't a heart attack. Poison or something, I don't know. She was so convinced that she started to do a little spying on her own and then enlisted the help of her ex-husband and a private investigator." I'm not too proud of the next part. I lick my lips, feeling dry. "But her ex-husband, Cyril, he's a real piece of shit. He cheated on Seraphine and married her for money, so it was no surprise when he won nothing in their divorce. And he's not the kind of man who likes his pride knocked around, so he went directly to my father the moment Seraphine contacted him."

"Revenge," Gabrielle says slowly, and those storm clouds roll in again, this time bringing disdain to her eyes, for my father, for my family, for me. "I'm going to guess this doesn't end well, or else Seraphine would still be in Paris."

"It ended as well as it could, thanks to me." If no one is going to pat me on the back for what I did, I might as well. "It could have been a lot worse. Then of course Blaise had to get himself involved, since he and Seraphine have had this quasi-incestuous relationship with each other since they were teenagers."

She raises her chin as if to say, *Ah*. "But they aren't related."

"Doesn't matter. Blaise chose her, and he disowned us."

"So he believed Seraphine."

"Yeah. He did. Still does. He loves her."

"And do you believe Seraphine?"

Our eyes lock for a moment; then I look away. "It doesn't matter what I think. It's what everyone else thinks."

She narrows her eyes thoughtfully. "Okay. But so far you've got Blaise and Seraphine who think your father murdered Ludovic. Anyone else?"

"Not that I'm aware of. Maybe Olivier, but I don't see him acting like that."

"And I take it you've talked to your brother?"

"I have. They didn't send it. I believe them."

"I do too. Seraphine seems like a smart woman; she wouldn't bother with this."

"Especially now that she's pregnant."

Her eyes light up. "She is?"

I raise a finger to my lips. "Part of your NDA. My parents don't know. I don't know if or when Blaise will ever tell them."

"I'm assuming they don't talk now."

"You have to understand my father," I tell her, and at the mention of those words, her eyes go even darker. "If you step out of line, if you betray him or the family name even a little bit . . ."

"You're dead to him."

I nod. "You're dead to him."

"And maybe you're just dead in general."

I don't say anything to that, but I coax her with my eyes because I'm curious as to what she's going to run with.

She taps her nails along the envelope. "Since you won't tell me what you think, or what you know, about whether your father had Ludovic murdered or not, do I have permission to tell you what I think?"

"Please do. Entertain me."

She gives me a bitter smile. "Before I do, let's revisit that whole NDA thing when it comes to what we're talking about staying between us."

I have to admit, I rather like having a confidante. Come to think of it, I don't think I've ever had someone I could confide in like this, even if this intimacy is all legally bound. "Agreed."

"Because the last thing I want," she says and then trails off, swallowing hard. Her eyes go wide and blank for a moment, as if remembering something.

"Gabrielle?"

Her gaze swings back to me, her jaw tighter, eyes harder. "The last thing I want is to get on your father's bad side. So if you repeat what I'm about to say . . ."

"I won't, I promise," I tell her, and I mean it. I've noticed the way she stiffens up whenever his name is mentioned. She thinks she's hiding it, but she's not. And though I can be very cruel at times, though I can act without thought and never suffer any consequences, I would never tell my father anything that would make him angry with her. For one, he would insist I fire her, and I need her help. And for two . . . I don't know. But it wouldn't be good.

My stomach sinks with unease at the thought. Maybe she shouldn't tell me anything, just in case. "On second thought," I tell her quickly, "maybe it's best we don't say anything."

Not to mention I live in fear that my office is bugged.

She frowns, on edge. "Why? Do you want me to help you or not?"

I exhale through my nose sharply and get up. "I think that speculating only gets people in trouble. Come to think of it, this whole thing is just silly. Let's forget about it and move on."

"What?" Her eyes widen as I go around the desk and put one finger to my lips to keep her quiet, the other holding out my hand.

She stares at my hand, hesitating, and then puts her hand in it.

It's soft and small and warm against my palm, and I wrap my fingers around it, just tight enough. I pull her to her feet and then lead her out of the office and down the hall, pausing outside my room. The feel of her hand in mine is rather nice and distracts me for a moment.

"Where are we going?" she whispers, and when I open the door to my bedroom, she balks. I tighten my grip on her hand and give her a pleading look, trying to get her to just trust me.

There seems to be a war going on in her head until she finally nods.

I bring her in the bedroom and lead her all the way into the bathroom and then shut the door, locking it behind me.

When I turn around, she's backed up against the sink, her hands gripping the corners, looking like a trapped deer. "What are you doing?" she says in a low, edgy voice.

"Gabrielle," I say softly, holding up my hands. "I'm not doing anything."

"Why are we here?"

"Maybe I wanted to do an inspection of your bathroom-cleaning skills."

She doesn't move, doesn't break her doe-eyed stare.

"Look," I tell her, putting my hands in my pockets. "I think I've grown a little paranoid lately. Sometimes I think my office could be bugged. Maybe even my bedroom. But I guarantee no one would put a bug in here."

"Who on earth would record you?"

My brow quirks up. She has to know.

The realization dawns on her face. "I see."

"After what happened with Blaise and Seraphine, after my father almost had her killed—"

"He *what?*"

*Ah fuck. Fuck, fuck.*

Maybe I've said more than I should have.

"Never mind that."

"*Never mind?* That's your cousin we're talking about. Now you're saying he tried to have her killed."

Well, down the rabbit hole we go. "At first he just wanted to scare her, so he says. Rough her up. I don't know, maybe worse. Maybe I try not to think about it. But yeah . . . I don't think he would have hesitated killing her to shut her up."

Gabrielle is staring at me with such intensity that it makes my stomach curl up in knots. "I can't believe you," she says quietly, shaking her head.

"What did I do?"

"What did you do? What . . . You live here, Pascal. And he's your father. You just told me that you think your father would have murdered your own cousin, and that's enough to tell me what you think really happened to your uncle. So fine, admit it or not, but you know what he's capable of, and yet here you are, living in his house, working for his company."

"It's my fucking company now," I growl. "I'm the one stepping in, doing everything. He does nothing."

"But in the end, it will still be his. Isn't that why he murdered Ludovic? To get everything? To put himself at the top and you right below him? Right under his thumb."

"Fuck you," I sneer, my blood running hot. "I'm not under his thumb."

"You can't be that delusional," she says snidely. "Or maybe you can. Maybe your ego is so out of control that it won't let you accept the reality, that you've spent your whole life trailing behind him, begging your father to be proud of you, doing everything you can to be just like Daddy."

I'm at her in a second, my hand on her throat, pressing the back of her head into the mirror while she gives a frightened cry. "You should know better than to say that," I tell her, my heart raging in my head, pushing my hand against her windpipe until her eyes widen and widen, until I feel her fear pulse against my palm, fear that once excited me, fear that now disturbs me.

As quick as it came on, my rage subsides, the black cloud that took hold of my brain and soul lifts, and I realize what I'm doing. I lost my temper, as I do, but I lost it in the worst way and with the wrong person. My issues are with my father. They aren't with her.

I quickly let go of her and turn around, not able to face her. I hear her coughing before she takes in a deep, wheezing breath.

"You just proved my point," she manages to say, her voice raw.

I glance at her over my shoulder and see her rubbing at her throat, brows knit together, her hand clenched around the edge of the sink until her knuckles are white.

Shit.

Fucking *shit*.

"I'm sorry," I tell her, even though these words don't come easy. "I shouldn't have done that."

"No, you shouldn't have," she says, straightening up. "But it's what you do. You're a Dumont."

And she's right. I am a Dumont, and I've been a slave to my temper and wicked ways for a long time. It's just never bothered me before.

It's bothering me now.

It's bothering me a lot.

I swallow the brick in my throat and take a step toward her. She backs up again.

"I'm really, really sorry, Gabrielle," I tell her imploringly. "I didn't mean to do that. It just . . . I lost control, and I'm sorry. I didn't mean to hurt you."

"*You* can't hurt me," she says, looking down at the tiles. "And believe it or not, I've had so much worse."

Fuck. That makes me feel even more terrible.

"I'm really sorry," I tell her again, and I reach out for her hand. She snatches hers away, holding it to her chest, warning me to stay away with her eyes that are full of fury.

We were doing so fucking well, and then I had to fuck it up.

Still, she didn't have to say shit in the first place, shit she knew would piss me off.

Stuff that's true, that I don't want to admit is true.

Oh fucking hell, she was baiting me, wasn't she?

I walked right into that one.

"You'll make it up to me," she says. "Then we'll be even."

"I guess you see my true colors now," I tell her.

"I always have," she says. "That's the magic of being someone's maid over the years, even if it was long ago. You see everyone's true colors. You see the sides of them they try so desperately to hide. My advice for you, Pascal, is don't be so offended. Own up to it. You know you're no good, and I bet you've been just fine with it for a long time. You don't have to change now because I'm here. You don't have to lie to me. I work for you. I'm nothing more than that."

I watch her for a moment, and I realize how right she is.

Still doesn't make me feel any less defeated, like shit at the bottom of someone's shoe.

"Okay," I tell her quietly. "I won't lie to you. I promise."

"Good," she says. "I know what you are, Pascal. There's no use in denying it." She clears her throat and straightens her shoulders. "Now that the pretenses are out of the way, let's go back to the matter at hand," she says in a clipped voice. "You want me to find out who is sending the letters, correct?"

"You don't have to . . ."

"Oh, come on, don't act like it no longer matters. It does. So while I do some sleuthing on the stamp and the postmark, maybe you can make a list of enemies for me, people who have wronged your father."

"What makes you think it's for my father and not for me?"

She blinks. "No reason," she says quickly. "Just based on what you just told me. But yes, it could be for anyone at this house, even your mother, but let's count her out for now. So if you think it could be for you, then it's probably someone who thinks you had something to do with your uncle's death. Think about your enemies, as numerous as they probably are, probably including ex-maids and -employees, if you treated all of them like you just treated me, and get back to me." She opens the door to the bathroom and looks at me over her shoulder. "You should get ready for your date tonight. Her name is Aurelie, by the way, and you're to send a car for her at six thirty p.m. All the info is in your agenda."

Then she walks out of the bathroom and disappears down the hall.

Fuck. The date. The last thing I feel like doing today. I think I'd rather stay and drink myself silly. I am my mother's son, too, after all.

I turn around and look at myself in the mirror, and it's not the first time that I barely recognize myself. It's not that I've physically changed at all. My eyes are still blue, brows are arched and black, my hair in need of a trim. It's that I don't think I know who I am anymore or who I'm trying to be.

I'm not sure I'll ever know.

Not at this rate.

# CHAPTER FIVE

## GABRIELLE

Marine et Olivier, the text reads.

I stare at it for a moment, trying to figure out what Pascal is talking about. He should be on his date right now with Aurelie; why is he texting me these names?

Then I remember.

His list of enemies.

Marine was his ex-wife.

Olivier is his cousin.

I'm not sure what he did to both of them, but I'm assuming it's something big if he thinks they might be the ones blackmailing him.

I text him back, What about your father? Do you know any offhand?

He texts back immediately, Too many to list. And I'm on a date, don't you remember?

I roll my eyes at that and put my phone away on my bedside table.

It's eight at night. He's on a date; I should be off work completely, not checking my work phone. I've at least changed out of that wretched uniform and am sitting on my bed in leggings and a V-neck tunic that's a little on the revealing side. I would never wear it around Pascal; his eyes linger on my body enough as it is. I most certainly wouldn't wear it around the house, either, but Gautier isn't expected until tomorrow night.

I've been trying not to think about it.

About what I'll feel when I see him.

What I'll say.

How I'll act.

I've planned for this so many times over the last eight years, and each time I imagine it, it's different, I guess depending on whatever I'm feeling at the moment.

I just need to hold it together the best that I can.

No matter what seeing him feels like, even if it makes me want to double over and vomit or burst into tears or run up to Pascal's office and grab his gun and shoot Gautier in the heart, I have to pretend that the past doesn't exist. I have to pretend that he didn't break me, even though I know that was always his goal.

My mind swirls back to Pascal earlier today in the bathroom. The way he looked at me with such anger, pushed me back, pressed his hand to my throat—it reminded me so much of his father. And yet at the same time, I wasn't afraid, because that anger came from a different place, and his touch was rough but not painful. He wasn't trying to hurt me; he didn't take any pleasure in it. He's just used to letting his impulses guide him, as bad as they might be.

And it was exactly as I predicted. I didn't mean to make him snap—that just came naturally—but the fact that he did snap was almost reassuring. It means he's shaping up to be the man I pegged him to be. It's one thing for someone to say they're without conscience; it's another to see it manifest.

Not that he wasn't sorry about what happened. I know he was, and I guess if anything that was the most surprising part of the whole altercation. He regretted the way he acted. He was remorseful.

But he's still Pascal, and I needed to see him with his mask off. I could tell all this week he's been playing the part he plays so well, the joker, the trickster, everything is for fun, nothing is serious. I needed to see the side he hides when he's trying to impress, the side the public gets, the side he believes sometimes. Like nothing can bother him when I know it does.

Now I feel we're more equal, and if not that, at least I have a better handle on him. I need Pascal to be the easiest part of this whole job. Play the part of the dutiful maid, indulge his whims when it comes to the letters, be a sounding board for things he wouldn't tell anyone because we have that contract protecting us both. I need to get that relationship sound—or as sound as it can be—so I can concentrate on why I'm really here.

A knock at my door snaps me out of my musings and not a moment too soon. My mind runs away on me at night, keeping sleep at bay, reliving horrors until I'm begging for sleep.

"Gabby," my mother says from the other side. "Are you sleeping?"

She has no idea. I never slept a wink in this house back then—why should I now?

I get up and go to my bedroom door. She's in her pajamas, silk. Probably Dumont, like everything is. There is no escape from them.

"Not sleeping," I tell her; then I notice the teapot she has in her hand.

She gestures to the couch and says brightly, "I've made some tea. Kusmi. That's still your favorite, right?"

"I haven't had it since I left," I admit.

"Oh, then you must have some now," she says. "Come on."

I'm not really in the mood to talk with my mother because, like she has all week, she'll just want to talk about superficial stuff, deflecting anything deeper with a blank look and then a cheery smile.

But she's part of the reason why I'm here.

I follow her out into our tiny living area and to the plush couch adorned with a copious number of pillows. The style in the house is different from what I remember—only my room remains untouched.

Everything before was bare and drab, and now it's all white and gold, with lots of ruffles and paintings and weird decor.

"Did you decorate this?" I ask, eyeing the walls as I sit down and she pours me tea.

"Me?" she says, looking around. "No, this is all Mrs. Dumont. She loves to come here and fix things up."

Something about that makes me so sad. I watch my mom closely as I ask, "Do you like what she's done with the place?"

My mother's lips quirk for a split second, as if she's unsure of whether to smile or not. Then she does, nodding enthusiastically. "Yes, of course. She has such excellent taste."

Hmm. That couldn't be further from the truth.

"I'm sure she could decorate your room if you'd like," she says. "We didn't want to change it, in case you came back."

I stare at her, puzzled. "You thought I would come back?"

After every fucking thing that happened?

She shrugs and blows on her tea. "Um, yes. Gautier always said you would return."

Gautier.

The bile in my throat rises. "He said that?" I say softly.

"Yes. He said that you left because you felt ashamed for what you did, that it was a misunderstanding. All is forgiven, you see. That's why you're back here."

No. No, no. I'm back here because I chose to be.

My heart is beginning to race, and my hands feel clammy. "I hate to break it to you, Mama, but I only decided to come here last month. I was going to stay in New York. No one had any idea I was coming here."

She tilts her head side to side like a bird, considering what I said. "If you insist. Sure. But Gautier knew you would come back and you would want to work for the family again. What I'm trying to say is that it's so good to have you home, where you belong."

No. This isn't my home. This will never be my home.

66

And it shouldn't be her home either.

I just don't know how I'm going to convince her of that.

"What else did he say?" I ask cautiously.

"You can ask him yourself," she says, and while I'm frowning at that, I notice that there is a third mug on the table.

And then a knock at the front door.

Oh my God.

I whirl around to check the door, and through the upper glass window, I see a darkened figure standing there on the other side.

"Who is that?" I cry out softly, hand at my chest.

"It's the master of the house," my mother says. "He came back early."

The master.

Oh fuck.

I'm not ready.

I'm not ready.

My mom is in the process of getting up to answer the door when the door opens anyway and Gautier steps in.

"Jolie," he says to my mother in a warm voice and with a stiff smile.

Then, as the door closes behind him with a loud *click* that sounds like the closing of a prison cell door, his eyes come to me.

The grin on his face widens, making him look like even more of a monster. He hasn't changed much, just more plastic surgery on his face, making him look like someone took him apart and put him back together, just with a touch more evil this time.

"My Gabrielle," he says in a rich voice. "You're here."

I freeze. I can't breathe, I can't smile, I can't make a sound.

I can only stare up at him.

I can only hope that he truly believes what he told my mother, that I'm here because I wanted to return home, because I wanted forgiveness for the things he thinks I did. I need him to think that, to have no suspicions about me.

"You're shocked to see me?" he asks when I don't say anything, and he comes around the couch so he's standing right in front of me, peering down at me. "Cat got your tongue?" His voice is lower now.

"I think she's just surprised that you're home early," my mother speaks up. "Please sit down. I have tea."

I still can't move. I can only stare at him with wide eyes, while my heart and lungs and every part of me inside cowers and shakes with absolute fear.

The memories.

The memories.

"Ah," he says, taking the seat right next to me, so close that I slide toward him on the cushion, my thigh pressing against him. "You must be tired from your first week at work."

Run, run, run.

His smell, that awful cologne, fills my nose, and the flashbacks slam into my brain like bombs going off, like I'm reliving a war, a war that I lost.

His cruel, depraved touch.

The merciless glint in his eyes.

The way he got excited when I struggled.

The day I found out I was pregnant, knowing I couldn't tell a soul.

Knowing I couldn't keep his evil seed inside me.

The trip to the doctor, all alone, so alone, to get the abortion.

The shame.

So much fucking shame.

Tears prick at the corners of my eyes, but I refuse to let them loose.

I look away from his awful stare and let the shame run its course and the anger come back to fuel me.

Anger has been my friend for so long now.

"She is tired," my mother fills in quickly when I don't say anything, and she pours him his tea. "She's not only cleaning up after Pascal, but she's organizing his life for him too. I don't know how you manage,

Gabby; that's a lot of work for one person. Always going above and beyond."

I glance at her curiously, since this is the first time she's said anything complimentary.

"Yes," he says slowly, his eyes skimming over my face and then resting on my cleavage. "I was so surprised to hear what Pascal had you doing." His eyes become more lustful, and then when he finally looks up at me, I see a smirk on his face, a smirk that tells me he thinks this is something we have, like this is some kind of secret.

This delusional motherfucker.

It's enough to bring the marrow back into my bones and let the feeling return to my skin.

I move over on the couch as far as I can go and give him a hard look. "I was surprised too," I tell him, and to my relief my voice is coming out clear and strong. "But I didn't want to waste my business degree."

And just like that, he seems bored. His eyes roam about the room. "Yes, I had heard from your mother that you were studying business. Seems to me quite a waste. You're far too pretty for that."

"Looks don't last forever," I tell him, hoping he feels the knife in that comment.

His eyes become slits for a second. Oh, he feels it.

"No, I suppose they don't," he says. Then he looks me over again. "Lucky for you, you're holding up very well. Such a pretty, pretty thing you are. I'm almost jealous that my son gets to have you all to himself."

My mother clears her throat, bringing our attention over to her. "Pascal needs her," she says. There's a hint of jealousy in her voice that devastates me. "If you ever need Gabby's services, I'm sure I could—"

He raises his hand. "It's fine, Jolie. Stick to making tea," he says dismissively.

The way her face falls breaks my heart and scares me to the bone, because she's that invested and in love with this monster, and the fact that he's paying attention to me like this is making her hate me.

"Now, Gabrielle," Gautier says, turning back to me with a sly smile, "we have so much catching up to do." I am so tired of these Dumont men and their need to catch up. "When are your days off? Is Pascal more selfish than I am when it comes to the help?"

"Sundays," I say quietly, pressing myself hard into the arm of the couch, as far away from him as possible, not liking where this question is going.

"Only one day?" he asks in mock surprise. "I should have a talk with my son. Sometimes I think he's a bit of a bad seed, you know." He picks up his tea and has a sip. "Perfect tea, as always, Jolie."

Then, when it feels like I've been holding my breath forever, he gets to his feet. "Well, I better get unpacked. I came to see you right away, you know. I couldn't wait. The moment I was able to take an earlier flight, I did, because honestly, Gabrielle, I didn't believe you were here until I saw it with my own eyes."

"But your tea," my mother protests feebly.

"It'll only keep me up," he says to her. "You drink it." He smiles down at me, and I swear I see fangs. "Keep your Sunday free. We need to talk. Perhaps a drive in the country. You've probably forgotten how lovely France is in the summer."

I don't say anything to that, I can't, I just watch as he walks around the couch and opens the door. "See you in the morning," he says and then leaves.

After the door clicks shut, all the air comes back into my lungs.

"You could have been a lot more appreciative," my mother scolds me, picking up the pot of tea and Gautier's mug and going back in the kitchen.

I'm tired of being so speechless this evening, but I really don't know what to say, so I follow my mother into the kitchen, bringing her the other two mugs, my legs feeling weak and shaky.

"I'm sorry," I tell her, knowing I have to be a sweet girl if I want to win this. I wash the mugs in the sink. "I'm just tired, you were right."

She makes a *tsk*ing sound. "He's the master of the house. He's the Dumont company now. After his poor brother died and then his son disowned him and moved, he's been through so much, and yet he's the one who has the whole company riding on his shoulders."

*Actually, Pascal does,* I think. I happen to know that the trip Gautier took had nothing to do with business at all. Something private. I'm guessing a whore he can beat up and toss around.

*He might be making fewer trips now that you're back in the picture.*

My stomach burns at the thought.

No matter what, that can't happen.

I can't go through that again.

I won't.

"It wouldn't kill you to be nicer to him," she goes on. "After all, he allowed you to come back."

"It wasn't up to him, it was Pascal."

"And do you think Pascal has the final say in this house? At any rate, you should be on your knees, groveling for forgiveness. Blame it on being a teenager and being stupid and emotional, whatever you wish. But you attacked him and slandered him, and he is such a good, good man to let you back here to work in this place."

I stare at her, trying to find something in her that is rooted in reality, the real one, not the one she's created in her head for herself. "Do you really believe that?" I ask quietly.

She looks stunned, like I slapped her. "Of course I do. It's not a matter of belief, it's just fact. You were a very troubled girl, Gabby, though I suppose that was all your father's fault. The things he would say to you were just awful."

"Mama, he beat you until you were bleeding, black and blue."

She gives me a stiff smile and pours the tea in the sink as she shrugs. "He did, but that's why it was so magical, so wonderful, that Gautier happened to see me at the hotel that one day. He saw the bruises. He wanted to know who did this to me. He promised us freedom, that we could escape from your father. And we did. He is our savior, and you can never, ever forget it. I know I never will." She pauses. "That's why I'm still here." Her gaze fixes me with a determination that's unnerving. "That's why I'll never, ever leave."

Then she turns away from me and starts to tidy up, even though there's nothing to tidy, even though that's all her life is now. Tidying up for the people she believes saved her when all they did was lock her up and throw away the key. Their trick was to make her think she deserved it.

"Good night, Mama," I tell her and then head back to my room, my heart heavy with all the impossible things. I'm too exhausted and strung out to even change my clothes, so I flick off the lights and head right to my bed.

I get under the covers and lie back, trying to process what just happened and how hopeless it's going to be to pull my mom away from the situation, when I notice movement outside the window.

I sit up and find myself looking right across the lawn at a lit window on the second floor.

Pascal's window.

And to my surprise, he's standing there.

Except he's not alone.

He's with some woman with long dark hair and big breasts.

I recognize her as the front-desk girl at the hotel.

Aurelie.

And she's completely naked, her breasts and the side of her face pressed up against the glass, palms wide and flat to brace herself as Pascal fucks her from behind.

I immediately look away, my cheeks flushing, knowing I saw something I wasn't supposed to see.

But when I get up to go close the curtains, I can't help but look again, more clearly this time.

I can see Pascal, the side of his hips, his legs, the taut ridges of his abs and his firm chest, skin smooth and tanned from the summer sun. His arm muscles sinewy and tight as they grip the woman's waist and he pumps in and out of her.

I catch his eye.

A hot, intense gaze flickering in them as he stares right at me.

For a moment, I'm actually turned on.

And then I'm equally as disgusted with myself.

I stare back at him, stone-faced, and shut the curtain.

Looks like his date went well.

# CHAPTER SIX

## PASCAL

"So how is your mother doing?" I ask.

Gabrielle seems to flinch at the question, as if she had forgotten I was in the same room as her.

I suppose it is kind of weird to be in my bedroom when she's trying to clean it, but it's Saturday morning, and I can't be bothered to get out of bed. Granted, I did get out of bed at the crack of dawn when I put Aurelie in a car and sent her home, but after a night of sex, I'm exhausted. I had remembered Aurelie as a bit boring in bed, but last night she completely proved me wrong.

"My mother?" she asks as she sprays cleaner on the windows. There are a fuckload of smudge marks left on there, courtesy of Aurelie. I don't normally bring women back here—just because it's so far out of Paris—but Aurelie gave me head on the whole car ride, and once we were in here, I had the devious notion of fucking her in front of Gabrielle.

I thought better of it when I realized that after the way I'd treated her earlier, it would probably be grounds for her quitting, and that's the last thing I wanted. But once I saw the lights on in Gabrielle's bedroom and could see straight into her room, I knew that was enough.

Was I trying to make Gabrielle jealous? Yes.

Did it work? Most likely no. The girl acts like she hates me even more than she did before, but that could be for many reasons, including the fact that I'm lounging in bed half-naked and pestering her while she cleans my room.

What it did do was ensure that when I came inside Aurelie, I was thinking about Gabrielle the entire time.

And I don't think I've come that hard in ages.

"Yes, your mother," I tell her, propping myself up on my elbow, the covers sliding down to my hips and barely covering my cock, which is standing at attention, as it seems to be lately when Gabrielle is around. "You said you were worried about her. That's why you asked to live here to begin with. Remember?"

"Oh," she says, pausing midwipe and then spraying the glass again and resuming. "Yes."

"So is she okay?" Getting information out of her is almost like a hostage situation.

I can see her reflection in the glass, the way she presses her lips together in thought, how she stares down at the servants' quarters. I'm guessing that no matter what she says to me, she doesn't think her mother is okay. "It's too early to tell."

"Do you mind telling me what the problem is?"

She glances at me over her shoulder, her face like stone. She gives a slight shake of her head.

"Okay, fair enough," I tell her. "Though you know you can tell me anything. I'm here for you. I aspire to be one of those cool bosses."

I added that last bit because I knew it would get a rise out of her, and it does. She rolls her eyes and gives me a slight smile before turning back to work, and it feels like sweet victory.

"You know, maybe you ought to have the day off," I tell her, feeling a little bad now for making her work. "It's sunny, it's hot. The weather is absolutely perfect. Go outside and relax with me." I pause. "Or come in here and relax with me."

She shakes her head and resumes cleaning. "I'm quite happy doing this."

"How could you be happy doing this? You're cleaning the rich prick son's bedroom while he's lying in bed, naked, if you must know, and watching you."

"I didn't need to know that."

"Ah, got enough of it last night, did you?"

She gives an exasperated sigh and then turns to face me. "Next time, try closing your blinds."

"Next time, you close your curtains," I tell her. "Besides, it's my house you're a part of. This is a workplace hazard."

"Seeing your dick shouldn't be a workplace hazard."

"And yet it is," I tell her. "Sorry I didn't include that in the job description."

Our eyes lock in a game of mental chess, and I'm starting to think she might enjoy sparring with me, though not as much as I do.

"I disgust you, don't I?" I ask when she doesn't speak.

Her brow raises. "If that's what you're going for, then no. You don't."

"Guess I'll have to try harder."

She gives me nothing in her stare and then turns to look back at the window. "I think I'm done in here."

She starts to walk away, but I call out, "Hey. Come back here."

Her gait halts, and her shoulders lower in defeat. Slowly she turns around.

"What is it?"

"Come here," I repeat.

She walks a few steps forward until she's at the foot of the bed, staring down at me with suspicion. The truth is, I don't know what I want from her, I just don't want to be alone. I'd rather be getting on her nerves if nothing else.

"Give me something," I tell her.

"What?" She crosses her arms with a sigh.

"Tell me something about yourself that I don't know."

"You don't know anything about me, Pascal."

"Then you should have lots of things to tell me. So tell me something. Anything."

"Fine. Birds scare the shit out of me."

I laugh. "Birds? You're scared of birds?"

She shrugs. "I blame Alfred Hitchcock and the pigeons in New York. Are we done?"

I decide that maybe I need to make this a little more businesslike. "Did you look into the names I gave you?"

Her eyes go round.

I press on. "Marine and Olivier. Did you look into them?"

She doesn't seem too impressed. She walks around the side of the bed, right up to me. She leans in close, the smell of her flooding my senses as she puts her lips at my ear. Heat generates from her skin to mine, and the hairs on my neck stand on end.

"What happened to your paranoia?" she whispers, and my eyes roll back in my head, my cock stiffening to the point of strain. Her face lingers beside mine for a hot and heady moment before she starts to pull back, and instinctively I reach up and slip my hand behind her neck, holding her in place, our faces just inches from each other.

I stare at her lips, then her perfect nose, then those eyes that are searching mine with curiosity. Not an ounce of fear. She doesn't even try to pull away.

Her gaze flicks to my mouth, and the blood running through my veins pumps hot and wild, my breath starting to catch in my throat.

I pull her down an inch, that inch that closes up so much space, feeling like I'm about to be overtaken by something very powerful and hungry and unstoppable.

"If you kiss me, I'm quitting," she says softly.

My eyes flick up to hers, and she's raising her brow in challenge.

Shit.

I can't afford to take that risk.

"You're a little tease, you know that?"

Her expression cools. "I'm sure everyone who doesn't throw themselves at your feet would be considered a tease to you." She leans in again to my ear. "If you want to talk about business," she whispers, and I swear to God I'm going to explode because her voice just became this throaty, sexy thing, "then come find me later. But I know your family and—"

A knock at the door makes us both jump, and she immediately straightens up just as the door to my bedroom opens.

My father strolls in with a newspaper in his hand and stops as soon as he sees us.

"Am I interrupting something?" he asks, his voice flinty as he looks between the two of us.

"Not at all," I tell him, sitting up and pulling the covers up as well, hoping they hide my erection, because this would look like something completely different otherwise.

I exchange a worried glance with Gabrielle, and she immediately puts her head down and quickly walks toward the door, giving my father a curt, "Sir," as she passes him but avoids looking at him.

"Gabrielle, stay," he says and reaches out and grabs her by the arm. He does this with such force and familiarity that it rattles something inside me.

Gabrielle glares at him combatively and pulls back as she stops, but my father doesn't let go of her arm. Instead, he smiles at her. It's wolfish. It's the smile you never want to see from him.

"Father," I say loudly, and my father looks at me in surprise. Then he drops Gabrielle's arm.

"There's no need for her to run off," he says to me and then smiles at her again. "I would prefer it if she stayed."

"I have work to do," she says stiffly, looking at the wall.

"Work?" He brings his gaze to me. "You're working her too hard, Pascal. It's her first week, and you're only giving her Sundays off." He twists toward her further and puts his hand on her shoulder. She eyes it, flinching a little. "Stay here with me, I insist. Perhaps I can take you for a drive today if your slave master will let you have the time off. Otherwise, we'll do it tomorrow."

Now I'm seeing pure fear in Gabrielle's eyes, fear I don't want her to feel. "Father," I say again, my voice firmer. "Let her go so she can work."

He eyes me like I've just ruined something spectacular for him, and the smile he gives me is as false as his teeth. "Do I get no say here? She is working in my house. In fact, I don't recall you even discussing her hire with me. Rather impetuous of you."

"Gabrielle," I say to her, ignoring him. "If you could prepare the files for Monday's meeting, that would be great."

I've never discussed any files with her before, but she nods gratefully and then exits the room, her feet moving fast.

"Monday's meeting?" my father asks, staring at the door for a moment and then looking back at me. "Which meeting is that?"

"The weekly meeting with the heads of the department," I tell him. I do have that meeting every Monday, and he should know that.

"Perhaps you're working yourself too hard too," he says, striding over to me, fiddling with the newspaper. He's dressed in his weekend outfit, which is always the same, a blue dress shirt and cream-colored pants.

"Someone has to do it," I say.

"Yes. Someone has to. I know what you're getting at, Pascal; you don't think I've worked enough. Perhaps I never did. There's a reason Luddie was around for as long as he was. But of course, even though he did it all, he did it all wrong. You have to learn, son, to delegate. Let someone else run the company. We're the CEOs; we're not expected to work. We pay other people to do that so we can sit back and drink and fuck whatever we want. That's the life, you know."

My nose twitches. It never sounds good when he says it.

"Now, was I interrupting something here? Because the two of you seemed awfully, well, close." He sits on the side of the bed, and I know that's a power dynamic thing, and I hate it. I'm lying down, naked, so I'm vulnerable and stuck, while he's lording over me.

"We were talking," I tell him, wondering if he saw my hand behind her neck, but I think we had broken apart by the time he came in.

"What about?" he asks, tapping the edge of the rolled-up newspaper against his thigh.

"Her maid duties. Is that all?"

The corner of his mouth twists into a smirk. "You're awfully defensive about her, Pascal. Don't go down this path."

"And what path is that?"

"Fucking the help," he says simply. "I know you've done it before."

He's not wrong. I slept with Charlotte in the beginning, before I realized she was overtly needy and couldn't separate us from her job (not that there ever was an us), and I did with another maid in the past. I can't help it. They throw themselves at me, and there are some things in life I just can't say no to.

"That's not what's going on," I tell him.

Of course, I wouldn't mind if that were the case.

"Then what is going on?"

I throw my hands up. "I don't know. Nothing. She's new. My life is fucking crazy right now. There's a lot to discuss."

He watches me carefully and then nods. "That I understand. But I may want to borrow her sometimes, just so you know."

His comment makes me uneasy, as does the glint in his eye. "Borrow her?"

"Yes. Sometimes Jolie is busy doing stuff for your mother."

No. I don't like this at all. I can't even explain why, but I don't. "Gabrielle is *mine*. I pay her salary from *my* pocket."

"And I pay your salary. So therefore . . ." He frowns at me and then lets out a sour laugh. "You should see your face right now, son. All red, all flustered. That's so rare to see. I rather like it, seeing something bother you for once. However, I don't like that it's happening on her behalf. You don't have history with her. I do."

"What history do you have?"

"I've always been rather fond of her," he says. "You know that. So I like to think of her as mine. Like a pet of sorts. Naturally, when your mother called me while I was away and told me that not only was she back in Paris but she'd be working for you, well, I wasn't very happy about that. I'm still not." He looks down at the newspaper and twists it around and around, like he's wringing someone's neck. "I just want you to remember that. Who runs the show here. I've raised you so well, almost too well, to the point where you think you're in charge of things when you're not. You don't have a say, son. You never will. Not as long as I'm alive."

He gets up and looms over me. I stare at him with hard eyes. Hatred spikes through my veins, something I've been trying not to feel toward him, something I've let lie beneath the surface like a dormant volcano.

"Now, I'm done being polite. If I require the use of Gabrielle, for whatever the reason, I'm going to take her. Do you understand?"

My jaw is locked so tight, I can't even talk.

"Pascal," my father says in a soft voice, mockingly. "You really must learn to share. What's yours is always definitely mine. That's never going to change." He gives me a smug smile. "Now, do we have any other business to discuss? I'm heading to the city for the day."

With my father gone all last week, I had been meaning to have a talk with him right away about the letters. I wasn't going to mention them outright, but I was going to ask if he had any enemies he could think of or if he thought maybe the things he did would ever come back to haunt him one day.

All these questions were another way of finding out whether the letters are for him or for me.

But now, after this, I simply don't care. If the letters are for me, I'll figure it out. If they're for my father, then let whoever the hell is sending them come for him.

Let them confront him with the terrible things he's done.

Let them destroy him.

I'll simply stand to the side and watch.

As if he can hear my thoughts, his gaze sharpens like a knife.

"More than that," he goes on, "you must learn to keep your guard up. This is very unlike you."

"What are you talking about now?" I ask, exasperated. He's talking in circles around me at this point.

"Do you trust her?"

I stare at him. "Trust her? Gabrielle?"

*I trust her more than I trust you.*

"Yes."

"I don't know. I guess so—she signed an NDA."

"Good," he says. "But sometimes that doesn't mean anything. Don't you find it odd that she's back?"

"Why should it be odd?" I'm not sure if I should say anything to him about Gabrielle being worried about her mother. In fact, I probably shouldn't. I'm not giving him any more information, because all he does is turn it around on people. And what if what Gabrielle is worried about involves my father and her mother together?

"You were what, twenty-three when she left? You were probably busy with work and your divorce; you wouldn't have been paying much attention. But she was eighteen, and she was a very troubled young girl. She was scared of everyone, especially men. I fear that something traumatic may have happened to her, but unfortunately she wouldn't let anyone help her."

All of this makes complete sense. "So why shouldn't I trust her?"

He shrugs. "I have no idea. She seems a lot better now. I would keep an eye on her, if I were you. Better yet, I'll keep an eye on her for you." He turns and heads out of my room, pausing in the doorway. "You're welcome."

# CHAPTER SEVEN

## GABRIELLE

Try as I might, I can't escape Sunday morning. It shows up with the rising sun, promising me a day of running and dodging, doing what I can to avoid Gautier.

I spend most of it lying in my bed with the door locked and the curtains closed, reading an old, dog-eared copy of *The Jungle Book* that was on my shelf, until my mother insists I join her for lunch on the terrace.

"You're too thin," she says to me as I set out of the back doors and shield my eyes from the blazing sun. To my relief, the table settings are for two, and there's a simple caprese salad and bread on the table, just enough for both of us. The backyard is teeming with flowers and birdsong and the buzz of insects, but none of the Dumonts is in sight.

"I am not too thin," I tell her. In NYC I got into the American mentality of working out. I did it a lot, boot camps and self-defense and the like, but I've also put on a few extra pounds. The weight—and bigger ass and boobs—doesn't bother me as long as I feel strong.

"I guess I'm just not used to seeing you as a woman," she says, dishing salad onto my plate. When I was younger, I was more on the pudgy side, a rarity in France. "You've changed so much."

Have I? I thought I became a different person when I moved, but I never put any of this behind me. Coming back here just proves it. I'm back to feeling lost and hopeless and scared. In some ways, it's like I never left at all.

*Except this time you have a plan,* I remind myself. *All you need is time and patience.*

Too bad it feels like I'm running out of both.

We eat lunch under the midday sun. My mother seems completely at ease, but I'm shouldering the feeling that a net is going to drop from above at any moment. I never saw Gautier again after he found me in Pascal's room yesterday. I did everything I could to make sure of that.

But he's mentioned twice now about wanting to take me for a drive today, and I refuse to get in any car with him alone. I'm just not sure how long I'll be able to avoid him or what I'll say.

"Where is everyone?" I ask my mother as I finish up the last bit of burrata cheese, olive oil dripping off it and onto the plate.

"Mrs. Dumont is out for Sunday brunch. Mr. Dumont is somewhere in the house. Maybe in his study. He was looking for you earlier, but you were sleeping." She gives me an annoyed look.

Fuck.

"And there's Pascal right now," my mother says, and I follow her gaze to the side of the house where his private entrance is. He's just opening the door, about to step inside.

"Excuse me," I tell her, and I bolt, dropping the fork in a clatter and running across the lawn in my bare feet until I reach him.

"Pascal," I call out quietly as he's about to close the door.

He pauses and peers around at me while I stop in front of him.

He's wearing aviator sunglasses that make him look like a model, though I rather prefer it when I can see his eyes instead of my own reflection. I feel I can read him so much better.

"I was wondering if I'd see you at all today," he says, leaning against the door with his arm propped up, all casual-like. "You enjoying your day off? You look relaxed."

I can't see his eyes, but I can definitely feel them as they coast up and down my body, causing heat to coil in my stomach. I'm wearing cutoff jean shorts and a demure tank top, something I threw on when I thought it would just be for lunch with my mother.

"I have something I'd like to discuss with you," I tell him, even though I didn't give it much thought, and the words are just tumbling out of my mouth.

He waves his hand at the door.

I shake my head. "I don't feel like having a conversation in your bathroom again."

He stills at that, and I know he's probably feeling bad about what happened.

"Where would you like to talk, then?" he asks, looking around.

"We could go for a drive," I tell him. He frowns, looking put out. I fumble on. "I know you just were out somewhere, but . . ."

*But please take me far away from this house.*

"My father said something about taking you for a ride," he says stiffly. "Is that not happening?"

I shake my head, giving him a tight smile.

He keeps frowning, and I know he's studying my face, chewing slightly on his bottom lip. "Okay. Sure. Wherever you want to go." He glances at my bare feet. "How about you grab some shoes."

How do I say the next thing without sounding pathetic? *Come with me, please? I don't want to go back to the house alone?*

But I don't say anything, because I can't tip him off that anything ever happened between his father and me. If he knew, he'd only question why I'm here.

I'm surprised Gautier isn't questioning me on that, either, but I guess that's what this Sunday drive was supposed to be. I have a feeling if he takes me away in his car like he wants, I might not come back.

So I just nod and turn around, running back over the lawn toward my mother, who is still drinking her mineral water outside. So far so good.

"What was that about?" she asks as I run inside. I grab some paper, an envelope, and a few euros I had kept between the pages of *The Jungle Book*, folding them over and slipping them in my bra; then I grab a pair of slides by the door, quickly slipping them on my feet, not wanting to spend an extra second in here in case Gautier shows up.

"I'm going out with Pascal," I tell her when I run back out. When she looks disapproving, I add, "We're talking business."

"Aren't you supposed to go with Mr. Dumont?" she asks. "He told me this morning that was your plan."

Well, it's better than ever that I thought of a new one.

"Duty calls," I tell her and blow her a kiss before running back across the lawn to Pascal, who is still waiting by his door.

I made it.

His glasses are pushed up on his head now, his dark hair flopping to the sides, and I can see his striking eyes as they take me in, his smile amused.

"What?" I ask.

"I don't know," he muses thoughtfully, still looking me up and down, and now I can *really* feel the heat in his gaze. "It's kind of nice seeing you like this. You looked so free and happy running toward me, I must have let it go to my head for a second."

"Well, don't," I tell him, but I can't help but smile back at him. "Your head would fall off."

He doesn't need to know that I was literally running away from something.

I follow him to his Audi, noticing that he's in his weekend clothes as well. Not exactly relaxed—just dark jeans and a black dress shirt—but at least it's not a damn suit. It also shows off his ass in a way that his suit jackets never let happen.

*Stop staring at his ass,* I tell myself, but then I decide, *why the hell not?* He's looking at my ass all the time. I actually like looking at him, just not when he can see me.

He's almost at the car when he stops suddenly, almost causing me to collide with his back.

"Why do I have the feeling you were staring at my ass?" he muses, turning around and taking a step toward me, staring down at me with a sort of lazy curiosity. Gosh, his eyes are pretty in the sunlight and on a Sunday. Must be a different Pascal than I'm used to.

"I would never be so disrespectful," I tell him, straight-faced.

His arched brows raise. "I wouldn't mind if you were."

"Staring at your ass or being disrespectful?"

He runs his hand along his strong chin in mock contemplation. "Both."

"Where are you going?" Gautier's voice bellows across the driveway, and my stomach sinks in response.

I look over my shoulder to see him stepping out of the house, walking toward us.

I glance up at Pascal, and he stares down at me, and there's something in his eyes that warns me, like he can read the fear inside me, like he'll handle it.

"I'm taking her to Paris," Pascal says casually, putting his hands in his pockets and striding toward his father with a casual ease that I know is a front.

Gautier stops and waves his arm at me. "Well, you're going to have to cancel. I told Gabrielle I needed to talk to her."

"You can come along," Pascal says, and even though it's a horrible idea, it at least means I won't be alone with him. "You can talk to her all you want."

"I wanted to talk to her in private," Gautier says, and the icy quality to his voice tells me that he does not want to elaborate.

Pascal glances at me. I give him nothing; I just hope he stays stubborn.

"Whatever you have to say to her, you can say in front of me," Pascal says, crossing his arms in a wide stance.

I was afraid to make eye contact with Gautier before, but now that Pascal is effectively between us and he's not backing down, I look him dead in the eye. Lift my chin, raise my brow, daring him. If he wants to take me, he's going to have to do it physically and with my mother and his wife home. That won't go over very well.

I don't even know if Pascal is being protective of me, or if he's just trying to rebel against his father, like he forgot to do it in his teenage years, but either way, I'm grateful.

"Fine," Gautier says, breaking away from my stare. "It's not important anyway. It would probably go over her head."

He gives me one last sharp look, a look that makes my blood pressure rise, and then he heads back to the house, shaking his head.

Pascal watches him until he disappears and then turns to face me.

"I think you and I definitely need to talk," he says carefully.

I just press my lips together and nod, my heart rate slowing.

I get in the passenger side as he gets in the driver's seat, and I'm barely buckled in before he's peeling out of the driveway and screaming past the trees down to the main road.

"Jesus," I swear as he whips the car around onto the country road, causing me to brace myself on the dashboard before he guns it from zero to sixty in about a second.

He's laughing as he does this, gleeful, his tongue sticking out like a crazy person. The glasses are slipping back down over his eyes, and he's rolling down the windows so the wind is blowing in and messing up both our hair.

"I take it that driving is your stress relief," I say, transferring my grip to the handle above the door.

"I'm probably the only person who enjoys their commute," he says. "Everyone wants to live in Paris and take the métro, but why would I want to cram my body among countless others and breathe in the stink and sweat when I could be doing this?"

He guns it again for emphasis, and I let out a little squeal, followed by laughter. I can't remember the last time I felt a thrill like this. Maybe never.

"You have a driver too," I remind him.

"Exactly. But I only use him when I'm drinking. It's not worth getting caught over, not for me."

"Hmm," I say, gazing at him. "I thought you'd flourish on all scandals."

"No, not all of them," he says, and at that his voice drops, and his expression becomes grim. "Especially a scandal that implicated my family in anything they couldn't run from." He licks his lips and shoots me a quick glance. "Or at least a scandal that implicated me in something I couldn't run from. Especially if it's something that I didn't do."

"You're talking about Ludovic's murder," I say. "I know you didn't do it."

His smile disappears as quickly as it appeared. "But someone out there might think that." He palms the steering wheel, switching his focus back to the narrow two-lane road that skirts along farms and clusters of oak trees. "Did you mean it when you said you wanted to talk business, or did you just want to get away from my father?"

"The first thing."

His brows knit together, and I know his eyes under his glasses are picking me apart for the truth. "You promise me?"

"Promise you what?" My throat feels parched at the way the conversation is going. I need it to go in the opposite direction, far away.

"My father seems to think he owns you."

I manage to swallow, but it's still like my mouth is packed with sawdust. "What makes you say that?"

"Nothing," he says. He bites his lip for a moment, then admits, "He said so."

"What? When?"

"After you left the room yesterday. He thought we were . . . a little too close for his comfort."

"Why should that matter to him?"

"Well, I'm glad to hear you say that, because it shouldn't matter to anyone."

I stare at him to go on. That was not at all what I meant.

"But it got him started," he continues. "He seems to think he owns you because what's mine is actually his."

*Your father is a fucking monster.* The words dance on my lips, and I have to bite down to keep them back.

"I'm not surprised, considering how you all operate."

"But . . . he really means it. He said you had history."

I give him a hard look. "In what way?"

He grimaces, looking uncomfortable, which is pretty rare for him. "I don't really know. He said you were a troubled child. Unseated by some deep trauma that happened to you but you wouldn't talk about."

A sour laugh escapes my lips. I can't help it. Oh, that is fucking rich. Of course he would spin it that way.

"What else did he tell you?" I ask once I've composed myself. I'm waiting to hear about the corkscrew stabbing.

"That's it . . . Is there something more?"

I shake my head. "No."

"Are you sure?"

I tilt my head as I stare at him. "Why does this matter to you?"

"Because I don't share."

My brows shoot up. Oh, of course he doesn't.

And yet, for reasons I can't explain, those words do something to me. They give me the same kind of thrill in my core as the reckless driving did.

"Because you're mine," he adds.

"I'm your employee," I point out.

"And you're mine. Whether you like it or not, you chose to work for me. You chose me, Gabrielle. You didn't have to."

"I didn't have a choice."

"We always have a choice. We lie to ourselves all the time and tell us that it's fate or it's destiny or it's in our blood. That who we are is predetermined by someone else. But that's not true. It's all a lie. We *always* have a choice. And you chose me."

I turn away and put my attention on the road. I don't like the way he's laid it out for me, though it seems he's the one who should be following his own advice. "I work for you, Pascal. Nothing else."

The lesser of two evils.

He just might be a lot less than I bargained for.

Regardless, I have to keep this a good relationship. I have to keep Pascal on my side because he's the only ally I have in that house. So if he wants to claim me as his, then fine. And I'm fucking relieved that he doesn't *share*.

"So what was the business, then?" he asks after a few minutes have rolled past. We've left the country roads behind and now are zipping along the highway heading into Paris, the smog getting thicker the closer we get. "What did you find out about the envelopes?"

I'm grateful to change the subject even though it feels a bit like walking on thin ice.

"Well, first I looked into the stamp and postmark," I tell him. "Both postmarks were from Paris, in the eleventh arrondissement."

That's a lie, though. The first postmark was from Paris. The second postmark was from Saint-Nom-la-Bretèche, the nearest town to the Dumont chateau.

"That doesn't tell us much," he says.

"No, it doesn't," I tell him. "And the ink and the paper are all pretty standard, and the stamps are of the new circulation. Which means if you really want to investigate this, you need to tell me why you think your ex-wife or cousin would be trying to blackmail you. I remember Olivier," I add. "He's a nice guy. Different side of the family, I suppose. I really don't see him doing that, but you did tell me he's your enemy, so let's start with him. What happened?"

"I blackmailed him," he says. He says it so simply, like he just told me what he had for breakfast.

"You blackmailed your cousin? Why? When?"

He stares straight ahead for a moment, then changes lanes to speed ahead of someone. "I was young. I was . . . I don't know. I followed orders, but I thought they came from me." He frowns. "I don't know if that makes any sense."

"What orders?"

"My father had an idea. A long con, if you know the term."

Do I ever.

He clears his throat and kneads the steering wheel lightly as he overtakes the vehicle and then cuts in front. "Do you mind if I smoke?" he asks.

I shake my head and wait patiently as he lights up a cigarette, putting the window back down halfway. The air whips the smoke out of the car as he puffs back. I find myself focusing on his lips for a moment until I remember what I'm waiting for.

"My father wanted to make sure that we ended up with the majority of the company," he says, smoke falling out of his mouth. "We had shares. My cousins, Renaud, Seraphine, and Olivier, had theirs. Olivier had the most. At the time, I was married to Marine, and my father thought it would work if we could get Marine to seduce Olivier."

I blink a few times, not sure I'm hearing this right. "You got your wife to sleep with your cousin?"

He nods. "It was easier than we thought. Goes to show, huh? Olivier gave in to her, and they had an affair, and then my father caught them. It was a setup. All Olivier ever cared about was saving face and trying to live up to his father's expectations, so we knew that he would never reveal what really happened. The shame it would bring him with his father. In some ways, I wish his father had known how imperfect his son really was. Besides, he didn't want to work for the Dumont brand anyway. Back then he already had plans to be a hotelier." He ashes out the window. "So we blackmailed him for the shares of the company. And it worked."

"And Olivier knows?"

"Oh yes, he knows." He shrugs. "That's how we got control after Ludovic died. That's why he fled with his tail between his legs to California."

I'm trying hard not to be so appalled by him, but I am.

"You're awful," I manage to say.

He glances at me and raises his glasses. His eyes are curious, but I'm not sure I see any remorse in them. "I never said I wasn't," he says, his tone low. "If you believe I have an ounce of good in me, that's on you."

"You don't seem to even care."

"Add that to your list of adjectives."

"Is that the worst thing you've ever done?"

*Please say yes. Please don't tell me you're exactly like your father.*

"Yes," he says after a beat. "I've broken up a few marriages. I've lied, cheated, stolen. I've committed fraud and embezzlement. I once hit a parked car, and I kept driving." He gives me a long, steady look, long enough to make me wish he were looking at the road. "But I've never taken candy from a baby, and I've never killed anyone."

"Were you an accessory?"

"Not knowingly."

I'm not sure I believe that. I'm not sure he believes it either. "So what about Marine, then? You said she was a suspect too."

He gives me a sheepish look. "You're not going to like this part either. After she had her affair with Olivier, I divorced her, citing her affair as cheating and proof that she didn't deserve a dime. She didn't get anything from the settlement."

"Jesus Christ," I swear.

"Watch your language, it's a Sunday," he chides.

"How could you do such a thing? To your wife, to your cousin?"

"Because I'm a Dumont," he says simply. "And I was raised to believe that it mattered more than anything else in the world. Money, power, greed. A legacy. All those things belonged to me; all those things were owed to me. And if I didn't succeed, I wasn't worthy of my name."

"Well, I'll tell you what I associate the name Dumont with," I tell him.

"You don't need to. I know. But if I'm not a Dumont, who am I?"

"You're you. You're Pascal. Your name doesn't dictate what you do or don't do. Your will does."

"And what does your will dictate, my little sprite?" he asks me, his eyes piercing me to the core. "What do you stand for? If money, power, greed don't mean anything to you, what does?"

"Justice," I blurt out. I don't even have to think.

*Revenge.*

Shit. Maybe I'm not much better than he is.

"Is that all?"

*Love.*

*Freedom.*

*A home.*

*Someone who has my back.*

*Security.*

*Safety.*

*And love again.*

"That's all," I confirm.

I can tell Pascal doesn't believe me, but he doesn't press any more. Perhaps because I'll just turn it around on him, and he's tired of talking.

Honestly, I'm surprised he was so forthcoming. He told me his deep, dark secrets, the worst of the festering bunch, like I was a long-lost friend and trusted confidante. This had nothing to do with the NDA; this was just him showing himself to me, every horribly gruesome bit.

He trusts me.

And now it's starting to bother me.

Because I don't want to hurt him.

*You're getting attached to him,* I remind myself. *Nearly one week working for him and it's already happening. You need to keep your head clear.*

Focus on Gautier.

Besides, the only reason at all I even feel this way is because Pascal is the person I am closest to in the house, and that doesn't mean a thing, not with him, not in *that* house.

We drive in silence for the rest of the ride into Paris. I have no idea where Pascal is taking me, and I don't particularly care until he parks around the corner from the Rodin Museum.

"Rodin?" I ask as I get out of the car. The air is both smoggy and sweet, the sun beating down on us from above and making waves on the pavement. Tourists are everywhere, and though they used to annoy me when I was young—purely because I was jealous that they were on a vacation, something I had never known—now I'm caught up in their infectious energy.

"Tell me you've been," he says with a charming smile, tucking his sunglasses into his shirt pocket.

I shake my head. "I don't think you understand how I grew up."

"That's because you don't ever talk about yourself," he says and holds out his arm for me. "Take it. Pretend I'm not a monster while we look at the pretty art."

I hesitate and then walk over to him and hook my arm around his.

He leads me into the museum, this sprawling grand hotel from the 1700s that now houses much of Auguste Rodin's art. It's light and airy, with large windows and marble floors and even with all the tourists, it still feels special, like we've stepped back in time to some hushed, soft place.

"What do you think?" he asks, peering down at me.

"It's gorgeous," I tell him truthfully. "I would have loved to come here as a child."

"You didn't at least come with school?"

"Not here. We went to the Louvre, I remember that day very well. But other than that and some others, I was pretty much kept at home." I give him a quick smile, wishing I could say more, but I don't particularly want to talk about my shitty childhood here.

"Just wait until you see my favorite part," he says. He leads me through the halls, past art that I recognize, a large marble statue called *The Kiss*, in which a man and a woman are in a very passionate embrace. I've seen it in books before, but in person it's breathtaking and impressive. Rodin's skill was supernatural.

"You can feel the chemistry coming off them, can't you?" Pascal says thoughtfully as he studies the statue. "As if they're flesh and bone, not marble. The strain of their muscles, the deep need and desire. It's palpable."

I look at him agape.

He gives me his crooked smile. "This surprises you."

"Didn't peg you for a deep art guy."

"I know you didn't. But I can be all those things that I am and still be this person too."

He has a point. I keep trying to put him in a box, good or bad, but he defies that.

"Are you even looking for redemption?" I ask him as he leads me outside and into the back gardens.

He lets his hand slide down my arm until he's holding my hand, taking me by surprise. "I don't know what redemption looks like. Maybe I'll know it when I see it."

I stare at our intertwined hands like it's an apparition. "Well, it isn't holding my hand, I can tell you that much."

He gives me a quick, slightly melancholy smile. "I know."

Then he lets go of my hand and walks off.

I follow. I hate to admit it, but I think I preferred it when he was holding my hand. It was something so harmless and comforting and gratifying all at once. A feeling completely foreign to me.

I catch up as he takes me past the long rectangular pond, past more statues, until we're squeezing through hedges at the back of the property. The land here has got to be at least a few acres, and even as far back as we are, there are still wondrous statues scattered about.

Fewer people, though. In fact, it's just the two of us in this little glen where there are a couple of benches and tables.

We sit beside each other on a bench, and he gestures to one of the empty tables. "Sometimes I come here when I need a break from the office. It's worth the drive over the river. I sit here, and usually there are a few older gentlemen playing chess and this woman reading and knitting at the same time. It's nice to just . . . forget for a moment. About everything." He nudges my arm with his elbow. "So when are you going to tell me all about your childhood? About your life? I opened up to you earlier, it's only fair. And you do believe in justice, don't you?"

"I will. I promise." I swallow and nod. I can tell him about growing up here in Paris, living a very different life from the one he lived. I can tell him some things about New York. I can tell him about boyfriends and school.

But I can't tell him everything.

If he knew what happened, how I really felt about his father, Pascal would see through me, see through this whole thing. He's smart enough to figure out the truth right away.

The truth of why I really came back.

Not just for my mother.

I came back to kill his father.

# CHAPTER EIGHT

## PASCAL

I can't remember the last time I was nervous (oh yes, it was when Blaise had a gun to my head during a rather intense workplace negotiation), but I'm feeling it as I dial Olivier's phone number.

*Get over yourself, you prick,* I scold myself.

I'm not even sure if it's still his number. He's been in California for the last year with his fiancée, Sadie; he probably has an American number now. My mother and father haven't kept tabs on him, or at least, my father hasn't talked about it. I have no doubt he knows exactly where Olivier is at any given moment, but if I were to ask for his information, my father would wonder why, and I don't want to get into it.

I also know that it ended on very bad terms between us, which isn't a surprise at all and was entirely my doing. I did threaten his girlfriend and her mother. I also threatened him. Some stalking was involved. I may have recorded them having sex as a way of extortion. And then there were all the years of blackmailing before then.

Suffice to say, I'm expecting Olivier to hang up on me.

The phone rings and rings, and I'm starting to think that either he's not around, or maybe he's sleeping, or even his number did change. It's

Tuesday evening here; I haven't a clue off the top of my head what time it is in California.

"Hello?" a woman's voice answers in English, a thick American west coast accent.

"Hello," I say, trying to make my voice warm and my English as fluent as possible. "Is Olivier there?"

There's a pause and then a muffled sound as if she's holding the phone away from her. "Who is this?"

"I need to speak with Olivier," I say and then revert back into old ways. "I promise you it's nothing bad, Sadie. I just have some questions."

A heavy pause. "Pascal?"

"Ah, I'm flattered you remember who I am."

"Fuck you, you piece of shit."

Well, I suppose I deserve that.

"I understand I'm probably not the most popular person right now or any time, but if you could be a dear and hand the phone to Olivier, that would be great."

"I'm going to hang up," she threatens.

"Who are you talking to?" I hear Olivier's voice floating in the background.

Sadie sighs angrily and says to him, "You'll never believe it. It's *Pascal*."

She says my name as if I were the devil himself.

"What?" he asks, and then there's another muffled sound.

"Pascal?" he asks into the phone.

"*Bonjour*, cousin," I tell him, switching to French. "How are you?"

"How am I?" he repeats both in English and in disbelief.

He doesn't take the bait. As far as I know, Sadie doesn't speak French (though maybe she does at this point), and our conversation in French would have been private.

"It's a question," I tell him with a sigh. "You don't have to answer it."

"Why are you calling me?" His voice is on edge. Guess I can't blame him.

"I just have some questions for you, and then I'll leave you alone." Though even this far into our conversation, I'm getting the feeling that Olivier didn't send the letters. He had as much reason to believe that his father's death wasn't an accident as his siblings, but he never pursued it the way Seraphine did.

"What is it?" he asks testily. "I'm rather busy. We're late for lunch."

"Ah, well, I'm glad I didn't wake you."

"You wouldn't have given a shit."

"You're right."

"I'm going to hang up now."

"Wait, wait," I tell him, wishing I knew how to play nice. He is family in the end, even if I've ostracized him and everyone else. "Just give me a second."

I hear an impatient huff of air. "What. Is. It?"

"Have you sent me any letters lately? Or should I say, have you gotten anyone to send me letters?"

"What the fuck are you talking about?"

I take that as a no.

I lick my lips, trying to put this in the right terms. "I think someone's blackmailing me."

There's a pause, and then Olivier bursts into laughter. It seems to go on forever.

"You done?" I ask, not amused.

"I can't believe it," he says, still laughing. "Someone is blackmailing *you*."

Now I hear Sadie screech, "Oh my God!" like some bimbo, and now she's laughing too.

"Yes, so obviously I have to wonder if it's you," I tell him, losing my patience at what a joke this is to them.

"Ah. Really? You can't be seriously thinking it's me? I don't know if you've noticed, Pascal, but I don't give a fuck about you or what you do. I have my own life here, and it has nothing to do with the life I had back there."

"You have to come back to Paris at some point."

"I *have* come back to Paris," he says. "On business. Surprised you weren't tailing me."

"I didn't know." Though I wonder if my father did. "Have you talked to your sister?"

He grows silent for a moment. "I have. I know everything you did, Pascal."

"Me?" I exclaim, squeezing the phone in anger. "I didn't do shit!"

"We both know your father doesn't work alone. You're his little clone."

"His Mini-Me!" Sadie pipes up in the background.

This phone call was a mistake.

"Seraphine is happier now," I tell him. "She got everything she wanted."

"Our father was murdered," Olivier seethes. "And whether you did it or not, you deserve to have whatever is coming to you. If this means blackmail, so be it. I hope this chases you for the rest of your goddamn life."

For once I'm speechless.

"And if you thought you could just phone me and confide in me and treat me like a long-lost friend, you're even more fucked-up than I thought. You have no one, Pascal. Not your brother. Not your cousins. *Everyone* hates you, and you only have yourself to blame. If you want to dig a little deeper, I think you'll find that even your mother and father would sell you out to the highest bidder. You're alone in this world, and it's exactly what you deserve. And the way it will stay. *Au revoir.*"

The line goes dead, and I stare at the phone in my hand for a moment, trying to process what happened. Normally I just shrug it off, let it slide. Any kinds of insults or conflict are brushed away because it's not important, it's just background noise.

But this cuts deeper, far deeper than it should. I don't know if Olivier knew the sword he was wielding today, but it did some damage.

That hurt.

It shouldn't have.

It was nothing new, nothing I hadn't heard before.

It was the truth and nothing else.

But the truth hurts this time around.

I truly do have no one. No one has my back, not a soul would stand by my side.

And I never thought that would be a problem, but now I'm thinking otherwise, a tiny seed of truth that's sprouting in the depths of my brain.

What am I even doing with my life?

I can feel the existential crisis pushing at me from all sides, the downward spiral that wants to open up and swallow me whole.

I think it's been waiting my entire life to take me.

I get up from my desk and head over to the bar in the corner of my office. I haven't been drinking much lately because when I get home, it's usually so late, but it's about half past eight now, and there's no time like the present.

I grab the bottle of Japanese whiskey and am about to sit back down at my desk, but the room is starting to feel stifling.

I peer out the window down at Gabrielle's room. Her curtains are open, and the light is on. I see her profile, sitting in bed cross-legged and bent over a book, her long hair in her face.

I feel a strange pain in my heart.

Olivier was right. I don't have anyone.

But maybe I could have her.

I know she's mine in the loosest sense. She's bound by contract, but she could quit at any minute, taking my secrets with her. She could cut out of this life as quickly as she cut out of it before. It didn't strike me until now that I would miss her if she were gone, that I've grown used to being around her, talking to her.

Looking at her.

I want her. Since the moment her big blue gemstone eyes gazed at me through the doorway in that hotel and she looked somewhere deep inside, seeing a part of me I'm not even aware of, that I'm still not, I've wanted her. In my bed, in my arms, anywhere. I want to not just tell her that she's mine, I want my cock so far deep inside her that she feels it. That she knows it.

That I know it too.

*She's not your redemption,* I remind myself. *There is no redemption for you.*

That may be true.

But if I could even feel it while I'm coming inside her, wouldn't that be worth it?

To just pretend, for a moment, I'm not a monster, that I'm more than my bloodline, that I can do more with myself than I do. That I can be a better man. If she can bring me that, even for a second, I think that might be worth everything.

I finish the rest of the glass of whiskey; then I take the bottle and head out of the room and down the stairs. I leave through my side door and cut across the lawn. I pass right by Gabrielle's window, close enough so that she'll see me, but I don't stop. I keep walking until I hit the gazebo, buried in the back of the yard.

I remember Blaise telling me once about when he was younger and that on his birthday, he and his friend were getting drunk for the first time in the gazebo. Father caught him, knocked him around a few times. While Blaise was telling me that, I know he was wanting me to say something that he could relate to. He wanted me to tell him that it wasn't just him, that our father beat me too. But I didn't say anything at all; I just let Blaise feel all alone, that Father picked on him and only him. That I was better than him. That I was exempt.

The truth is, my father did the same to me. He was frustrated that Blaise wasn't like me, so he took it out on him. When it came to me, however, he was angry that I wasn't like himself, so he took that out on me. I've been smacked around, punched—even kicked, once. It all stopped when I became a teenager, became taller, stronger, bigger than him.

But the shit he did I still carry with me. It's no wonder that Blaise went on to study martial arts. As for me, I just put up a shield, and I've never set it down. I let that shield deflect the things my father did and the horrible things I've done. I don't think I could have survived without it.

"Here's to you, Blaise," I say, spilling some whiskey onto the gazebo floor before I sit down in the corner. "Sorry I couldn't have been a better brother."

"He's not dead, you know."

I look up to see Gabrielle standing at the edge of the gazebo, covered by shadows. Something in my chest tightens in a way I can't explain.

"What are you doing here?" she asks.

I raise the bottle. "Feeling sorry for myself. It's a new thing I'm trying out. Not sure I like it."

"Am I intruding?" She gestures back to her quarters. "I saw you walk past with the bottle, and I figured this can't be good."

"It's better now that you're here," I tell her. I pat the floor next to me. "Here, sit."

She walks into the gazebo and takes a tepid look around. "It's dirty. And you're still wearing a suit."

"I'm not sure if you've noticed, but I have an endless supply of suits. Now, sit. As your boss, that's an order."

"Technically I'm off duty." She puts her hips to the side in a ta-da moment. "See, no uniform."

"What are you wearing?" I peer at her, trying to see through the shadows. I can't remember what I saw when I looked through her window. "If you don't spend your leisure time lounging around in a braless T-shirt and booty shorts, I'm going to be very, *very* disappointed."

"Sorry to disappoint you," she says and then sits next to me, leaning back against the gazebo wall. She's in leggings and a T-shirt, which somehow aren't that disappointing. Then she holds her hand out for the bottle.

I pass it to her. "Rough day?"

"Yeah," she says, having a sip straight from the bottle. She doesn't even wince. "My boss likes to work me really hard."

My cock twitches, heat building slowly. "Tell me more about how hard he works you."

She gives me a wry sidelong glance and hands me back the bottle. "Why, so you can have fodder to jack off to tonight?"

I can't help but grin. Just the fact that she said that gives me a full-on erection. "I don't need any help in that. Unless you wanted to help me. I could always use an extra hand."

She stares at me for a moment, and I can't quite read her eyes with the way the shadows are falling on them. I swear to God I see something like lust glinting in them, but I always see what I want to see.

Then, to my complete surprise, she leans over and places her hand between my legs on my cock that's tenting up in my pants. She gives it a firm squeeze, which elicits a low, unguarded moan from my mouth.

"Are you always this hard when you're around me?" she asks, leaning in closer, her tone more curious than anything else.

I'm so taken aback, I don't know what to say. I can only press my cock up into the palm of her hand, letting heat wash over me like a fevered man.

"I take that as a yes," she says.

Then she removes her hand and resumes leaning against the wall.

"What the fuck was that?" I ask, bewildered and breathless.

*It's a trap. It's got to be a trap.*

"Should I not have done that?" she asks. Her tone is mock innocence. I have no idea what's going on with her.

I swallow, the pleasure in my cock now turning to pain without her to relieve me. "You can do that all you want, but—"

"I was just curious," she says mildly. "I wanted to see if you had a reason to have the ego that you do."

"And?" I prompt.

She shrugs.

Wow. Talk about automatic deflation.

"You sure know how to talk up a man."

"You're a man who needs to be taken down a few pegs."

"Well, believe me, I have been," I tell her, taking a larger gulp of whiskey this time. I shake the bottle at her. "Why do you think I'm drinking in the gazebo?"

"You called Olivier?" she asks.

"I did," I tell her as I hand her the bottle and bring out a pack of cigarettes. I'm really trying to cut down to just a few a day. In France, that's pretty much the same as quitting.

I light it and then inhale, hoping the cigarette takes the weight off my shoulders.

"And so . . . ?" she prods.

I blow the smoke away from her. "Well, nothing. He didn't send them. I never thought it was him anyway. That's not his style. He's too *good* for that."

"So then that leaves Marine."

"She does seem to have every reason to do this. We also haven't talked in many years. Last I heard, she married a rich man and has a few kids. She has the means for revenge, but I'm not sure if money is something she needs."

"The letters never mentioned money. They also never mentioned you. So, since your list of enemies is accounted for, I think we should concentrate on your father. The likelihood of the threats being for him is high."

"Too high. Where do you begin?"

"Figure out who would want him dead."

"Whoa," I tell her, coughing. "Dead? Who said they wanted him dead? So far it's just idle threats."

She shrugs, seeming uneasy. "I don't take idle threats lightly, and neither should you."

"But extortion and murder are very different things. Why would anyone want my father dead?"

"Maybe he hurt them," she says quietly, looking away. Then she glances at me. "You said that he was going to kill your cousin and has a hit man working for him. You can't pretend that she was the first person he had that done to. Nor can you pretend that your uncle was the first person he murdered. If he were able to do that to his own brother, he'd be able to do it to anyone. And if that's the case, perhaps someone wants revenge for something he did. It could be someone who was close to Ludovic, someone we're missing, or it could be someone else from years ago. The fact is, your father has done things, horrible things, and now someone is going to make him pay."

I run my hand over my face, trying to ease the tension that's building inside me.

My father really is this horrible.

I've been complicit this whole time.

His lackey. His minion.

All his.

I'm nothing of mine.

"Anyway," Gabrielle says, getting to her feet. "I'll let you think about it."

"Where are you going?" I reach out for her, but she steps back out of the way. "You're just going to grab my crotch, drink my whiskey, and leave?"

Even with shadows on her face, I know she's smiling. "You did call me a tease, didn't you? Good night, Pascal Dumont."

"Good night," I call after her, my voice disappearing in the darkness.

I stare at the bottle in my hands for a moment before I have another drink. I wish she'd stayed out here longer with me. I wish I'd found the balls to kiss her earlier when she was touching me, touching me in ways I'd only dreamed of. I wish a lot of things. It's very unlike me to be caught off guard, and it's even more unlike me to hesitate in taking what I want.

But the only way out of this wishing and wanting is at the bottom of the bottle.

I drink most of it sitting alone in the dark in that gazebo, trying so damn hard to drown the turmoil inside me. There's a shift happening, deep within whatever blackened soul I have, and I don't know what the shift means.

I just know that it scares me.

And I *hate* to be scared.

When I'm good and drunk, I stumble back across the lawn and up to my room, where I collapse onto my bed, swept away into the din.

I dream about Gabrielle.

In my dreams, we are back in the gazebo.

This time she's completely naked, and though it's dark, she shines bright, like diamonds are lighting her from within.

She unzips my pants, takes my cock out, stiffer and harder than it's ever been, like she's grasping hot steel in her hands. Her legs spread as she straddles me and slowly lowers herself until it feels like my world is blown right open, until whatever pixie dust is lighting her up is taking over me.

I run my hands up the soft skin of her sides, staring at her bright and shining, lost in her beauty, in her power, the power I feel running through my veins like I've been poured with radioactive dye.

It feels like I have redemption in my hands, slowly grinding herself on me, squeezing my cock until I can't breathe, until I can't think.

In my dream, she drives my demons out.

◆ ◆ ◆

Two days later, I'm standing bleary-eyed in the kitchen, getting my morning coffee when I feel a poke in my side.

I flinch and look to see Gabrielle has sidled up next to me, staring at me with something on her mind.

"Good morning," I tell her, surprised. "You're up early. And stealthy."

She's not even in her maid uniform yet; instead she's wearing a loose flannel shirt and black leggings, no doubt some H&M stuff again, but she wears it so well, it could almost be high-end. Maybe it's because she seems completely comfortable in this, and it feels like I'm seeing a magical creature in her element. Doesn't hurt that she doesn't have a lick of makeup on her face, her freckles are popping through, and her platinum hair is long and loose and messy around her shoulders, the faint glow from the sky lighting her up.

She looks so beautiful, it's catching me off guard as much as the fact that she's here at this hour. The sun rose only twenty minutes ago.

"I wanted to give you something," she whispers and then opens my suit jacket, sliding a letter into my inside pocket. I have to fight the impulse to put my hand around her lower back and keep her close to me. Then I have to fight an even greater impulse to not lean down and kiss her. For some reason, it feels like the right thing to do, the only thing to do.

After the dream I had the other night, she's all I can think about.

I'm becoming a man obsessed.

"Aren't you curious?" she says softly.

I can barely move my lips, I'm so fixated on hers. "About what?" My words come out thick, and my cock is getting hard.

"About the letter?" she says. "It was under the pile in the hallway. I went through it last night because no one else did. You're lucky I found it."

"Did you read it?"

"Yeah, I . . ." She trails off and looks up when she hears footsteps coming from upstairs. "I have to go," she says, and then she very quickly, very silently scurries away across the kitchen to the back door and then runs to the servants' house.

Moments later, my father steps into the kitchen and looks around. "Is Jolie here?"

I shrug and take a sip of my coffee. "I haven't seen her."

"Hmph. I thought I heard you talking to someone."

"I often talk to myself. Nothing to be ashamed of." I shrug again, my face giving him nothing. "You're up early. Trying to beat me to the office?"

"I have a meeting in Lyon, have to make the train," he says. "Give me a ride into the city."

I stare at him. No manners at all. A *please* would be nice.

"All right," I tell him. You would have thought we would have made a habit of carpooling from the start, but the one time I suggested it (mind you, this was years ago), he told me that it went against what we stood for. We weren't about saving anything, we were about spending. The excess was what drove us. Besides, the both of us go to and from the office at different hours, and he definitely isn't putting in the hours I am.

Also, there's the fact that these days I can't stand to be around him, even for a little bit.

I also doubt that this is a business meeting for him.

I wonder if he ever thinks he'll get caught. Even though my mother knows he's stepping out, and even though it's expected of men with power and money, if the tabloids got wind of it, it could be pretty embarrassing for us.

Most likely he thinks he's above it. Above the law, as the letters said.

Am I a bad son for now wishing he would get caught?

Probably.

But he raised me that way.

I go to my car, and while I'm sitting there, waiting for my father to join me, I take the envelope out of my jacket pocket. In some ways it feels like a clandestine love letter from Gabrielle, a secret only the two of us keep.

The envelope itself looks the same as always, the same stamp, same markings. Except this time the letter is no longer addressed to The Dumonts.

It says *Gautier Dumont* on the front.

Relief floods through me like a raging river. Not only am I relieved that the letter and the blackmailing aren't addressed to me, but that Gabrielle was quick enough to retrieve it from the mail last night. It's hard to say what would have happened if my father had gotten it. There's a chance he would have confided in me, and there's a bigger chance he wouldn't have, depending on what he's done.

And what hasn't he done?

My gaze goes to the door, making sure my father isn't there, and then I deftly open the envelope, taking out the letter.

*There's no place to hide. Soon the letters will end and I'll be coming for you.*

A little more of a threat this time. Something tangible. Someone will come for him, in what way I don't know.

There's something else different about this one. I'm not sure what. The ink looks the same, but the way it sits on the paper is somehow different, maybe because the paper is different. I flip it over a few times, but I can't glean anything else from it.

It doesn't really matter anyway.

There will be another letter.

# CHAPTER NINE

## GABRIELLE

"Pack your bags, little sprite. We're out of here."

I look up from Pascal's desk in his home office, where I was entering some things on his spreadsheet, to see him standing in the doorway, a large leather duffel bag slung over his shoulder.

I glance at the time and date on the computer. It's Tuesday, July 16. I've been working for Pascal for two weeks now and have been really getting into the swing of his schedule. There's nothing on his agenda about going anywhere this week, let alone with me. Plus, he should be at work right now.

"When did you get home?" I ask. "And what are you talking about?"

He puts his bag down by the door and strides on over to me, his eyes dancing mischievously. "We're getting the fuck out of here, darling."

"I gathered that," I say, glancing once more at the calendar. "And how long have you been planning this?"

"Since lunchtime, when I almost punched my father in the face at the office."

I want more details on that, but I don't press him. I've done such a good job of avoiding Gautier ever since I saw him last, and so far he's not sought me out. Helps he's been traveling on "business" as well. The less I hear about him, the better it is.

"Bad day?"

"Bad few months, more like it." He sits on the edge of the desk and reaches over, shutting the screen of the laptop. I barely get my fingers out of the way. "I need a break. I need a vacation. Fuck it, I deserve a vacation. And you're coming with me."

A vacation? A chance to get away from this place? I mean, I would be going with Pascal, so that's obviously a con, but damn it if I don't feel a bit of weight lift for the first time since I got here. Still . . .

"You're not worried about any letters?"

"All taken care of. I told my mother to put them aside in my office until we return. She'll keep an eye out for them."

"And you trust her?"

He shrugs. "The letters are addressed to him, so if the worst-case scenario happens, then fine. But no. My mother is not a fan of my father."

"What exactly did you tell her?"

"I said that there might be a letter addressed to him that he shouldn't see, and that I'll deal with it when I get home."

I watch him carefully. He seems to believe this. "You're not worried she'll open it out of curiosity?"

"She might. But she'll come to me first, not him. Look, my mother and I aren't close, but the older she gets, the more she leans on me. My father has become her enemy of sorts." He runs his hand over his jaw, appraising me. "You're awfully worried about those letters."

"I'm not," I say, maybe a little defensively. I pull it back. Smile reassuringly. "I'm not. I was just thinking about you."

"Thinking about me for once? How sweet."

"Pascal, it's my job to think of you."

"That very well may be, but you don't need to burst my bubble. Anyway, are you interested in getting away? Don't pretend you don't want to go," he says. "I can read you like a book."

*Don't be so sure about that.*

"Where are we going?" I ask.

"Have you been to Mallorca?" he asks, and then he catches himself. "Sorry, I forgot. Poor-girl childhood. But you did say you were all over Europe after you left here."

"No, I haven't been."

"Well, we have a place there, and I haven't been in a long time. It's on the beach. For a week we'll have nothing to do but laze around and drink and get tan lines." He bites his lip as he stares at me with raised brows. "Or no tan lines, if you're into tanning naked. I am. Just so you know."

I roll my eyes. "Of course you are."

"Don't roll your eyes at me, miss. You're the one who got handsy with me last week, let the record show."

I feel a flush burn on my cheeks. He's right. I'm still not sure what the hell came over me the other night in that gazebo. I guess I just wanted to see, feel what effect I had on him. And I wanted it to be on my terms, not his.

He slaps his hand down on the desk. "So let's go before anyone finds out, or I change my mind. Go get out of that uniform and pack a bunch of bikinis or something."

Another roll of my eyes. As if I even have a single bathing suit. "What am I going to tell my mother?"

"You're going with me on a business trip. That's all she needs to know. You're twenty-five. You can do what you want, can't you?"

"And you're thirty-one and you almost punched your father at work," I point out. I add under my breath, "Though I'm sure he was asking for it."

"He was. It doesn't matter, though. We have a plane to catch."

When Pascal said we had a plane to catch, I was expecting your typical commercial airline, probably business class. But when we get to the small airport just outside Paris, I realize we're talking about a private jet.

"Are you kidding me?" I ask as he takes me through the gates and over to the small waiting lounge, stocked with champagne and finger foods, the sleek jet parked outside. "This is how you travel?"

He shrugs and shoves a piece of bruschetta in his mouth before taking a swig of champagne. "Why not? I have the means, I might as well use them. What else would I spend my money on?"

"Hookers and blow," I joke.

But from the curve of his lips, it's probably not a joke.

"Whatever," I tell him quickly. "As long as I don't hear about it."

"We tell each other everything, though," he says knowingly. "Remember the contract."

"How could I forget?"

"You still owe me some stories." He picks up a glass of champagne and hands it to me. "How about I'll spare you from mine if you tell me yours."

"Deal," I say, clinking the glass against his.

The private jet is everything I've seen in the movies and from a select few lucky influencers on Instagram. It's narrow, lined with shining wood, with plush cream seats and a smiling hostess who caters to your every whim. This particular hostess looks like she could be a model, and she seems to be awfully chummy with Pascal. I have zero doubt that he's slept with her, and for once, I feel a pang of jealousy in my belly.

I don't like it.

Jealousy is a foreign and most unwanted feeling.

And that feeling definitely wasn't part of the plan, not even a little.

Makes me wonder how I'm going to get through this. I'm here for a reason, or at least two, and neither has to do with Pascal.

I need to get my mother out of the house. This is a long shot, but I know I have to try. I know she seems happy there, I know she *thinks* she's happy there, but I have no doubt that Gautier treats her like a toy, that she's got an extreme case of Stockholm syndrome and she'll never truly be safe or free until she leaves.

That's my first priority, and in some ways, that's the trickiest one. All this time I've been gone, I've been fixated on how to get my revenge on Gautier. I've fantasized about his death. I've planned so many different ways. Poison. A gun. Stabbing him while he sleeps. Compared to convincing my mother to leave, it all seems easy.

But as much as I've thought about it, my mother will have to come first. If I can convince her to go, if I convince her of what a monster Gautier is, then I won't have to kill him at all. Sure, there will be no justice for what he did; he'll get to keep on living, free, since there's no way anyone would convict a man of his wealth and power over the word of an unstable and lowly maid.

However, if my mother won't come with me, then I have no choice. I can't live my life knowing she's there in his clutches.

If she won't go, I'll make to make sure he goes.

And with a man like Gautier, there's only one way to do that.

Thoughts like that have me wondering if perhaps I'm a little unhinged.

I glance over at Pascal, who is sitting across the aisle, a glass of whiskey in his hand, staring out at the clouds.

Maybe I'm not much better than he is.

What a terrifying thought.

◆ ◆ ◆

My first impression of Mallorca is that it's an absolutely magical island. If Pascal keeps calling me a sprite, then perhaps this is where I come from, born of the clear aquamarine water that seems to beckon me from each winding turn the car makes as we drive toward his villa.

We're in a rental Mercedes convertible, and the top is down, and the sun is just starting to set behind us, turning the blues into golds.

I close my eyes and take my hair out of the bun and let the wind whip it around into a blonde tornado. I laugh, I smile. I soak it all in. This feeling of freedom I've never had before.

When I open my eyes, Pascal is staring at me with an expression I can't quite read.

"What?" I ask, but I'm unable to stop grinning.

"Nothing," he says after a bit. "I'm just admiring the view."

I look to the right to see stark cliffs dipping into the sea with sail-boats plying the waters. The view is beautiful, but I have a feeling he may have been talking about me.

My heart does a skip and a jump, and I try to knock that feeling away the best I can, but the freedom of this island and the open air are infectious.

So I let myself enjoy the compliment. I ignore the fact that Pascal is a smooth talker, that this is part of his shtick. I know he wants me, and I know exactly in what way. It's a way that could fuck things up for me royally.

*Eyes on the prize,* I remind myself, but those thoughts drift away with the sea breeze.

It's not too long before we pull down a narrow gravel road, the car bouncing between olive groves until a sprawling ochre villa appears, the sea behind it.

It's not as big as the Dumont house near Paris, but it's still beauti-ful all the same, down to the terracotta tiles on the roof and the bright goldenrod-painted door.

"Wow," I say breathlessly. "I can see why you wanted to come here. I already feel at peace."

"Good," he says. "That's all I ask."

We get the bags, and he gives me a quick tour, pointing out the reading nooks, the living room, the dining room, the breakfast area, and the kitchen, plus the terrace and the rocky cliffs that lead down to a cream-colored beach, the shining gold sea beyond it. Then we head up the gleaming wood staircase adorned with colorful tiles to the second level.

"Which one is my bedroom?" I ask.

"You mean you don't want to sleep with me? Oh, Gabrielle, you're breaking my heart." He presses his hand to his chest in mock despair.

"If only you had a heart to break," I comment, looking down the hall. "Which room is mine?"

When I don't hear an answer, I glance back at him, and a line has set between his eyes. Not exactly angry but . . . not happy either.

"It's your choice," he says in a clipped voice. "I'll be down here." He heads off down the hall, bag slung over his shoulder.

I watch him go and then wonder what that shift in mood was about. I'm exhausted from the travel anyway, so I don't venture far. I poke my head in the nearest room and see that it has a sea view, and I'm sold. I drag my suitcase in and then flop down on the luxurious bed with glossy wooden bedposts and a vibrant yellow-and-white crocheted duvet.

I must fall asleep, because when I open my eyes again, the room is dark, and it takes me a moment to remember where I am. In that moment, fear rushes at me like a lion pouncing from behind. I fear the dark, I fear the men who lurk in it.

But when I sit up in the bed, I see the faint glow of the lights outside making the room less and less dim as my eyes adjust, and I remember I'm in Mallorca.

I'm safe.

I have to be.

And yet I don't feel safe. Not alone like this.

I get up, use the attached washroom, and then open my door, though I don't remember closing it after me. I look up and down the hallway and hear nothing but silence.

"Pascal?" I call out softly.

I think I hear stirring from downstairs, so I slowly head down the stairs and make my way to the kitchen.

There's no one there.

But the wide back doors of the breakfast nook are open to the terrace outside and banging lightly in the soft breeze, so I step outside and see lights coming from the beach. I'm in bare feet, so I carefully make my way through the terrace to where a stone staircase is carved into the rock, leading in a slight curve down to the sand.

On the sand is a table with two candles lit, two places set.

Not a soul around.

My paranoia takes hold of me again and makes me stop and study the area before I venture any farther. I inspect the corners of the rocks and the shadows, wondering if it's a trap or Pascal's doing. Seems a little too thoughtful for his liking. Still, I'm convinced I'm alone.

The sand is soft on my feet, and I walk over to the table and see a note hanging off a bottle of white wine. Dumont label, of course.

The note says, *Have a seat and pour yourself a glass.*

I look around and then pull out a chair and sit down. The wine is already uncorked and perfectly chilled as I pour myself some. Even though I'm still woozy from the nap, the wine is going down easy. Maybe too easy.

But Pascal is nowhere to be found. Did he mean for me to eat by myself or . . . ?

Or is this him trying to be nice?

Trying to impress me?

I can never tell with him.

The faint sound of a car door slamming can be heard above the soft crash of the waves, and it's not long before I see Pascal leaving the house and walking down the steps toward me, holding a big paper bag in his hands.

"You're up," he says to me. "I thought you might be down for the count all night."

I blink at him for a moment, illuminated by the candle glow and the soft landscape lighting around the terrace and steps. He's dressed in tan pants, and his shirt is white and silk and slightly undone, hinting at his bronzed chest beneath. His hair is equally mussed, and he looks the epitome of rich French guy on vacation, and yet it's such a change from the Pascal I normally see. It's not just that he's not in a dark suit and tie, it's that he looks fresh and free.

Or maybe I'm just projecting myself on him.

"What is this?" I ask, gesturing to the table.

"Dinner?" he says. "I thought if you did wake up, you were going to be ravenous. At least I was." He plunks the bag on the table and then removes the contents, two foil takeout containers. "And of course there is no food in the house, so I drove to my favorite seafood restaurant next town over and got them to make us some paella to go."

"I don't think I've ever had paella," I admit, surprised at how thoughtful he's being.

"Not even when you were traveling Europe?"

The thing is, I wasn't so much traveling as I was running from Gautier. I had only saved up so much, so when I fled, I just hopped from city to city, looking for work and wishing I spoke better English.

I shake my head. "No." But I leave it at that.

He watches me for a moment, thinking something I'm not sure I want to know, and then starts to dish out the food onto the plates. Though I haven't had paella, I know what it looks like, and this looks and smells divine. Saffron-colored rice, red chorizo, fresh prawns.

"This is all amazing," I tell him as he sits down across from me.

"Good. I'm glad you're impressed."

"Fresh authentic paella, wine, a candlelit table on the beach. If I didn't know any better, I would say you were wooing me."

"I am," he says, covering his smile with his glass of wine.

Heat flares in my core, my belly doing flips. There I go again, feeling things for him I shouldn't be feeling. I have some more wine to try to drown the feeling, but all it does is make me want to revel in it.

"Are you being wooed?" he goes on with a hopeful tone.

I give him a shy smile. "Maybe . . ." I pause. "Do you do this for all your employees?"

"I don't even do this for my dates," he admits with a shrug. "A trip to Mallorca, food on the beach. I would have cooked all this if I knew shit about cooking."

"I'm actually surprised you don't have a cook anymore." If I recall correctly, they did back in the day. Francis or something like that.

"Your mom cooks most of the time now. I suppose I should be putting you to the test. I wouldn't mind you serving me breakfast in bed."

The mention of my mother is a cold knife into my chest, making my breath hitch. For a moment there, I had kind of forgotten what we both left behind when we came here.

"Okay, how about this," he says, and I meet his eyes. "We don't mention anything about back home. Not your mother, not my father, no mother or brother or cousins or blackmail or murder or anything. Not for the whole trip. Sound good?"

I raise my wineglass. "I will definitely drink to that."

"So with that shit out of the way, let's talk about you like you promised."

Oh jeez.

"Let's start with your childhood," he says, swirling the wine in his glass.

"Hmm, not an overwhelmingly broad topic at all."

"What was your life like before you moved in?"

"Well, let's see," I say, taking a bite of the paella and letting the orgasmic taste distract me for a second. I swallow reluctantly. "I lived with my mom and dad outside Paris in a shitty neighborhood you would have never heard of. People shooting up on the street, prostitutes, smugglers, the whole lot. Our apartment was one bedroom, and my mom often slept on the couch with me because my father would kick her out of the bedroom. He beat her—a lot. She . . ." I trail off, refusing to bring up images. "It was pretty bad."

Pascal winces, his eyes downcast. "Okay, this was the worst subject to bring up. I'm sorry."

"Don't be. It's okay. I mean, it's not okay, but it's done. It all made me stronger. It should have made my mother stronger, too, but . . ."

"She met my father."

"She met your father. And he offered us protection from him. My mother thought he was her savior . . ."

"I thought we weren't supposed to talk about them."

"No, it's fine." I manage a quick smile. "My father's out of my life. We never heard from him again, so if he exists still, I don't really know, and I don't really care." There are more people to fear than him.

"Did your father ever beat you?"

"No, actually," I say, remembering the smell of booze on his breath, how red his face was when he was enraged. How scared I was, but it was more for my mother than for me. I could handle the insults. "He was cruel, but he didn't touch me."

"You're lucky."

"I'm guessing yours did?"

Pascal nods. "I've never admitted this before to anyone, not Blaise when I know he went through the same thing, not my mother, because I felt she wouldn't care, that she would blame me somehow, that she would make an excuse. But yes. He hit me. Hurt me. A lot. And I just took it. Like a fucking wimp."

"Because you had no choice."

"What did I say about choices again?" he asks, his voice low.

"You didn't have a choice in that," I repeat, hoping he can at least understand that. "No kid does." God, I hope he doesn't blame himself, but if he grew up thinking he deserved it, then it explains a lot.

My blood starts to run cold at the thought of Gautier ruining Pascal's psyche in that same way. Pascal is a smart man, funny, cunning, charming. And he can be kind when he wants to be. Sweet, even. Raised by someone else—say Ludovic, for example—Pascal probably wouldn't have turned out the way he did. Nature versus nurture at its finest.

"You're feeling pity for me," he says. His eyes seem a shade darker now, or maybe it's the candlelight throwing light and shadows.

"I don't feel pity for you, Pascal," I say to him. "I just . . . *feel*."

He stares at me for a moment, our gazes locked across the table with the flames dancing in between. We're alone on this beach, and it feels like we're alone in this world. Alone but still together.

I'm getting in over my head.

He breaks our gaze and has a sip of his wine. Clears his throat. "I like that you feel. It's probably my favorite thing about you. Those eyes of yours hold so much, but they don't hide so much. I see you taking everything in, every scene, every word, every look. You take it in, and you feel it right away, good or bad. Even when you try to control it, it's there all the same. Do you . . ." He rubs his lips together, seeming to think about something.

"What?"

"Nothing," he says after a moment, shaking his head. "It was nothing." Then he smiles at me. It's not quite genuine, it's more shaky than anything else. "So this is pretty fucking awful dinner conversation. If this were a date, you'd be asking for the check by now."

"If this were a date, I would have worn something nicer," I tell him, looking down at my linen tunic and leggings.

"You look beautiful to me," he says warmly. Then he narrows his eyes. "And before you roll your eyes at me, because that's what you do every time I try to compliment you—"

"Making sexual comments isn't the same as complimenting," I interject.

"Every time I try to compliment you," he repeats, voice louder, as if he's trying to be heard above something, "you just brush it off. So don't do that. Please. I mean what I say. You know I do."

But I don't. I don't know when Pascal is being honest or when he's just being a womanizing flirt. I trust him to some extent, and he's been extremely open with me before, but when it comes to that sort of thing between us, I just don't know where he really stands.

He wants to fuck me, that's a given.

But then what?

Every woman he's been with who has ever wondered *then what* has been thoroughly disappointed. Discarded like yesterday's trash.

"What are you thinking about?" he asks.

"You don't want to know."

"I don't? Or you don't want me to know?"

I don't say anything to that; instead I busy myself with the rest of the meal.

"So since we've discussed your childhood, from your deadbeat dad to my father discovering your mother at a hotel and whisking you and her off to the paradise of the Dumont chateau, let's move on to something a little . . . juicier."

I freeze, my glass of wine almost to my lips. Oh God. He's going to ask about the night I left again.

"How many boyfriends have you had?"

I stare at him agape for a moment, then laugh, relieved at how inappropriate and yet harmless the question is. "Why do you want to know that?"

He gives an elegant shrug with one shoulder and starts to peel one of the prawns. "I would like to know if I'm bigger and better than them."

"That's not a fair comparison."

"You felt my cock weeks ago. You can judge it based on that, though if we really want to make it fair, I think you should probably take a look at it too."

I scoff, trying not to laugh but failing. "You're unreal."

"I'm very real. You felt so yourself. So tell me, how do I compare?"

"You're my boss, not my boyfriend."

"Semantics."

From the wicked, determined look in his eyes, I know he's not going to drop this. I cock my brow and say, "You're bigger and better."

He breaks out into such a wide grin that it gives me chills. The good kind. The kind that cascade down your spine and make you shiver because you're feeling so damn much. "That's exactly what I wanted to hear. Almost makes up for that shrug you gave me the other week."

I shovel rice into my mouth and smile at him.

He chuckles. "Okay. So who was your last boyfriend?"

"Oh my God," I say through a mouthful and swallow down my food. "What's with the questions?"

"I want to know you, Gabrielle. This is one way."

"You just want to use this as an excuse to talk about all your sexual conquests in return."

"I promise you, I don't. They're pretty much all the same anyway. Girl wants me, I fuck her, she leaves, and I never call her again."

"And I bet you're so proud of this, aren't you?"

"No," he says with a shrug. "I'm not proud. It just is what it is. I don't have time for relationships. You know how busy I am."

That comment shouldn't bother me, but it does, like I was actually thinking for a moment that we had a relationship, when in reality, not only is that the worst idea in the world, it couldn't be further from the truth.

"People make time for what's important."

"And what could be more important than money?" he says, wiping his mouth with his napkin and sitting back in his chair. He locks me in his gaze. "So tell me."

I sigh into my wine, briefly closing my eyes. "I haven't had any boyfriends. I've had some flings. That's it."

His forehead creases. "Really?"

"I have . . . issues."

"You don't say. Perhaps you have the same issues as I do."

"I highly doubt that."

"I take it you don't want to talk about it?"

"With you? No."

"With anyone?"

He's got me there. I shake my head but don't elaborate. I know I'd probably be a much healthier, fully functioning human being if I talked about my trauma with someone, but the thought of even opening up, not just about what happened but what I want to do, my thoughts, my life in fear and those dark, restless nights, makes me feel like I'm bleeding dry.

"How about you, then? Let's talk about your love life. Your ex-wife in particular."

He squints at me and has a long sip of his wine. When he finishes, he settles back in his chair, the angle off-kilter because of the sand, and sighs.

"What do you want to know?" he asks calmly.

"Did you love her?"

He shakes his head slightly. "No."

"Not even a little?"

"No," he says, more adamant this time, nostrils flaring.

"Then why did you marry her?"

"I guess I was young and stupid."

"Young, yes, but definitely not stupid. Was it all part of a long con? Did you marry her just so that you could blackmail Olivier?"

"No. I didn't. It hadn't even occurred to me at that time. I mean, my father hadn't . . . It doesn't matter. It's in the past."

"Right. But we can't get to know each other unless we share our pasts. That's what you said."

"I did *not* say that."

"Not in as many words, but you can't expect a one-way street here. Why did you marry her? For real? Was it what you wanted at the time, or was it all your father? Your mother?" *Just give me something to work with here, Pascal.*

"I married her because I was told to," he says sharply, spitting out the words in distaste.

I stare at him a moment. I suspected as much.

He runs his hand down over his pinched features. "It's not an easy thing to admit."

"I'm sure it's not."

"It was both my parents' idea. Marine came from a good family, and she was beautiful, so my mother wanted those good genes and that good money to be passed along, even though we had so much more money than her family did. Enough so that it was pretty obvious Marine only wanted me for that reason."

"So she never loved you either?"

He takes a large gulp of wine and clears his throat. "No. She couldn't love anything. I guess we were well suited in that respect." He pauses, his eyes seeming to count the grains of sand in the flickering candlelight. "She had no problem seducing Olivier. She thought it was great. She thought she was going to benefit from it all, as if she didn't already have everything she ever wanted."

"And then you showed her the door."

He frowns. "Look. I'm not proud of it."

"I never said you were. And what did your father have to do with this arrangement?"

"He said it was the right move. I was young, but it was good to show the world that I was ready to settle down . . ."

I raise my brow. "You don't think your father had this all planned from the start? That he wanted you to marry Marine so that he could blackmail your cousin?"

He sighs and runs his fingers along the tablecloth. Oh, how the tables have turned here. He thought he could get me to bare all and he'd be exempt. "Maybe. Probably."

"Just another pawn in his game."

His eyes blaze as he glances at me, but he doesn't say anything.

We lapse into silence, occasionally glancing at each other, until all the food and wine is gone.

"How about dessert?" he asks me, pushing back his chair and getting to his feet.

I look around. I don't see any dessert.

Oh. It's sexual, isn't it?

I give him a wry look as he comes to my side of the table and holds out his hand for me. "Just trust me."

"I'm no one's dessert, Pascal," I warn him, but I feel shaky inside, as if I might go back on my word.

The corner of his mouth curls into a grin as he stares down at me. "You don't have to tell me twice. Come on."

He gestures with his open hand and cautiously places mine in his. He wraps his strong, warm fingers around me and helps me to my feet.

He doesn't let go as he leads me away from the table and to the beach, right to the water's edge.

"We're going swimming?" I ask.

"Tomorrow," he says. "Come this way."

Still grasping my hand, he takes me along the water past the cliffs and bare rocks that slide into the sea until we round a corner and come to another long expanse of beach. There are a few houses at the water's edge here and there, but farther down there is a low building right on the sand with disco lights, and I can hear the soft thump of EDM music.

"Are you taking me to a rave?" I ask suspiciously. "You know I'm still in bare feet."

"Just getting dessert," he says.

We walk down the beach for what feels like forever until the music is louder and the building is upon us. It's a beach bar with a casual vibe and only a few patrons. Most of them are in chairs sprawled across the sand, drinking beer, while a few girls are dancing around them, lit up by the colorful rotating lights. There's a DJ in the corner who looks like he's giving it his all, even though the crowd is small.

Pascal leads me over to the bar, where we take a seat on high stools that sink a little into the beach. *"Dos sangrias, por favor,"* he says to the bartender.

"You speak Spanish?" I ask him.

"Barely," the bartender says in English. I look at him and see he's got a twinkle in his eye like they're longtime friends. Pascal obviously frequents this place when he's on the island, although this doesn't strike me as Pascal's scene either.

"What?" Pascal says to me, reading my face. "Beach bars are my favorite, and Manuel is the best bartender on the island, isn't that right?"

I'm not sure that Manuel understands Pascal's French, but I think he gets the gist anyway because he pours an insane amount of brandy into each of our glasses.

Pascal then puts his hand on my knee and leans in closer to me, and my heart seems to stop, because the closer his eyes get to me, the more arresting they are. They hold me in place until I can't breathe, can't move. "You should let me surprise you every now and then."

He gives my leg a light squeeze and then backs off, taking the drinks from the bartender and handing me one. "Here's to this part of the night. No more talking. Only dancing."

I bite down on the straw to keep from laughing. "Excuse me. It sounded like you said dancing."

"You don't think I can dance?"

"It's not that I don't think you can, it's that *I* can't."

He sucks back on his drink thoughtfully, and I have to tear my gaze away from his lips before he catches on. "When was the last time you went dancing?"

I try to think. Eventually I admit, "Never."

His brows go up. "Never?"

"My school wasn't a party school," I tell him. Actually, it was an online school that I did out of my own shitty apartment in the Bronx. It was all I could afford. But he doesn't have to know that.

"You didn't go out with friends? You're young, Gabrielle."

I glare at him. "Not every young person cares about friends and partying. *You* don't have any friends."

He blinks and moves his head back in surprise. "Were you trying to make that a low blow?"

"Was it? Does anything hurt you?"

The bartender clears his throat, and we both look at him in unison. He quickly starts wiping down the counter, pretending to mind his own business.

I suppose it does look like we're a bickering couple who might just have a throw down in his bar.

I give Pascal a sheepish, quasi-apologetic smile and suck down the rest of my drink.

"I can't tell if alcohol is making you more relaxed or more angry," Pascal muses after a moment.

"You have that effect on me," I say under my breath.

"We'll see." He turns to the bartender and says something in Spanish. Before I know it, I not only have another sangria, but there's a shot in front of me.

"What is this?"

"It's either going to make you like me more or make you like me less."

I pick it up and sniff it. It smells strong with a hint of sweetness. "That's quite the gamble."

"A risk I'm willing to take."

Shots are never a good idea, but I'd just given Pascal the very accurate impression that I haven't had a lot of fun in my life, and I'd like to show him otherwise.

Hell, I'd like to show myself otherwise.

I raise the glass and take back the shot in one go. It burns beautifully, and I immediately feel the warmth of it encompass me.

"You took that like a champ," he says once he's done his, wiping his mouth.

"Maybe I'm stronger than I look."

"I might call you a little sprite, but I know you're stronger than you look. You said you're harmless until threatened, and I don't take that mildly." His eyes rake over me. "I don't take any of you mildly. You're a force to be reckoned with."

I'm not sure if he's saying that because he knows that kind of comment means something to me and I'll eat it up like candy, but either way, I needed to hear it. And I needed to hear it from him.

Shit. Maybe the alcohol is making me like him more.

*You're going to sleep with him, aren't you?*

I try to bat that thought out of my head.

But it doesn't surprise me.

And more than that, it doesn't scare me.

It should. He's Gautier's son. Yes, he's also my boss, but that part is so minor, since I only took the job for one thing. The fact that he's Gautier's son, that he's nearly as wicked, that his vile blood runs through Pascal, that should terrify me beyond all hope.

And yet as more drinks come and the music gets louder and I start feeling looser, with my actions, with my feelings, the fear drifts away. I let myself look at him longer, not caring that I'm being blatant about it. He seems to enjoy it. He seems to enjoy all things that involve me.

*What happens after you sleep with him?* The voice comes back. *What happens when you sleep with him and then you leave with your mother, never to return?*

Better yet, what happens if I sleep with him and then kill his father?

He wouldn't survive that.

I might not survive that.

I'm no assassin. I don't know what I'm doing. I know I'm a little bit crazy and in over my head. I know how wrong this is, how risky it is, how if I'm not careful, it's poised to fail in a way I'll never get out of. I'm just driven by this obsessive, debilitating need to make Gautier go away, to erase my whole past, to erase everything I was and start anew. I need it in order to breathe, to live. I can't spend my days in fear—the only thing that has kept me going since I left is the very fact that I planned to take care of him. That's probably the only reason I'm alive.

"Uh-oh, you're going to the dark place," Pascal says, getting to his feet and grabbing me by the elbows, hauling me up. "There's only one way out of the dark place."

"You know about the dark place?" I ask, almost whispering, and it's then that I realize, holy fuck, I'm drunk as a skunk.

"I'm the mayor of the dark place," he tells me. He leads me away from the bar to the middle of the dance floor, which is just a patch of sand with disco lights on it. There's no one else around. The bar is empty except for the DJ and the bartender.

"A few more songs, down tempo," Pascal yells at the DJ. "You know I'll make it worth your while."

The DJ shrugs and puts on a new track, something with a very heavy, low beat.

"This is how we get out of it," Pascal says to me, wrapping his arms around my lower back and holding me close to him, his lips going for my ear. "This time we can get out of it together," he murmurs, and I feel a rush shoot down into my core.

This is a bad idea.

This is danger.

Or maybe I'm the dangerous one?

"Put on some Rüfüs Du Sol," Pascal yells at the DJ. Then he smiles down at me. Lopsided, kind of sweet. I think I'm seeing double of him. "And you, you put your arms around me."

I do as I'm told.

As he holds me tight, his hard-on pressed against my thigh, I put my arms around his neck and let him grind into me, moving to the music with each heavy, bass-loaded beat.

This feels nice.

Not just the evidence of how much he wants me but the way our bodies meld together so seamlessly. It doesn't feel awkward. It feels real. Like all this time, this was what was supposed to happen.

"Do I dare ask what's going on in that head of yours?" he says, his forehead resting against mine as we sway.

I close my eyes and drift with the movement. "I'm not quite sure myself."

Everything starts to get just a little bit swimmy, a little bit dizzy. My feet feel like they're sticking to the sand.

I sink into his arms.

Down.

Down.

Down.

# CHAPTER TEN

## Pascal

Ow. Oh God. My head.

Motherfucking Manuel.

That Spanish bastard should have cut us off when he had the chance. All that extra brandy in the sangria is creating a punishing jackhammer in my head that triples in pain every time I open my eyes.

I should have stuck to whiskey.

But whiskey didn't feel right last night. I wanted to drink whatever Gabrielle was drinking, and I wanted her to enjoy it. Seeing her enjoy something has given me life.

The moment she stepped off the plane in Palma, it was like seeing the sunrise for the first time. She just lit up from within, and every bit of darkness that hid in her deepest parts was banished away, if only for a few moments.

It caught me off guard a few times, stole the breath from my lungs, made me feel something I'd never felt before. Something for her. It was in her smile, the way she literally let her hair down in the car and let it dance free and messy and wild.

I want to be the man who makes her like that on his own. I want her free and messy and wild in my bed. I want to see that sunrise again, that blinding light, to feel the joy move through her.

Last night, I was sure that was going to happen.

It wasn't my plan, per se.

Yes, I was trying to woo her. Impress her, at any rate. If we'd ended up having sex, that would have been an added bonus. My main goal was just to get her to open up to me, to let me see the things she deems too dark for me to know. You'd think after all that I've told her, every depraved and wicked part of me, she would have felt comfortable enough to finally tell me who she really is and what she really wants.

If what she wants happens to be me, well, I can't say I'd be disappointed.

That's kind of what this whole trip is about, if I'm being honest here. I wanted to get her out of that house, away from what's holding her down and putting that fear in her eyes, the way she's on edge when she's in a darkened room, how she's always tense and looking over her shoulder. I don't know what it is; maybe it has something to do with her mother, maybe something to do with my father, maybe the letters are freaking her out—I don't know. But here I was hoping she could let her guard down, if only just an inch.

Speaking of the letters, I roll over, wincing as I do so, and grab my phone. I text my mother to remind her about the mail. I wait for her reply and close my eyes as I lie back down with my head on the pillow. Sun is spilling through the window, which makes my headache worse.

I swear I hear clatter from downstairs.

I really hope it's Gabrielle, though I have no idea why she'd be up so early. Then again, it's nearly eleven in the morning.

Last night, my plan to get her to relax and open up morphed into getting her ridiculously drunk. I got drunk, too, hence the headache. But then while we were dancing, she practically passed out in my arms, and I had no choice but to pick her up, sling her over my shoulder, and carry her back like a caveman.

Of course, if I truly were a caveman, I would have brought her into this room with me. But even though I've done some despicable things, I draw the line somewhere. I have no fears in being forward with Gabrielle, but I'm not going to take advantage of her like that either.

My mother texts back, telling me that nothing came for my father, and with a sigh of relief, I get up and head to the washroom, then go downstairs, where the smell of coffee and food frying gets increasingly stronger.

Gabrielle is in the kitchen, bent over the stove and flipping some eggs. She glances up at me and gives me a shy smile. "I hope I wasn't making too much racket, but if I didn't eat something, I was going to die."

I stop where I am and admire the scene. She's wearing just shorts and a V-neck T-shirt, her hair pulled back in a low bun, and when you combine that with the fact that she's cooking, well, all those caveman instincts come flooding back. It takes a lot of effort not to go over to her and kiss her in the crook of her neck where her shirt has started to slip off the shoulder.

"Are you hungry?" she asks, standing on her tiptoes to grab some plates from the shelves, giving me a very nice view of her ass.

"Very," I tell her, my voice coming out low and gruff. Her ass looks juicy enough to bite.

She glances at me over her shoulder, and if she notices me staring, she doesn't seem to care. "You're not curious where I got all the food from?"

"It's hard to care about anything else other than you in those shorts, little sprite."

Her lips twist in a dry smile as she starts sliding the eggs onto the plate. "Last night we talked about how you don't have a cook anymore, so I thought, since I'm technically working here, I might as well make your dreams come true. Plus, I'm ravenous, like I said. So I took the car and drove to the nearest town, Cala something or other, and went shopping. I was hoping to bring you breakfast in bed, since you mentioned it, but now that you're up . . ." She holds out a plate for me.

"Breakfast in bed?" I ask, coming over and taking it from her. I remain in her space, not too eager to step away. Beyond the delicious smell of the fried eggs is the sweet coconut scent of her shampoo. "I don't even know who you are anymore."

"Don't get carried away," she says, brushing past me to take her food over to the breakfast table that's already set up with cutlery, a coffee press filled with steaming coffee, mugs, a basket full of bread, as well as cold cuts and cheese. A very Spanish-style breakfast.

She sits down and gestures to the food. "Don't be afraid. Sit. I didn't poison you."

"If you did, I'm sure I would have deserved it," I tell her, taking the seat across from her.

I thought the comment would have been amusing to her, but instead her brows furrow and she seems to busy herself with the bread. "Anyway," she says, tearing off a piece, "I felt bad for how nice you've been to me, so I thought I could repay the favor."

"Consider it repaid," I tell her, reaching for the coffee. "Hey, how come you don't have a hangover?"

She shrugs. "I'm younger than you." Then she gives me a quick smile. "I felt like garbage this morning. I couldn't sleep, though I barely can anyway. I went for a long walk on the beach, past the bar we were at last night, the scene of the crime. I have to say I don't remember that much except dancing with you."

"You passed out in my arms, and I carried you home. And yes, before you ask, I was a perfect gentleman."

"*Pascal* and *gentleman* are two terms that don't really go together," she comments, pretending to muse over it. "Anyway, I thought about going swimming, but I don't have a suit, and it was so early, it didn't seem inviting."

"Then that's what we'll be doing today," I tell her. "The perfect hangover cure is a jump from the cliffs into the water. I know just the spot too. We can stop by in town and get you a suit."

"Is this part of the official work schedule?"

"As you know, this is a vacation, and there is no schedule. But yes, it's part of it, and you have to do it."

"Or what?"

"I'll fire you?"

"For not going swimming?"

"Yes, and for hiding your culinary skills from me for too long. These eggs are amazing."

Truly, it's one of the best breakfasts I've had in a while. Usually I'm just having cigarettes and maybe a croissant. Sitting with her like this, just the two of us, in a bright and airy villa with the sun streaming in and the waves crashing below us, I could be tricked into thinking that this is my life now.

That's the point of a vacation, isn't it? A chance to pretend to live another life for a bit until you have to go back to the one you have. The funny thing is, deep in some part of me, I know I have so much ability, so much privilege to change everything. Maybe that's what makes it worse. Knowing I could maybe have a life like this one day, quiet moments with someone I care about in some sunshiny place, a new way of existing that isn't born of deception and greed, and yet I don't have the balls to change any of it.

After breakfast, we grab some towels and head out in the car. There are a lot of cliffs in Mallorca that are popular for jumping off, but there's one in particular I used to go to a lot as a child, when we'd spend summer vacations here.

First we stop by the nearest town to get some water and find Gabrielle a bathing suit. We luck upon a swimwear boutique, but to

Gabrielle's embarrassment, all the suits are of the teeny-weeny bikini kind.

Gabrielle's embarrassment is my victory, of course, and she doesn't have a choice.

"Let me see," I call to her from outside the dressing room, where she's been struggling and swearing at a suit for the last five minutes.

"No!" she yells back. "It's too small."

I give the salesperson, an older and overly tanned lady, a look, and she shrugs. "It is not too small," she says in Spanish. "It is her size. She has a great figure; tell her to come on out so we can see."

"Did you get that, Gabrielle?" I yell at her. "Get out here so we can see."

"Up yours," she says.

I grin.

She eventually comes out—not in the bathing suit—though she plunks it down on the cash register, about to pay. I gently shove her to the side so I can finish up the transaction.

"I'm not letting you pay for this," I say, nodding at the suit, which the salesperson is sliding into the world's tiniest bag. "I'm going to get a lot more pleasure out of it than you are."

Gabrielle grumbles something in return. I'd like to think it was a thank-you.

We get back in the car, and it's not too long before I've pulled off the main road and we're bouncing down a dirt one among a scrub forest of fragrant rosemary and sage until we come to a tiny spot for parking. Luckily, no one else is here.

"Are you sure we're not on someone's property?" she asks as we get out of the car.

"Relax. The island has a lot of secrets that tourists don't know about."

I grab the towels, and we walk through the scrub, honeybees buzzing around us, until it opens up to a wide expanse of limestone cliff.

I drop the towels on the ground and then proceed to pull off my shirt.

I know I'm giving her a good show, because she's trying her hardest not to stare blatantly at me.

"You can look, it's okay," I tell her with a grin. "If you didn't, I'd fear all my hours at the gym every week weren't paying off."

A flush goes to her cheeks, and she looks away as I start to undo my jeans. I'm just in my black boxer briefs, which sometimes make for a better swimsuit than board shorts do. They're also a hell of a lot more revealing, which is great at making her uncomfortable in the best way possible.

"Your turn," I tell her. "Put on your suit."

She shoots me a look over her shoulder and frowns as her eyes rake up and down my body, concentrating on my bulge. "You're in your underwear," she says, aghast.

"Have you ever asked yourself what's the difference between underwear and a swimsuit?"

"The fact that I can see . . . um, everything?"

"Just be glad I'm not in a Speedo."

"You might as well be."

She reaches down for a towel, giving another glance at my crotch as she does so, and then attempts to wrap the towel around her chest.

I watch her struggle for a few minutes, trying to get her T-shirt off while still being covered up by the towel. Whatever modest game she's trying to play, she's losing at it.

I can't help but chuckle.

She glares at me, her hair all messy, her face flustered with her shirt half-off. "You could help me."

"I could," I tell her. "But this is so much more amusing."

Her eyes turn to slits, but she doesn't scare me. I reach over and grab the edge of the towel by her chest.

"Don't look," she warns, as if I'm not going to see nearly every inch of her body once that suit is on.

"I wouldn't dream of it," I tell her. "I'm a gentleman, remember?"

"Then close your eyes."

I sigh and close my eyes, trying to keep the ends of the towel together. "You know, I could just drop the towel, and you could get changed in the open, and it would be so much easier."

"What if someone comes along? I'd be naked."

"If I don't mind, I'm pretty sure they wouldn't mind either."

I hear her struggle for a few more minutes and then the snap of spandex, and true to my word, I keep my eyes closed, though the temptation to look is beckoning.

Finally she says, "Okay, I'm done."

I open my eyes and take the towel away from her so I can get a better look.

She's literally stunning.

Her skin is pale, touched with gold from the sun, her breasts and hips heavenly full with a dip at her slim waist. The bikini she's wearing is tomato red and leaves very little to the imagination, but I happen to have a huge imagination, and seeing her displayed in front of me like this, vulnerable and strong all at once—achingly beautiful, undeniably sexy—my mind floods with all the things I crave to do to her.

"I feel like I'm naked," she says quietly.

"I'm glad you're not," I tell her. "I don't think my heart could handle it."

Her eyes drop down to my crotch, where I know my cock is extremely rigid and extremely visible. I grin.

"Looks like your cock can barely handle it either," she says.

"Look, if you want to get all handsy with me again, I'm not going to complain," I tell her. One of her straps on the side of her bikini bottoms is twisted, so I take a step toward her, hands out. She stills, holding her breath, but she doesn't move as I reach down and slide my fingers against the warmth of her skin, luxuriating in how soft her skin feels on her hip. Ever so slowly, I untwist it, overwhelmed by how close I am to her, the heat between our bodies rising, becoming thick and heady, unaltered by the breeze off the sea. My cock grows bigger, thicker, until it's almost painful, making it hard to breathe or think straight.

Gabrielle has been focused on my hand at her side. She now gazes up at me through her long lashes, and I see a whole other world in her eyes, a million feelings swimming in the depths. I see what I want to see—lust—and it's wild and ripening before me.

My other hand drops to the other side of her hips, and I slowly drag my thumb up and down her skin, bracketing her in. I want so badly to pull her into me, to feel her flesh on mine, but I know the moment I do so, I'm going to lose all control. I wasn't kidding when I said I was barely holding it together. For the first time in my life, I want a woman who has more power over me, power she doesn't even know she possesses, power that would completely change me.

And *fuck*, how I fear that change.

How badly I want it.

"Gabrielle," I say in a murmur, my words coming out thick and wanting. "I *need* you."

I say it without even thinking of what it means, what the consequences are, ignoring the vulnerable state it puts me in. I say it because there's nothing left to say.

She gazes at my lips; then her eyes skirt to mine again, and now I see those dark storm clouds roll in, turning the lust into fear, and I think I might have fucked everything up.

Suddenly she sucks in her breath and takes a step away from me, shaking her head back and forth, avoiding my eyes, and I have no idea what to do or say.

"Hey," I say, reaching for her, but now she pulls out of my grasp, and with a quick look that's full of shame and sorrow, she starts running along the cliff.

I'm so stunned, it takes me a moment to realize what she's doing, but by then it's too late. She runs along the rocky cliff top, her bare feet lithe and quick, her hair flowing behind her like a platinum cape, until she leaps into the sky and dives over the edge, disappearing from my sight.

"Gabrielle!" I yell and start running after her. I have no idea where she landed; she just ran and jumped, not knowing if there was deep water below us or rocks.

*Shit, shit, shit.*

I can't even think. I just keep running, a prayer on my lips until I come to a stop at the edge and look over. The water is rippled where she dived, but I don't see her anywhere.

"Gabrielle!" I yell again, though it's pointless. Without hesitating, I do as she did and swan dive into the blue sea below.

I hit the water with minimal splash, diving deeper and deeper into the blue, then opening my eyes, wincing at the salt. Through the blurry mess of bubbles, I see Gabrielle's shape, suspended in the water. I quickly swim through the haze until I get a better look.

She's just a few feet off the bottom, just floating there.

For a moment I think she hurt herself or worse . . . that she's dead.

But when I approach her, she turns her head to look at me with those round eyes of hers, and it feels like I've stumbled upon a part of her I wasn't meant to see. She's choosing to be down here, holding her breath, not moving at all.

Jesus, she's fucked up.

She's perfect.

I reach out and grab her arm and start kicking to the surface, pulling her up with me until we break through.

We both gasp for air, and I have my hand around her waist, holding her up in case she wants to sink back down. "Are you okay?" I ask, spitting out seawater, brushing the wet hair from my eyes, which sting from the salt and the bright sun.

She shakes her head and then inhales, brash and deep, that fear coming through again. Maybe over whatever spooked her earlier, maybe because she had practically drowned herself.

Still holding on to her with one hand, I start swimming for the shore, the tiny patch of sandy beach that's pocketed by high cliffs, a scraggly trail leading up between them to the top.

Once on shore, I collapse on the sand, rolling over, trying to regain my breath. I'm a strong swimmer, always have been, but I'm not used to hauling people around.

When the air returns to my lungs and my heart slows, I sit up and peer at Gabrielle. She's sitting, staring off at the sea, her knees cradled against her chest as she hugs her legs. I ache to reach out and touch her spine, to let my finger follow the beads of water that drip down her back. But I don't want to set her off again, so I just watch and wait.

Moments turn to minutes. There's just us and the silence and the blue sky and even bluer sea and the sun beaming from up high.

Finally, I have to ask. "Do you want to talk about it?"

She doesn't say anything.

"You scared me," I admit, taking in a deep, shaking breath. For some reason, it's easier to unload on her when she's not looking at me. "I thought I lost you for a second. I didn't . . . I didn't realize how painful that would be. To lose someone. I've never had someone in my life to lose. I've always pushed people away. Shoved, more like it. I've acted unfettered by rules and morality. I've done as I pleased, and what pleased me was to make sure no one could ever get close to me. I'd been taught that letting people in meant letting your guard down, and when you let your guard down, that's when they stick in the knife. Why would I risk it? How could it ever be worth it?"

I start drawing lines in the sand with my forefinger, aimless, as everything I've kept locked away and buried is starting to surface, as if it's found the key.

Gabrielle is my key.

The key to becoming a better man.

She's the one who is worth it.

Silence falls on us again save for the crashing of the waves and the occasional cry from a gull up ahead, wondering if we have anything to eat. I'm not sure if we should continue to sit here or head back to get the towels and water, but then she starts to stir. She doesn't face me, but her head drops to the side, resting her cheek against her knee so I can see her profile. Her eyes are searching the sky.

"I was raped," she says, and the stark admission makes my heart free-fall in my chest. "When I was young. Several times. All by the same person."

I swallow the thickness in my throat, feeling livid that someone did this to her. "I'm sorry," I manage to say. I don't know what else to say. But it explains a lot.

"I'm sorry too," she says quietly, still avoiding my eyes. That's okay. "I thought it was my fault for a long time. I thought at first maybe I led him on. I was young and stupid. He was . . . older. He paid attention to me in ways that no one else did, and after my childhood, it felt good. But I never thought of him in that way. I thought maybe he was a friend. Except he wasn't." She pauses, licks her lips. "I never told anyone this. I never went to therapy for it. I know I should have, but it's too late for that now. It's too late for a lot of things. I think maybe I'm beyond saving."

"You don't need to be saved," I tell her. I've always questioned the existence of my own heart. It never seemed to beat or bleed for anyone, not even myself. But now it aches, a full-on pain in my chest, like it's opened up and bleeding me dry for her. I try to compose myself, but it's hard against the pull of emotions; they grab at my ankles like an undertow.

"I do need to be saved," she says, her voice taking on an edge. "You have no idea. I need to be saved from myself. I'm the thing most dangerous, and it's not in a way you'd expect. I have revenge on my mind. I think that's the only way out of this. I dream about killing him, I fantasize about it. And I know I'm an awful human being for even having those thoughts."

"You're a normal human being. He probably deserves it."

She closes her eyes for a moment. "I think he does. That's the only thing that keeps me going."

"Who was he?" I ask, even though I know if she tells me, I'm going to have to do something about it. I'm already making fists in the sand, the anger running through my blood hot and fluid.

"It doesn't matter," she says tiredly.

"It does. Tell me who it is so I can go and kill him myself."

Finally she looks up and meets my eyes. "Not if I kill him first." Our eyes are locked, and in our stare, I can feel everything she's feeling. How serious she seems. For her own sake, I hope she's not. Then she looks away again at the horizon. "The first time it happened, it took me by surprise. I was too shocked to feel anything, and then after I felt nothing but shame. In a way, he seduced me, and even when I said no, it sounded like I was saying yes. The second time"—she takes in a deep breath—"the second time I said no again, and that time he hit me."

It feels like I'm about to crush this fist of sand into glass. "You don't have to tell me this," I say through grinding teeth. If she keeps going on, I might end up punching something.

"I want to tell you, Pascal. I want you to know. I want you to understand. And I've never told anyone before. I need to tell someone, and you're the only one I trust in this whole wide world, this world that only wants to hold me down. And yet you're there, holding your hand out for me, trying to help me up. I know it shouldn't be you. It *really* shouldn't be you. But here we are."

I press my lips together and wait for her to go on.

"He hit me, but he did it in such a way that no one could really tell. After that, I knew what I was up against, and I did everything I could to avoid him, but sometimes that was impossible."

"When was this?"

"It doesn't matter," she says again, and now I know that it does matter, at least to her. "I know you want to play hero, Pascal, but this has been my story and mine alone for so long, so trust me when I say it really doesn't matter. Please."

"Okay," I say quickly, nodding to show her I'm dropping it.

"He was brutal, and he took pleasure in it, like a fucking psychopath. He tortured me with fear, and he only inflicted pain and suffering. He ruined me, over and over again, and it was only later that I realized I had to be the phoenix, that I had to rise out of the ashes. I told you I have issues, and these are my issues. I . . ." She exhales shakily. "I don't know who I am without them, you know? It's been my identity for so long."

"So I take it they never caught him?"

She shakes her head.

"Why didn't you press charges?"

"I was too young and . . . I figured it wouldn't work. He's the type of man who would get away with it. Besides, I didn't want to go to trial. I didn't want to be put on a stand and have to look him in the eye and relive it. I didn't want the world to know my shame."

"You must have told your mother?"

She nods. "I did tell her. And she didn't believe me. I laid myself bare and admitted the truth, and she looked the other way. After that, I had no choice but to leave her."

"Is that why you suddenly left us? You couldn't be around her anymore?"

"Mm-hmm," she says, turning her head slightly so that her wet hair falls over her face, obscuring it from view.

"My father told me that you left because you had issues, that some traumatic experience happened to you once but he didn't know what it was."

She goes still at that. I swear she stops breathing.

"Did he have any guesses?" she asks quietly.

"No. None. But he also said he was only guessing. You never opened up. I can understand why."

She's breathing again. Her back rises and falls with deep breath after deep breath, like she's doing a breathing exercise.

I know I shouldn't touch her, especially after everything she just admitted to me, but I feel like if I don't, she'll move further and further away from me. I can feel the connection between us severing somehow.

I get to my knees and slide over to her, gently placing my hand on her back. She flinches slightly, and goose bumps erupt on her skin.

"It's okay," I whisper, though it feels like such a trite thing to say. "You're a strong fucking woman. And even though you don't need a man—especially a man like me—to have your back, I have it. You are not alone, Gabrielle."

She raises her head and turns it toward me.

I reach out and brush the hair off her face, tucking it behind her ears, my fingers then resting on her jaw.

Her eyes search mine wildly, but the fear in them has changed once more.

"Kiss me," she whispers.

"Wh-what?" I blink, wondering if I heard her right.

Before I can process it, she puts her hand at my cheek and leans in and brushes her lips against mine softly, just for a moment, just enough time for a jolt to pass from her to me, all the way to my toes. I'm lighting up like fucking firecrackers.

I kiss her back because that's all I've wanted to do from the moment I first saw her. I kiss her, flush and warm, and though the kiss is still heating up, I fear where it could go.

I don't want to hurt her.

Not after everything.

I pull back slightly, lick my lips, try to breathe. "Are you sure about this?" I murmur, my voice thick with desire. "I don't feel right after . . . after . . ."

"I'm not damaged goods," she whispers, staring into my eyes with such intensity that I don't dare move. "I'm just a little broken. Maybe I need you to put me back together again. It can't hurt to try, can it?"

God, I hope she's right.

# CHAPTER ELEVEN

## GABRIELLE

*What are you doing?* the voice says. *This will ruin you.*

But I'm determined not to ever hear that voice again.

Not right now, staring at Pascal, breathless, still feeling the hot buzz of his lips on my mouth. He's staring right back at me, his mouth open and wet where I kissed him. There's wonder in his gaze, and I feel lost in that same feeling, too, hypnotized, his eyes so blue and intense, they rival the sky and the sea.

I can't believe I kissed him.

I figured it might happen at one point, but never did I imagine it would happen now.

Not after everything I told him about his father.

Even if he doesn't know it's about his father.

I just had to see, had to know for sure, how different he was. What he felt like.

His lips were like heaven, soft and seductive, and every part of me is on fire, begging me to go back for more.

I want to be more than what was done to me.

I want to prove to myself that I'm not damaged beyond repair.

That I'm still a woman with wants and needs and urges.

He's the man I shouldn't want, the son of the devil.

And he's staring at me like I'm the only woman in the world for him, the only one he really, truly needs. Salvation, maybe.

Whatever it is, I want more.

I want all of him.

I lean in slightly, staring up at him with a look that should be undeniable.

He reads that look.

Desire washes over his face like the incoming tide.

He grabs my face in his hands, pressing his fingers into my cheekbones, searching my eyes like if he doesn't find what he's looking for, he might just die.

He catches me in a hard, long kiss, his lips having their way with mine, our tongues clashing wildly with each long pull. He tastes like the sea, and I want to drink all of him.

His fingers slide back into my wet hair, and I'm suddenly conscious that we're making out on the beach in just his underwear and the world's smallest bikini. Anyone could see us if they approached from a boat or the cliff above, but I don't care.

It feels so good to just not *care*.

Pascal pulls me in closer, his kiss deepening, and my mouth opens up in kind, wanting this, needing this. Our kiss turns into something hot and messy, teeth and lips and tongues that dance with each other like in the depths of a fever dream.

He nips at my bottom lip, eliciting a groan that falls into his mouth.

"You have no idea," he murmurs into my mouth, pulling back just enough to rub his nose against mine. "No idea how much I've wanted to do this, to know what you taste like." He pauses, lips going to my jaw and leaving tiny wet kisses. "I want to taste all of you, every inch. I want to do it until you can't handle it anymore, and then I want to do it some more."

A thrill runs down my spine, the kind that shoots out into every nerve in every crevice in my body. A heat builds between my legs, a pressure that's both foreign and familiar to me. I want this more than I can admit.

His lips now suck along my neck, and his moan sends vibrations down my spine. I put my hands on his shoulders, on his back, feeling the taut strain of his muscles, the heat of his body, and the sun beating down on us.

"Pascal," I whisper, though I don't want to say anything more than his name. I want to keep saying it, keep reminding myself that this is him, this is him. My boss, son of the devil, the one person I want to get closer to and the one person I shouldn't.

Those thoughts would normally be enough to shake me out of it, but this time they don't. This time they disappear in a flurry of lust as Pascal makes a gentle fist in the back of my hair with one hand—I can feel the water trickling down my back from it, making me shiver. His other hand goes to my bikini top and slips under.

His thumb brushes over my nipple, and I gasp, my nails on his back digging in. His touch is electric. Whatever I was feeling before was just kindling, and now this is the fuel he's poured on top. I am so fucking alive, so damn turned on. I've never felt this way before. I've never had anyone touch me and make me feel the way he's making me feel now.

"Don't stop, ever," I manage to say, my heart starting to beat in my throat. His lips come down to my pulse, sucking and licking until they rest in the corner of my neck. The way his thumb keeps passing over my hardened nipple shoots rays of pleasure out of my breast, washing over the rest of me. I'm starting to become impatient. I'm starting to need more, like some rabid animal.

His mouth comes back up to mine again, and I gasp into another kiss. I open my eyes enough to see him staring back at me, those endless blues reflecting my own lust to me. "Lie back," he whispers, and one hand goes to my shoulder, gently pushing me onto the sand. He reaches down and carefully spreads my legs, then gets between them.

He could be rougher. I get why he's not. He's been as easy on me as he can, and I don't blame him. It's thoughtful. It's endearing. It's a side of Pascal I never thought I'd see when it came to sex. I thought he would just take, rough and wild, and discard. This is different. This is gentle but commanding. It's slow but it's decadent. It's borderline torturous.

I gasp again as he briefly hovers over me and licks up the sides of my breast, swirling his thick tongue around and around until I'm fidgeting, the pressure inside me building again with nowhere to go. The need to get off is greater than anything else right now. I'm being driven mad.

He glances up at me, his damp dark hair falling in his eyes, and he gives me his trademark crooked grin. Though the want on his face is written clearly, the way his pupils are dilated, how tense his jaw is, the way his lips are open and wet, I also see something else in his eyes. The feeling that no matter what happens next, he's got me.

With a hard, slick pull, he sucks my nipple into his mouth, and my hands shoot up to his thick hair, grabbing on tight. I know how fussy he is about his hair, and I don't blame him. He's got the perfect hair to hold in times like this.

Then he moves back, his lips leaving my breasts and trailing down the middle of my stomach, making light little kisses down and down and down.

I tense up, nervous and excited and desperate all at once.

I've never had a guy go down on me before.

Suddenly I'm glad that I'm still wet from the ocean, though perhaps that's my own desire as well.

Pascal slips his finger under one side of my bikini—the same side he was untwisting earlier, when the intimacy got too much for me—and instead of pulling them down over my hips, he undoes the ties until the bikini falls to the side.

"Jesus," he says in awe, and when I raise my head, I see him between my legs, staring at my pussy with the kind of eagerness that makes me feel like I'm about to be devoured. "You're fucking perfect, you know that? Absolutely perfect. I think I might stare at you all day."

I swallow hard, trying to think of something witty to say, but I've got nothing. I just want his face between my legs. I want to know what that strong, skilled tongue of his feels like there.

He grins at me, biting his lip. "You're absolutely soaked. It's beautiful."

While he keeps eye contact with me, he slips his finger down over my clit, through the slick folds, and back up. My back arches, my clit screaming for more of that, more of him. "You're beautiful. Just like this. Raw and drenched and begging for it. Are you begging for it?"

There's the dirty talker I knew would be in him. "Yes," I manage to say, the word choked.

"Tell me you're begging for it. Tell me you want my tongue to lap you up, again and again, until you can't take it anymore."

I let out a frustrated groan in response. I don't even know what he said, so I can't repeat it, all I can think about is that finger, the calloused tip of it sliding back and forth, the sound filling the air, competing with the waves.

*Jesus, I really am that wet,* I think. I'm almost proud of myself, though I know it's all Pascal's doing.

"I'm going to give you what you want," he says, moving back more and lowering his face until I can feel his breath on my pussy. "And then I'm going to give you more."

He touches my clit with the tip of his tongue, and I shudder, my hands tightening in his hair. His tongue takes its time moving up along my clit and back down, just as achingly slow as his finger, but now he starts plunging his tongue deep inside me, fucking me that way.

Oh fuck.

My back arches again, and I raise my hips, trying to get more purchase, to get more of everything.

He continues to fuck me with his tongue, and it's both amazing and not enough. I clench for more. I crave his cock. I want to be split open by him, I want him driven in deep, I want—

He moves his mouth up a few inches, and now I'm clenching without him there. His tongue and lips slide over my clit, and the feeling spurs a need in me so great that I cry out, "Oh fuck!"

He murmurs something against me, but I'm not sure what it is. It doesn't matter. Nothing matters except my hands in his hair and his mouth on my clit, swirling and sucking and licking until, until . . .

"I'm going to come," I say, though the words leave my mouth in a ragged cry.

I don't even have time to think about what it's going to be like, to prepare.

The pressure builds and builds, and then suddenly there's an explosion, a balloon popping, stars of confetti bursting through the air.

"Oh, Pascal!" I cry out, screaming, bucking my hips up into his mouth until I fear I might break his jaw.

His tongue slows, and I come back down to earth, trying to remember where I am. It feels like I'm a bird, soaring far above the sea, higher and higher until I'm just floating down like a feather. I know where I am. On the beach with Pascal. My hands are grasping his hair so tight that it actually hurts to undo my fists.

"You know what you taste like?" he says to me, and when I lift my heavy head to look at him, he's wiping my shiny desire from his lips and sliding his finger into his mouth. "You taste like something I've dreamed of but never had a word for. You taste like Gabrielle."

I blink at him, at his words, at the sight of him enjoying my taste, his messy, mussed-up hair falling in his eyes, but that look is still the same, the one that's both wild and full of wonder.

He gives me another wanton grin, and then he gets to his knees between my legs. His cock is practically bursting out of his boxer briefs, the darkened tip of it sticking out of the top of the waistband.

"Careful," he warns playfully. "If you keep staring at my cock like that, I might just come right now."

"I want you to come in me," I tell him. My boldness should surprise me, but it doesn't anymore, not when it comes to him.

"That can be arranged," he says, reaching down to take his cock out of his briefs. It's thick and long and impressive in his hands, seeming even bigger, larger than life, than I had felt before.

I swallow as he starts to prowl over me, but I don't want to have him like this.

"No," I say and try to get up.

He stops dead, wide-eyed and worried.

"I mean, I want to be on top," I tell him. I gesture to the sand. "Your turn to lie back."

His brows rise, as if to say, *Are you sure?*

I don't want to explain to him that I want to be in control. He had all the power just now as he ate me out, leaving me raw and vulnerable, spread open wide for him. Now I want to take him, and I want to be the one to do it. I want to see him succumb to me.

I nod at the sand, and he quickly gets back down, rolling over.

I stand up, letting the bikini bottoms slink down to the sand, and then I straddle him. His hands are at my ankles as I reach behind my neck and untie my top until my breasts are completely bare. I throw the top to the side and smile at him.

"Jesus," he swears again. "I've done nothing in my life to deserve this."

"Maybe you can make up for it after, then," I tell him and then drop to my knees, my thighs on either side of him, his cock jutting out in front of me like a joystick. I move up slowly, grabbing on to his shaft, feeling the heat and immense power pulse into my palm. He feels good, too good. I can't think about anything but us, right here in the moment. No future, no consequences, just *this*.

I lift myself up slightly, positioning his cock just right before I slowly, cautiously lower myself down.

I'm not going to lie. It hurts. There's a pinch, and I'm so tight that it takes a bit for my body to loosen, no matter how wet I still am.

"Go as slow as you want," Pascal says in a thick, throaty voice as he grabs the sides of my hips to help lift me up a bit. His hands look so tanned and large against my pale skin.

I nod, breathing through the tightness until I start to relax. I lower myself back down, my muscles straining as I do so. In and out, up and down, I ride him torturously slow, letting the thick tip of his cock slide over every bit. From the look on his face, his brows knitted together, his eyes pinched shut, the moans that are grinded out of his mouth, he's feeling the torture too.

His hands dig into my soft sides, and I start moving faster, rocking back and forth. He tries to reach up for my breasts, giving them a hard pinch, which makes me throw my head back and moan.

I don't know who I am in this moment with the sea and the sand and the sun, but I like this woman. I like the pleasure I'm feeling, I like how he's giving it to me, like it's a gift, like he knows how rare and precious it is for me.

I close my eyes and let every single feeling sink into me. The heat of the sun on my back, the feel of his hands as they slide back down my sides, the slide of his cock as I move up and down, feeling so full and lush.

"I want you to come," he says through a grunt, rocking me faster and faster before slowing down. It's like the both of us are trying to be in charge, but in the end it's clear we'll both be winners.

"If that's what you want," I tease, as if that wasn't in the cards. Though it's slightly awkward, I reach down to touch my clit, feeling kind of shy about doing this in front of him, but he bats my hand away.

"I want to make you come," he says again with emphasis and twists his hand to start rubbing my clit in circles.

Fuck. Me.

"Don't stop," I cry out softly, rocking him deeper and harder.

He grunts again in response, and I watch as he concentrates on getting me off with feverish intensity.

The way he's looking at me almost makes me come by itself.

And then the pressure starts to build, thick and hot and sweet, and I know I don't have long. I lean forward, and he raises his head, capturing my mouth in a wet and sweaty kiss. My tits bounce harder, and he slaps one of them, a beautiful spike of pain that makes me cry out and brings me so close to the edge. Then, when I don't think I can ride him any harder, sweat pouring down my spine and into my eyes, I lean back, exposing my chest to the sky.

"I dreamed this," Pascal says thickly. When I look down at him, he's staring at me like he can't decide if I'm real or not. "I dreamed this very thing. You fucking me like this, filled with light. All this light that came onto me." He trails off and closes his eyes, biting back a groan.

Then he dips his fingers to where I'm wet, rubbing the edge of his cock, and circles my clit hard.

That's all it takes.

"Oh fuck, oh fuck, oh fuck," I cry out as the orgasm crashes over me like a tsunami. I'm drowning in it, goose bumps and sweat covering my skin as I'm brought to another place again, up so fucking high.

It's enough to make me stop rocking—I can't feel my legs—but Pascal has a strong hold on my hips, and he keeps me moving up and down, fucking me into his cock, and it's not long before his thick throat is arching back and he's coming with a long and helpless groan.

"Jesus," he grunts. "*Oh fuck* is right."

I can't help the lazy smile on my lips, watching as the orgasm rolls through his body. It's a dream to see Pascal come undone like this, his torso slick with sweat, his hair messed up, his chest rising and falling with the power of his orgasm.

But I can't sit like this all day. I slowly ease myself off his cock, his cum running out of me, and then collapse on the sand beside him, catching my breath.

I'm not sure how much time has passed, but he rolls on his side to look at me. "Are you okay?" he asks.

I turn my head and give him a small smile. "I'm more than okay."

He reaches for me, brushing the hair off my face. I love it when he does that. "I didn't want to hurt you . . ."

"It was fine, Pascal. It was better than fine." I pause, licking my lips, my heart still knocking around in my chest. "I don't know how to process it. But I'm glad it happened."

The corner of his mouth quirks. "It was about time, if I'm being honest."

"If you're being honest," I repeat. "You don't realize how honest you actually are with me. I don't think you give yourself enough credit."

He raises a brow as if to say, *I don't?*

I laugh. "Okay, maybe you do."

Then his smirk flattens out, and a serious look comes across his brow.

"You've made a huge mistake," Pascal says, and my heart slows to a loud *boom-boom*, fear creeping back in. I stare down at him, at his sated, heavy-lidded eyes that are sparking with intensity, the firm determination on his jaw. "You're mine now. Every single inch of you is mine. That just sealed it. There is no escaping this."

I swallow the sawdust in my throat. I can tell he means it. I've never had anyone look at me the way he is, like I'm a possession, something he's dreamed of and finally has. I wouldn't mind it, either, if only . . .

If only he had been part of the plan.

And this is why I should have listened to those voices instead of letting my hormones guide me. Because there will be consequences for what we've done; I just don't know what they are.

But I know they won't be good.

"I didn't mean to scare you," he says, running his thumb over my cheek. "But I'm not backing off either."

I manage a smile, closing my eyes at his touch. "I know." I hesitate. "I don't want you to back off."

And that's the truth. No matter how messy this is going to get, no matter how much this might hurt the both of us, I don't want him to back off.

At least not while we're here.

I'm good at pretending.

I can pretend that there's no other world beyond this.

# CHAPTER TWELVE

## Pascal

The sins of the father don't determine the sins of the son.

I heard that somewhere, once upon a time.

I never took it to heart.

But now . . .

Now I have this woman sitting in the car beside me. Her shirt askew, her cheeks still flushed either from the sex or from the sun, her blonde hair back in a wet, tangled braid. She's smiling to herself, arm out the car, tapping to an imaginary song. I have this woman, and I have to wonder if this is what I've been missing out on my whole life.

Not that it's too late. I'm only thirty-one. I just feel I've done so much damage to so many people's lives that I was set to follow in that path, my father's footsteps, until the day I died.

Gabrielle has changed everything. I just don't know if it's too late for me to change.

"Are you hungry?" I ask her.

"I wouldn't mind a bite to eat, sure."

After we fucked on the beach, we went back in the water to cool off, clean off. It was fun, I have to admit, just splashing around with her, like a couple of teenagers. Occasionally I would be able to kiss her, other times she'd act shy. In the back of my mind, I kept thinking about what she told me; then I thought about the way she dived off the cliff and sank to the bottom of the sea, and both those things had me hitting the brakes when I got those vibes.

Truthfully, I don't know what I'm doing with her. This is brand-new territory for me. I'm the type to sleep with his maid, but I'm not the type to give a shit about her, and with Gabrielle, it's completely different. I give a shit. I care. I want more of what happened back there, not less. I don't want us to go back to the way it was, but it's going to get messy going forward. I'm not sure how long I'll be able to hide our relationship.

Because that is what this is, what this could be, anyway. I meant it when I said she was mine. She is mine, and I am hers, and perhaps this is completely out of character, but I don't want to share her with anyone else, and I don't want to be with anyone else.

For the first time in my life, I'm a one-woman kind of man. Maybe this is my new character.

It's hard to say, when most days I don't know who I really am.

Since the only food at the house is what we scarfed down for breakfast, we stop at a tapas bar in the nearest town. We both order small glasses of white wine and *patatas bravas* and chorizo and sit on the patio overlooking a small square. Mallorca in the summer is busy everywhere, but it's a nice change of pace from the remoteness of the villa.

"So, since you're the big fancy CEO of the Dumont label," Gabrielle teases, "how about I test your knowledge about clothes."

"A game? That's fun," I say, popping a spicy potato in my mouth. "What do I get if I win?" I wag my brows at her like a sleaze.

She laughs into her wine. "You'll get something. I'll make it worth your while."

"Is this for every time I get it right? You're going to run out of body parts to suck."

Her cheeks flush bright red, and she turns her head away from me. After a moment, she looks back, trying not to smile. "Okay, it'll be out of five."

"Fine. But do you know enough about fashion to know if I'm right or not?"

"We'll see," she says and then nods at a woman walking past the restaurant. "Her. What label is her bag?"

"Easy," I say, having noticed the distinctive chains and faux leather finish. "That's Stella McCartney. High-end vegan shit. What a waste of a design."

Gabrielle rolls her eyes. "Fine. You won that. How about that man there in the suit. Name something he's wearing."

The man is wearing a light-tan linen suit. I have absolutely no idea who makes it, but the belt is a no-brainer. "Gucci belt."

"Okay, I suppose that was easy." She looks around the restaurant and then lowers her sunglasses when she spots something. I turn to look at a fiftysomething woman and her husband having sangria. They're both dressed nicely, though the man is more on the touristy side. Dear God, I won't get this one right.

"Them," she says, nodding at them. "Anything."

I flip my aviators down over my eyes so I can stare at them without being a major creep. I have zero idea. They're both in matching khaki. The man's shorts could also be my shorts, except mine come almost to the knee, are impeccably woven and tailored to fit me, and cost $500.

"I give up," I say. "Walmart?"

She laughs softly. "Well actually, that woman's top is from H and M. Part of the African safari without having to go to Africa collection."

I tilt my head at her and flip up my glasses to give her an imploring look. "Please tell me you have shopped at somewhere other than the H and M sales rack."

"You are such a snob," she chides, reaching over with a toothpick and spearing one of my potatoes.

"I *am* a snob," I admit, trying to pull my plate away. "And I told you, I don't share, whether that means you or potatoes."

"You don't share. How could I forget," she muses.

I also told my father that.

When he was in my bedroom and somewhat threatening me over Gabrielle.

A trickle of uneasiness comes over me, though I can't quite place why.

If my father finds out about Gabrielle and me, this isn't going to be good. I don't know what his deal is with her and why he's so damn possessive, but the fact is, I know he'd have no qualms in punishing either of us for this. He may fire her; he may do worse.

What I do know is that I'm not going to go through any of that without a fight.

"Potato for your thoughts?" Gabrielle says, leaning across the table with a piece of potato for me. In the time I've been locked in my head, she managed to steal all my food and eat most of it.

I open my mouth and snatch the potato from the toothpick, giving her a reassuring grin. "I'm just thinking about what I'm going to do with my prizes. I won, didn't I?"

"We only did three."

"Fine."

We order another round of tapas and wine and play some more. I'm able to pick out a Chanel bag, a Tom Ford suit, and a Dolce & Gabbana sundress before I'm declared the winner.

"I guess I really had no chance," she says, leaning back in her chair, hands clasped at her stomach and smiling at me.

"No," I tell her. "Unless you thought everyone was wearing H and M. This tells me two things, of course." I tick off my fingers. "One is that you wanted to lose, and I get that. Why wouldn't you want to suck my cock later?" She snorts at that. "And two, you need a new wardrobe."

"Oh, is this the Cinderella part of the story? Because no thanks. I'm not touching anything Dumont with a ten-foot pole."

"Well, you were more than willing to touch this Dumont's ten-foot pole."

She coughs out a laugh. "Oh, come on. You wish."

"I don't wish, I know. I watched you ride me this afternoon with your fantastic tits bouncing up and down, writhing on top of my cock as it brought you to new planes of existence you didn't even know were there."

"*Pascal,*" she says in a hush, her body stiffening. I know she's worried about someone overhearing, but hell, everyone should overhear what a lucky fuck I am.

I shouldn't delight in making her uncomfortable like this, but I do.

After we're full, we head back to the villa. I should have been proactive and gotten something to make for dinner, but let's face it—Gabrielle would have done the cooking, and I didn't want to impose on her. Seems like the moment she stripped, her duties went with it. I can't complain; it's a fair trade, and I tell her I'm taking her out for dinner tonight.

"On a proper date," I add as we get out of the car.

"A date?" she asks. "Isn't it uncouth to date the maid?"

"No more uncouth than fucking her."

"You are so crude."

"Yeah," I tell her as I open the front door to the villa. "But I think you like it."

She shakes her head and steps inside. I'm exhausted, so I figure lying by the lap pool at the side of the house might be in order, but she heads for the stairs and says, "I'm going to take a nap."

I have to admit, I'm disappointed. I *hate* being disappointed.

I watch as she disappears, and I hear the door to her room close.

Hmm. I have no doubt she's tired, but I was hoping for a little more time together. Not exactly sex but . . . yeah. Sex. Sex would be nice.

But she's got issues, as she says, and she might need some time to figure it all out.

*Slow your roll, Pascal.*

It's just that I'm not used to that at all.

So while Gabrielle naps, I jerk off outside in the stark daylight, replaying what happened earlier in my head. Why not?

I think I actually pass out right after because when I come to, the sun is lower in the sky and Gabrielle is standing over me, shaking her head with a tiny smile on her lips.

"Huh?" I say, my voice thick with sleep. I look down and notice my cock is out, just as asleep as I was, my hand beside it.

"Am I interrupting something?"

"No, no," I say, sitting up and putting my cock back in my pants. "The something is already over."

"It's getting late." She gestures to the house, and it's only now that I notice that she's changed. She's wearing a pale-peach strapless sundress with ruffles along the bust. A little bit Spanish-looking, it makes her look extremely beautiful, especially when paired with glossy peach lips. I'm not going to ask her where it's from.

"You look beautiful," I tell her, getting to my feet. "I suppose I better dress to impress."

"I don't care what you do," she says, turning to walk back to the house. "As long as you're quick. I don't know what it is about this place, but I am absolutely starving."

"Sea, sun, and sex, baby," I tell her with a wink, following her inside.

I quickly shower and get dressed into tan linen pants and a dark-blue collared shirt, putting just a little bit of product in my hair and slipping a couple of condoms into my pocket. I observe myself in the mirror and again I'm struck by how distant I seem from myself. But this time it isn't a bad thing. I may not know who I am, really, when it comes down to it, but the guy in the mirror is a handsome fucker, and he has lightness in his eyes that was never there before. It's not quite peace, but in time it could be.

We're back in the car, and I'm taking her on the road to the city of Palma, where one of my favorite sushi restaurants is.

"I hope you don't mind," I tell her. "If you don't eat sushi, there are plenty of options."

"I like sushi," she says. "There was a great place near me in New York. A total hole-in-the-wall, but the fish was fresh and it was cheap. I would fill up on cucumber rolls and miso soup when I was broke."

"Did you work in New York?"

"Of course," she says, frowning in a way that says, *Come on.* "I had to. Who would have paid for me? I had saved up some money working for you guys, and then I just worked my way around Europe. Renting houses and apartments with tons of sketchy people, sleeping on couches, living out of a suitcase. Once I was in New York, it was the same deal. I had multiple jobs all the time and barely had enough to get by. I'm a connoisseur of ramen noodles."

"Well, you're in luck, because this restaurant has the best ramen noodles in the world."

"We'll see."

"By the way, about the letters," I say, and I can't help but notice her stiffen out of the corner of my eye. "I texted my mother earlier. There's been nothing."

"Well, that's good."

"Is it? It's been over a week since that last letter was sent, and it was the most threatening out of the bunch. They could be waiting."

"Does it make a difference, though?" she says. Then she twists in her seat to face me better. "Does it even make a difference at all? The letters are for your father, not for you. You're keeping the letters from him . . . why? Because you want him to get what's coming to him."

This isn't exactly the conversation I want to have with her, especially if we're on a so-called date. It's funny how we've only been here twenty-four hours, and yet any mention of the reality back home feels like a harsh intrusion.

"If you don't mind, I'd rather we talk about something else."

"But we're going to have to come back to this subject sooner or later."

"Then let it be later. Please."

She seems to hear the strain in my voice because she sits back. "Sorry."

"That's fine. Now, can we go back to me wooing you again?"

"Pascal," she says affectionately, a slow smile creeping onto her lips. "You know you don't have to woo me. I'm already wooed."

"I don't know about that. We got home, and you went straight to have a nap."

"And you went straight to have a wank."

"Because you were napping!"

She shrugs and looks down at her hands. "I just need time to figure some stuff out."

"That's what I thought."

"It's all moving so fast."

My heart sinks as I say, "We can pull back if you want. We can go back to the way it was."

She gives me a furtive glance. "Do you really believe that?"

"No," I admit. "But I could try. For you, I would. Anything to make you comfortable, anything to make you happy."

Gabrielle watches me for a moment and then places her hand on top of mine on the steering wheel. "Thank you for that. But when I'm with you, I am happy. Even if I don't seem it, even if my brain is stuck on worrying about other things, I'm happy. Or it's the closest thing to happiness I've felt."

"You didn't seem very happy when you jumped into the sea today."

She sighs and gives my hand a squeeze. "Like I said, I'm figuring things out. Just be patient with me."

"I am," I assure her, and in that moment, I know that if she wanted to call it off, if she wanted to wait forever, I might just have to do the same. There's truly no one else. Either she's my future or it's nothing at all. "Take all the time you need. I'll be here."

The subject in the car switches to lighter topics. Even though we're not supposed to talk about work, I have been ignoring calls and emails from the company all day, so I work through some troubleshooting with her. She's smart. Either that business school paid off for her, or she's just that bright. By the time we reach the restaurant an hour later, I feel a million times lighter.

The sushi place is big and spacious and completely modern—you'd think you were in Japan, not an island off the coast of Spain. The hostess recognizes me, either because I've been here many times before or because of the Dumont brand, and we're seated at a table at the back, facing the teppanyaki chefs in the middle and the rest of the restaurant.

I decide to sit on the other side of the table beside Gabrielle so we can both watch the chefs do their tricks together. She *oohs* and *aahs* in delight at everything they do, her pixie face alight with this joyous, buoyant enthusiasm as she watches them.

"I take it the sushi restaurant you went to didn't have this entertainment?" I ask, murmuring into her ear. There's no need to whisper, I just like to do it. Gives me a chance to smell her, too, that rich coconut scent. It's almost as good as the way she smelled earlier, legs wide open, pussy in my face.

She shivers and turns her head to me slightly, gazing into my eyes. "No. Nothing like this." Her gaze drops to my mouth, and I can feel the heat on my lips. Then she looks back to the chefs. "They're amazing."

"You're amazing," I tell her, sliding a hand down her thigh to the edge of her dress.

"You're going to give me a big ego if you keep paying me compliments like that," she says. For a moment I think she might bat my hand away, but instead she parts her legs a little more.

"Maybe you deserve it," I say to her. "Maybe you deserve everything."

I bring my hand up her thigh, slowly, slowly pushing up her dress and making my way up and up until my fingers graze the decadently soft skin of her pussy.

Fuck me. She's not wearing underwear.

She wanted this to happen.

"You little tease," I say into her ear, nipping the bottom of it. Needless to say, I'm turned on as fuck, and I was already turned on.

"I don't know what you're talking about," she says primly and then clears her throat, eyes forward. I see the waitress approaching with our bottle of cold sake, but I don't move my hand.

Instead I subtly slide my finger between her folds, finding her wet.

She tenses up, especially as the waitress does the grand display of showing us the bottle and then asking who wants to taste it.

"She wants to taste it," I say, nodding at Gabrielle. "She's the one with good taste."

"Very well," the waitress says with a big smile just as I start to rub my fingers in circles around Gabrielle's clit. As the waitress pours, Gabrielle tries her hardest to keep a normal face, but I can see the tick of her pulse in her neck, the way she's holding her jaw like she's trying to keep it together.

"Here you go," the waitress says as she pushes the glass closer to her before stepping back with the bottle in hand and waiting for Gabrielle's approval.

Meanwhile, Gabrielle gingerly reaches for the glass, and her grip around the stem tightens as I keep rubbing and rubbing and she keeps getting wetter and wetter. She somehow manages to bring the glass to her lips, and just as she takes her first sip and swallows, I gently thrust my finger up inside her.

"Oh God," she cries out softly, her eyes closed, mouth open.

"That good?" the waitress asks, looking amused.

The sake in Gabrielle's glass is starting to spill from her shaking, so she opens her eyes and quickly puts it back on the table. "Yes," she says in a hoarse voice as I continue to thrust my finger in and out. "Yes, it's excellent."

The waitress nods and then gives me a bemused look before retreating.

Once she's out of earshot, Gabrielle turns to me and hisses, "She knew what you were doing."

"I'm still doing it," I tell her, getting her wetter and wetter. "You're going to make a mess all over the seat. You better come with me to the restroom so I can get you all cleaned up."

Before she can protest, I remove my hand and then grab hers. I lift up our hands until they're at her lips, and then I probe her mouth with my finger. "This is the appetizer," I tell her, watching as she tastes herself. I don't think I've ever been so turned on, and I'm not sure how long I'll hold out. The blood in my head is pumping harder and hotter until I'm almost dizzy from it.

I get to my feet and pull her up with me and then lead her through the restaurant to the restrooms.

"What about the waitress? She'll think we've left without paying," Gabrielle says as I check the door. It's vacant.

"She knows exactly what's happening," I tell her, opening the door and hurrying her in there.

Once inside, I lock the door, and then I ravage her.

My hands grip her face, driving her backward toward the wall until she's pressed up against it. My mouth devours her, lips hungry for her lips, tongue thrusting into her mouth, playing with hers. She moans into my mouth, and I feel it all the way to my toes.

I'm in a frenzy. Hot-headed, skin tight and on fire, cock begging for release. I reach down and hike up her dress until it's bunched at her hips; then I slide my hands under her ass and lift her up so that her legs are wrapped around me.

In a flurry, I spin her around and place her on the edge of the sink as she braces herself from falling with her hands on the black tiled wall. I crouch down and immediately bury my face between her legs, licking up and down her, drinking in every drop, careful not to waste any.

"Oh fuck," she cries out, legs spread wider for me while she grabs my hair like she did earlier. I fucking love it, fucking her with my mouth, tasting her, feeling her pulse beneath my lips, the way she pulls at my strands, sending sharp shards of pleasure and pain until I'm almost coming in my pants.

Just before she's about to come, her body tensing, I pull back and straighten up, quickly unzipping my pants and taking out my cock. It's nearly painful to handle, I want her that badly. I can barely get the condom on quickly enough.

I grab her around the small of her back, holding her there, and guide my cock into her. There's a split second where all that anticipation and lust and raw, primal need hang in the air, and then I'm driving myself inside her, to the hilt.

She cries out loudly, and I move my hand to her mouth, trying to keep her quiet. I don't care if the waitress here knew I was finger fucking Gabrielle under the table, but it's different if the whole restaurant knows. People can be gossips, and everyone has a cell phone now. Many, many times have I ended up in the tabloids and papers and internet sites because of my carelessness with women in public.

I don't want that to happen with Gabrielle. We have too much to lose now.

Gabrielle nods beneath my hand, looking trusting, and I remove it as I continue to pump into her harder and harder. The sink digs into my hips as I fuck her against it, and her legs wrap tighter around my waist, holding me in place. Her hands move up and down my shirt, nails digging into my muscles and working their way down to my ass where she takes a hard hold, pulling me into her until I'm driven so deep inside her pussy, the breath is knocked out of my lungs.

"Fuck," I swear, grunting with each thrust, the sweat beading on my forehead and rolling off the tip of my nose and onto her collarbone. "Fuck, I'm not going to last long. I need you to come with me."

"So make me," she says in a thick, throaty voice, leaving quick bites along my neck. "Make me come, Pascal."

Jesus. I've never heard anything sexier before.

I start arching up, driving my cock up at an angle, trying to get her coming from the inside, and then when I realize it's only making me want to come, I slip my fingers over her clit.

The combination is all it takes. She comes, biting down on my shoulder to muffle her cries, her legs shaking as she convulses around my dick, squeezing and milking me until I have no choice anymore but to come.

Almost there.

*Fuck.*

The release slides up my spine, and it's like a bomb going off, blowing my mind and body apart as I come, shooting straight into her as my pumps begin to slow. I groan loudly, lost to the feeling, lost to the sensation of her around me, feeling her deep inside. All her secrets seem like they've been brought to the surface, for me and me only.

If she's not my salvation, if she's not my redemption, then she's something better and greater than that.

I think I might be finding a better version of myself in her.

A better man.

"Fuck me," she whispers, her hands coming to the side of my face. She holds me in her grasp, sliding her thumb around my chin in a blissed-out, thoughtful way.

"I think I just did," I manage to say, my voice rough.

She smiles at me sweetly, the kind of smile that radiates joy from her eyes.

I lean in and place a soft kiss on her lips, smiling against them.

Because I'm happy.

I'm fucking happy.

"We should get back to the table before our food gets warm," I tell her with a smirk, grabbing my cock and pulling out of her.

"Ha-ha," she says in a goofy way, and I grab her by the waist and lift her off the sink. Her legs are a bit shaky as we quickly adjust each other, making sure we both look presentable.

I kiss her on the forehead before we leave. "Let's go have the second course."

# CHAPTER THIRTEEN

## GABRIELLE

For the first time in a long time, I wake up rested, like I actually had a full night's sleep. The feeling is so strange to me that it takes me a while to wonder who I am and where I am.

And then . . . who I'm with.

I'm lying naked under the covers in a bedroom that wasn't the one I passed out in on our first night.

It's Pascal's room.

And he's sleeping in bed right beside me, on his back, head to the side. His eyes are closed, and he's snoring ever so slightly.

The sight of him makes me stop and stare.

I still can't really believe it.

Yesterday was such a blur, full of things I didn't dare imagine or dream for, that I'm still unsure if this is a dream right now.

I mean, he's here. I'm in his bed. We're both naked.

After he fucked me in the restaurant bathroom, we went out and had an amazing sushi meal. Then it was a long drive back to the villa. You'd think we would have gone straight to sleep, but instead he brought me to his bed and I went willingly.

I wanted him.

I want him.

The more I have him, the more that need builds, that need that's making me crazy, that's clouding my thoughts and judgment and blowing it all into the wind.

I adjust myself carefully on the bed, ignoring the inner voices, the ones that are warning me and telling me I'm going to screw up somehow. I mean, the fuck-up is imminent.

But then there's Pascal lying beside me.

So fucking handsome. And in sleep, a bit more boyish, almost innocent. His high cheekbones are softened somehow, his lips even fuller and rose pink. I've never had the chance to stare at him like this before; usually his eyes are so intense and arresting that they steal the focus. They demand you look at him, and he holds eye contact like it's a sport.

He looks like all his sins have been stripped away.

Which makes all my sins even worse.

How can I go through with what I'm supposed to do when I'm sharing a bed with him? Pascal hates his father, but that doesn't mean he'd turn a blind eye if he found out what I want to do.

*Focus on your mother first,* I remind myself. *When you get back next week, you do what you can with her. Maybe even ask Pascal for help.*

But how do I do that without telling him what happened?

"Are you watching me sleep?" Pascal asks, his voice groggy, eyes still closed.

I can't help the smile spreading across my face, and I reach over and let my fingers trail up from his flat belly, through the hard ridges of his abs, to his firm, golden chest. The man has a magnificent body, the kind that makes you wonder why he's not modeling Dumont underwear instead of cologne.

"Maybe," I tell him.

He opens his eyes and looks at me.

There they are.

Those saturated blues, that gaze that could launch—or destroy—a thousand ships.

Even in the morning, he's looking at me with the confidence of a man secure in what he has. Me. I'm his possession. And as much as that scares me, I also need it to be true. Just for this week, perhaps, until we return to the reality that's going to drop-kick me to the ground.

"How did you sleep?" he asks softly, reaching up to touch my cheek. "Better question is, am I still asleep? Because I had the most wonderful dream . . . I was fucking your brains out on the beach, in a restaurant restroom, in this bed . . ."

"That's funny," I say as he runs his thumb over my lips, my eyes locked with his, sleepy and seductive. "I had the same dream."

He grins at me salaciously and reaches down, pulling the sheets off him, exposing his very large, very hard cock pointing straight up at his stomach.

Automatically, I lower my hand on it, relishing the feel of him, how hot and rigid and soft he is. There's a warm flutter of want between my legs, even though I'm a bit sore everywhere from yesterday.

"This isn't a dream, is it?" he asks as I gently start stroking him, my palm sliding over him, my grip loose to start.

"I wouldn't think so," I tell him. "Unless I'm sleepwalking."

"Sleep fucking, that's a new one," he muses, and I tighten my grip, causing his eyes to roll back in his head, his mouth to drop open and let out a moan. When he opens his eyes, his brow is knit together in stark determination to have me.

I don't have time to react. He's on me in a second, flipping me over so that I'm on my back and he's on top of me, his cock pressed against my pelvis, his hands taking hold of my wrists and pinning them above my head. I watch the strain in his biceps as he holds me, transferring the weight to one hand as he reaches down with his other and slips his stiff cock between my legs.

"Condom?" I ask. It was a major momentary lapse of judgment that we didn't use one the first time we slept together. Out there on the beach, it was like all logic and reason went out the window, and I was a slave to my desire for the very first time in my life.

He pauses and nods, reaching over into his bedside table to take one out. He slowly slips it on, and I enjoy watching him do it until he's ready.

I smile up at him in anticipation, spreading my legs for easier access.

"No," he says, bringing his mouth to the spot below my ear and giving it a long lick, causing me to erupt in an explosion of shivers. "Keep your legs together."

I do as he says, and when he tries to push his cock inside me, the tension between my legs only makes me throb and ache harder for him.

"Oh." I let out a small gasp as he slowly, deliberately pushes in. I feel myself trying to expand, but the harder I hold my legs together, the tighter it is. "I don't know if you'll fit this way," I say, my heart starting to whoosh loudly in my ears.

"I appreciate the compliment," he says, his lips coasting down my neck. "But the fun part is trying. Just breathe."

So I do, willing myself to relax while still making it tight for us. He's able to push in deeper, though the fact that he has to go so slowly is making him shake with tension, his neck corded, his jaw grinding together as he drives in to the hilt.

"Fuck," he swears, hair falling over his eyes. Whatever innocent Pascal I saw this morning is gone and has been replaced by someone wild, primal, raw, and I'm trapped in his feral stare. "You feel so fucking good, Gabrielle. I am all but lost to you." He slowly pulls back out with a groan, but his eye contact doesn't break. "I'm not sure I want to be found."

"I don't either," I tell him, and as he pushes in again, I have to close my eyes. The intimacy is too much, and it feels too good. My proverbial heart is starting to rise and fall with his words, with his look, his touch.

I am losing myself to him, body and soul, and it scares me that I may never get the me I know back.

What if I belong to him forever?

Would it be so bad? To be fucked like this? To be wooed like this? To have such sweet words from a bad man? If he's only good to me, does that make him good?

"Stop thinking," he says roughly, and when I open my eyes, his face is inches from mine. He's searching me with a raw intensity, determined to find something. I just don't know what he's looking for. "Stop thinking and start feeling. I know you feel, Gabrielle. I know you feel me." He slides his hand over my clit, which sends sparks out along my nerves, like I'm constructed of live wires. "*Feel* me."

"I feel you," I say through a groan, my voice throaty, breathy, lost in his touch.

"Don't stop."

"I won't if you won't."

He pistons his hips into me harder, a bit faster, the force causing my legs to come apart. His grip tightens around my wrist, and he takes his hand off my clit for a moment to slap my breasts as they bounce up and down. "Keep them together," he grinds out. "Feel me."

I feel nothing but him.

Every stroke of his cock as it drags along each sensitive spot inside, the feel of his hips as they slam into me, the way his hand feels around my wrist, keeping me bound and in place. I would have thought this type of sex would have triggered me in some way, but with Pascal it's cathartic. It's something that's real, about bringing me pleasure, making me feel wanted, needed, desired.

Respected.

"Come on, little sprite," he says, placing his lips on mine in a quick and messy kiss. "I want to hear you come undone."

I moan into him, the sound becoming louder, wilder as he starts stroking me again, fingers slick and slippery against me.

I'm coming.

"Oh God!" I scream, the orgasm taking hold of me, making me feel open and new. My head goes back, my back arches, my legs fall apart as it rides through me, wave after wave. "Fuck, fuck . . . oh, Pascal . . ." I trail off, unable to keep the words from coming from my mouth.

"God, that's so hot," he says, and he starts driving in deeper, deeper, every muscle in his body shaking from the exertion. "I'm going to come just from you saying my name."

And he does come, driving in so deep that I can't breathe and I cry out, my body still throbbing around his cock as he shoots into the condom. He grunts out a string of expletives as his body finishes, and then he slows, sweat dripping off his body onto mine, his abs straining.

"Jesus," he swears, pumping once, twice, and then nearly collapsing on me. His sweaty chest is rising and falling against my breasts, and he brushes the hair off my face, staring at me with a sated expression. "Tell me I'm yours. I need to know it. I need to feel it."

I don't hesitate, though maybe I should.

The words just come out.

"I'm yours."

◆ ◆ ◆

"I don't want to go home," I say quietly, staring at the glowing blue pool, the dark sky with endless stars above us.

Pascal reaches for the wine from the small table in between us and nods, having a sip of the cold, crisp chardonnay. "I know."

It's ten o'clock at night, and we're lying on the lounge chairs by the small lap pool at the side of the house. We're covered up by towels from the slight chill that comes off the sea some evenings, but we're both completely naked underneath. We've been here in Mallorca one week now, and we've lapsed into just being naked around each other all the time. It's absolutely freeing, being able to do this with someone, plus we're screwing twenty-four hours a day. It's just a lot more efficient this way when you don't have to worry about taking off clothes and putting them back on again.

Tomorrow morning, we go back home.

Home, even though it's not my home.

I've been dreading it. It's been a wonderful cocoon being here with Pascal. My nightmares have ceased; I've even been able to sleep. I know the life we've built here this last week isn't a real one, but it's the one I want, the one I never thought I'd have. Having someone by my side who cares for me, has my back, makes me feel the kind of pleasure and bliss that should be downright illegal. He's my eternal high.

When we leave, I don't know if what we have will last. I'm not sure how it can. How can I be free around Pascal when his father watches me like a hawk? How can I feel comfortable when I still live in that house, when I have to get my mother out, when I still might have to do the unthinkable?

Yes, unthinkable.

But I'm still thinking about it, here and there.

I'm not sure what I'm going to do.

"I wish we could stay forever," Pascal admits, staring at me with kind eyes. "And I really mean that. I mean . . . I really do. I'm not looking forward to going back any more than you are. But I have to. Like it or not, if I don't run the company, someone else will have to, and I don't feel like being replaced right now."

"Do you love the job that much?"

He shrugs, pressing his lips together in thought. "I don't know. I don't think in terms of love."

*Oh.*

"I just know it's mine. And it's my job to do. You have to understand, my whole life has been gearing up to this, to being in charge of the Dumont label."

"But is that what you want or what your father wants?"

He has a look that says, *Shit*. He hadn't considered that. "I don't know," he says after a moment. "I never thought of it that way. I just knew it was something I wanted."

"But maybe you just wanted power and approval. Maybe it's not actually the job that you do."

He puts his wine down and sighs, leaning back in his lounge chair. "Maybe. But then what the fuck do I do? I don't even know what I want from life, I've either been told what to do or I've had something to prove." He glances at me, frowning. "If this isn't what I was born and raised for, why did I do so many horrible things in order to obtain it? If I throw away my career, it means all the people I've hurt have been for nothing."

I swallow hard, feeling his anxiety rolling off him. It's never easy to question yourself. It's why I don't make a habit of it.

If all I thought I was isn't who I'm supposed to be . . .

Who am I?

My obsession with Gautier has been my whole life. If I were to drop it, if I were to let it go, I'm not sure I'd even recognize myself.

"I know how you feel," I tell him quietly. "When you're afraid of really looking at yourself. What if you don't like the person you find?"

"All I know is that I've found you," he says. "The rest doesn't really matter."

"But . . . ," I say and pause because I really don't want to approach the subject, I really don't want any truth or reality. I want to keep this life here on this island going forever. But I know it's not possible. Not even a little. "What's going to happen to us when we go back? Is there even going to be an us? Am I . . . am I reading too much into this?"

He sits up, spearing me with his gaze. "You think you're reading too much into this?"

I shrug, looking back at the pool and feeling on the spot and a bit stupid. "Maybe. I mean . . . you and me. Here. It's perfect. But is it just supposed to be for here?"

"Is that what you want?" His voice gets low and sharp.

I could tell him yes. Put my shields back up and end it. But I can't do that. So I choose to be vulnerable. "No. It's not what I want."

"What do you want?"

"I want you." I sneak a glance at him.

His features soften slightly. "You have me, okay? You have me. This doesn't end here. It continues. I told you that you were mine, and I'm yours too. I'm not backing down. I'm not letting go. I may be a wicked man in many ways, but I'm not stupid. I know when I've got something good for me in my hands, and, little sprite, you are perfect for me. In every single way."

"You deserve someone better than me," I tell him.

"I don't think that I do," he says.

"I'm . . . I'm not perfect. I've got . . ."

"Issues. Yes, I know. You have daddy issues, I have them too. You've been through trauma, I have too, though not to your extent, not even a little. But I get where you're coming from, because I've come out of a similar place. I deserve you and you deserve me because we're more alike than you think."

"You mean both of us are slightly off?"

"And I wouldn't want it any other way. How boring would it be if we were normal?"

He says that, but he really has no idea.

If I stay with Pascal, how can I possibly go through with what I have planned? Even if he doesn't find out, even if it goes so perfectly that I'm not caught, how can I live with myself, knowing what I've done?

"Listen," he says, swinging his legs over the side of the chair, the towel dropping to his waist. He reaches out and takes my hand in his. "I know you're worried, but I've got you. What we have here, we will have there, I promise. Maybe we'll have to hide it for a while, but what I feel for you won't go away."

What he feels for me?

What does he feel for me?

"I don't think your family will ever understand," I tell him carefully, trying to convey so much by saying so little.

"They don't really matter."

"Your father will care."

His jaw sets firmly as his eyes grow sharp. "Believe me when I say, I've got you. My father has no say."

"But your father has ways of correcting things when they don't go his way."

His brow furrows. "Are you afraid he's going to hurt you or me?"

"Both," I whisper.

"You're like his favorite . . ." He trails off.

"Pet?" I fill in. "I know. Believe me, I know. And what happens to me when you try to take me away?"

"He's not going to touch you. He wouldn't do that."

*Oh, he wouldn't, would he? Pascal, you are so blind sometimes.*

I have to wonder how long it took for him to admit it to himself, what his father did to Ludovic, especially after his own brother came to the same conclusion.

"I'm afraid of him," I admit.

"I know you are. But you shouldn't be. Do you have any reason?"

The words are on the tip of my tongue, just begging to come out.

"He's a *murderer*," I eke out.

Pascal exhales through his nose in a huff and looks down at my hand in his, shaking his head. "I know he is. And I know . . . I know." He lets go of my hand and drags his palms over his face, anguish on his brow. "Fuck, I know I have to do something about it. That I just can't live with him anymore knowing this. That it isn't right. It isn't fair. That if I let him get away with it, then I'm just as bad as he is and, Gabrielle, baby, I don't want to be like him anymore. I . . . I've seen what redemption looks like. I've felt it when I'm inside you, looking into your eyes, into your heart. That's what I want now. And I'll get it through you."

I feel a pinch of relief in my chest. Even though I know I can't be his redemption because my veins run hot with revenge, I'm so glad to hear him say this, to hear him admit it to himself. That he can't be his father's son anymore. That the cycle has to stop, and it will stop with him.

"Gabrielle," he whispers, leaning across to grasp my chin between his fingers. He looks deep inside my eyes, to my heart and bones. "I'm not letting you go, no matter what. We're going to get through this, through all of this, together."

His eyes flutter closed, and he places a soft kiss on my lips, a kiss filled with longing and lust and something deeper than that.

I think I've fallen for him.

It might be the biggest mistake I've ever made.

# CHAPTER FOURTEEN

## Pascal

"It's my day off, for fuck's sake, find someone else to figure it out." I hang up the phone and cover my face with my hands, letting out a low growl.

We've been back from Mallorca for more than two weeks now, and I know that I've had a shit ton of catching up to do, but it seems that instead of the work being delegated to the heads of the departments like it should be, everyone keeps coming to me.

The fact that I'm at home and it's a Sunday doesn't seem to matter. I've had to field call after call of people inquiring about the upcoming spring fashion show (yes, the spring lines debut in the autumn). Our head designer is the one who is in charge of that; we've had the location in the Grand Palais booked since last year. I have little to no say except clearing the budget, and yet everyone keeps calling me.

*Because everyone is new; because your two best people, Seraphine and Blaise, left; because you're a dick, and your father is a murderer.*

I know that's true, but it doesn't stop it from stressing me out.

I sigh and get up, looking out the window at the lawn beneath. Gabrielle and her mother are having lunch on their patio. They seem to be arguing about something, something I'm not privy to. Suddenly

Jolie throws her hands up in the air and storms into the guesthouse, and Gabrielle follows, shutting the door behind her.

I know that when Gabrielle first wanted the job, she said it was because of her mother. That she was worried about her. When I've broached the topic before, Gabrielle got that look on her face, the one she gets when you want her to open up and she's nowhere near ready. It reminds me of a cornered animal, and because I know she can lash out from fear, I don't want to provoke her.

But if she's still worried about her mother, I'm worried about her.

I knew it wasn't going to be an easy transition coming back here, and I knew that Gabrielle didn't want to come. I don't blame her. It didn't take long for us to fall back into our familiar patterns, me stressed about work, her walking around like she's being followed all the time. When we pulled up in front of the house, it was like I saw the joy sink from her eyes. In that moment, I wanted nothing more than to turn the car around and drive far, far away.

But we can't run from our problems forever.

I know I can't.

And since Gabrielle said she was going to have a meaningful talk with her mother, maybe she's facing them head-on too.

I sigh again and turn from the window, heading out of the office and down the hall. I can hear my mom on the phone with someone in her room, giggling in a high voice. If she's smart, she's got a lover on the line, hopefully someone a bit nicer than my father.

I hear my father stirring in his room, his door slightly ajar, so I hurry down the staircase to the first floor. The last thing I want today is to talk to him. I haven't been able to avoid him at all this week—he's been at the office more than normal, telling me that he's trying to pick up after my slacking—and most of the time, he's downright sinister. I don't know what has come over him, but I know it has to have something to do with Gabrielle.

Which is why I don't want him to know anything at the moment. We're sneaking around, trying to be extra careful. I'm still paranoid about bugs, so we don't talk inside, except in the bathroom. That happens to be where we fuck a lot too. Also in the car, in the woods behind the house, in the gazebo. The other night, she came to my room and we had sex in total silence, which was also extremely hot.

I just don't know how to approach it. I shouldn't be afraid of my father. I want to stand up to him and be defiant in my feelings for her. I want him to know that I will choose her over him every time.

I know I need to play my cards right, though. Because this isn't just your normal father-son relationship.

I remember what he said earlier this year when I made it clear that I wasn't going to hurt Seraphine or collect her for his own revenge. He told me he has every means to turn around and pin Ludovic's death on me, even though there isn't a shred of evidence, even though I had nothing to do with it.

The truth is, I didn't even know what he was going to do that night at the masquerade ball. I was under the impression that Father just wanted to sabotage things, make Ludovic sick and unstable so that he could take over the company, so that I would rise in the ranks with Olivier's shares gone. He had told me he had a plan to take his brother out of the picture "for now," and the thought of him murdering him didn't even cross my mind.

But then Ludovic dropped dead in front of my eyes, while my father was grinning at him like a fucking skull, and then I knew. I knew immediately what my father had done. Whether it was poison or other means, who knows. The autopsy was no doubt paid off. I just knew that my father had murdered his own brother in cold blood, and I had no choice but to stand by and look and pretend that this didn't really happen. Pretend that Seraphine's wild accusations were part of an overactive imagination. I had to pretend that when I was helping my father, I was doing it for the good of myself, the good of the company.

So much pretending. It's like the mask I wore that night Ludovic died had never come off. It hadn't come off until I let Gabrielle into my life, and she removed it with her beauty and vulnerability and strength. And she liked the man she saw underneath, a man I don't know.

A man I want to know. A man who is still looking for something to stand for.

There is a change coming now, the same change that I felt before. It's unstoppable. And when it happens, I will never be the same. This family will never be the same. The Dumont brand will never be the same.

In the end, that might just be a good thing.

It's a cloudy day, so the halls are dark as I make my way into the kitchen. As I head toward it, I think I hear a noise from the study.

I go over and peer around the corner, seeing Gabrielle standing by the books, running her hands over them as if in a trance.

I stand there in the doorway, watching her for a few moments. Usually she's so aware of her surroundings, it surprises me that she hasn't seen me yet.

Then I realize there are tears running down her face.

Immediately, I spring across the study toward her, having to step back just in time before it looks too intimate.

"What happened?" I whisper.

She's holding the book with the bullet hole in it. "Did your gun do this?"

I blink at her, shake my head absently. "No, it was Blaise's gun. Or Seraphine's. Mine was in the desk."

"This desk?" she asks and opens the drawer. The gun is gone.

"I had it there just in case. It's upstairs now, you know this. Why are you crying?"

I glance over at the hall and the staircase, but I see no one. I reach for her, cupping her beautiful, ethereal face in my hands and wiping away her tears.

"It's nothing," she says softly, her eyes downcast.

"I've never seen you cry," I tell her, and it's true. It's breaking my heart. "It has to be something. Please tell me."

She swallows loudly. "It's my mother."

"Is she okay?"

She shakes her head, still avoiding my gaze. "No. And she'll never be. But there's nothing I can do. I have no choice."

"No choice for what?" I ask her. When she doesn't answer me, when another tear drops to the floor, I put my hands on her shoulders and shake her slightly. "No choice for what?"

"I need to fix this, Pascal," she whispers, finally looking up at me through wet lashes.

"Fix what?"

She clamps her mouth together for a moment, staring at me with such hopefulness that I feel my heart crack, just a little, and then she reaches up and kisses me.

I kiss her back, tasting her tears, wanting to take away whatever pain she's feeling. I want to be that one for her, the one to make her nightmares end. I know she has them—we've slept together enough times that I've seen her thrashing all night, crying out, and when she's not having a nightmare, she's sitting up in bed, staring at the wall in the dark for what seems like hours.

She talks about wanting to fix things, and I get it, I really fucking do, because all I want is to be able to fix *her*.

"I have to go," she says when she pulls away.

"Where are you going?" I ask, grabbing hold of her hand.

"I need to try again with my mother," she says.

"Will you ever tell me what this is about?"

"I'd like to," she says, giving my hand a squeeze while another tear falls from her eyes. A noncommittal answer but I let it go for now.

Then she stands on her tiptoes, reaching up again to kiss me on the mouth.

"I love you, Pascal," she says quietly. "Always believe that." Then she quickly drops away and hurries out of the room.

I stand there, stunned.

Her words feel like a slap in the face, but there's no pain in them, only pleasure, only this searing, warming convergence around my heart.

She loves me.

For some stupid, ill-advised reason, she *loves* me.

I've always thought of myself as a man too wicked to love and too wicked to be loved, and yet she loves me.

I don't even know how to deal with that. I don't even know how I feel. All I know is that I do feel; I feel more than I ever have before in my whole entire life.

It took thirty-one years to hear it.

I wonder how much longer it will take for me to believe it.

I don't know how long I stand there in the study, staring at the empty space where she once was. Eventually I have to move, to process, to make sense.

I'm going to need her to open up to me in every way possible.

If she truly loves me, there are to be no secrets between us, not even little ones.

I head out of the study and grab my keys. I exit the house and get into my car and drive off, fast. I need to feel the rush of air, the thrill of speed, something to make sense of what I'm grappling with.

But as fast as I go on the narrow country roads, I can't escape what she told me.

She loves me.

I can't outrun that truth.

She loves me.

I don't know how long I drive for, but suddenly I have to pull over into a farmer's lane, thrusting the car in park and putting my head on the steering wheel, trying to breathe.

She loves me.

I need to let that feeling—that it's real, that I deserve it—into my heart, even just a fraction. I need to be able to accept it, or what we have is never going to work.

I need to figure out how I feel about her, and I need to tell her with the same conviction that she told me.

But how do I know if I love her? How do I know what love is? All that I've seen of love has been the mask over the lies. Love is a pretty cover-up. Love is what a father denies his son. Love is what a mother gives, but only when you're good enough. Love is what you tell your wife, knowing she's playing exactly into your plan. Love is a game, and it's up to you to stay on top, playing everyone until you're the only winner.

I have no idea how much time has passed out there on the side of the road until I notice storm clouds rolling in from the north and the sky growing darker. I glance at my watch and see that it's already six p.m. I should go back for dinner soon, though I don't have an appetite at all. Besides, it's Sunday, which means my mother is cooking, and even I have better skills than she does. She's just probably going to drink vodka.

I drive back and make it home just as rain starts to fall, a late summer thunderstorm rumbling in the distance.

It matches my chaotic mood.

I enter the house and go up the stairs to my office. I can hear my mother and father discussing something in the kitchen, something I don't want any part of, so I sneak past them.

Even though work was pissing me off earlier, I could use the distraction now. Maybe if I shove everything that just happened to the back of my mind, my subconscious can go to work on it and figure it out. Seems it can be a lot smarter than I give it credit for.

I open my laptop and see that more emails have piled up. One of them has a Word attachment I have to open, some bullshit for the HR department (seriously, again, it's a Sunday—since when are the French workaholics?).

I open up the document, read it through, and then do a virtual signature, only it's not working.

I have zero patience with computers. I'm always one second away from either putting my fist through it (which doesn't work when you have a laptop) or hurling it across the room (which does work very well when you have a laptop).

Taking a deep breath to steady my patience, I decide to print out the document instead.

Of course, the printer says there is a queue, though I don't know how that's possible, since I don't remember the last time I printed something out. I'm surprised I even have paper, to be honest, though I figure maybe Gabrielle refilled it for me. She might have been printing out my schedule as well.

I push the rest of the backed-up documents to print, and they start to go through the machine, feeding out blank pages first until it starts to print something. I barely have time to read it before it falls to the floor, but in that brief glance, I see something that makes my skin crawl.

No.

It can't be.

Holding my breath, I crouch down and pick up the corner of the paper, almost afraid to look at it, for it to tell me the truth.

I flip it over.

The paper has the following words printed out on it:

*There's no place to hide. Soon the letters will end and I'll be coming for you.*

The letter that was addressed to my father was written on my computer.

But that's not the end of it.

Another letter prints out, and I grab it before it falls.

*Await my instructions or you will lose everything.*

I stare at the papers in my hand, my mind grappling with the truth. I hadn't seen that last one before. What the fuck?

What the *fuck*?

The third paper falls from the machine, the HR document, but it seems so foreign and trivial to me in light of all this, I let it stay on the floor.

I take the papers over to my desk and then start going through my Word files on the computer, trying to find the source of them. I don't find it anywhere in the Word documents, but I find a few in the trash, some of them ones I haven't seen.

Who is doing this?

But the question is futile, because even though I'd like to think my father is the one behind them, even though I wouldn't know why, there's only one other person who has access to my computer via password.

Just then the door to my office flies open, and I have just enough time to slip the papers in my desk and close the documents on the computer.

It's my father, dressed in a black suit, like he's going to a funeral even though it's Sunday night.

"Pascal," he says to me with a stiff smile. "I need to have a word with you."

"Now really isn't a good time," I tell him, no smile in return. "And there really is such a thing as knocking."

"Manners have to take a back seat sometimes," he says, standing on the other side of the desk and staring down at me. "This is one of those times."

His eyes look black, cavernous. It takes a lot to hold his eye contact these days. I know what he's capable of, and looking into the eyes of the devil is hard when he's your father.

"I received some letters," he says simply, and my heart stills in my chest. I watch, unable to breathe, as he reaches into his suit pocket and pulls out folded slips of paper.

He places them on the desk and waits for me to unfold them.

One of them is the one I discovered earlier.

*Await my instructions or you will lose everything.*

Another is the first letter that was sent.

Then the next.

And everything that was sent in between, everything I intercepted, everything that wasn't addressed to anyone.

Finally, the last one says:

*1692 Rue Saint-Jacques, Sunday 8 p.m.*

"When did you get these?" I ask, hoping my hand isn't starting to shake.

"Almost every single day last week." He pauses. "Since you got back."

"Were they addressed to the house?"

"No. The office."

*Gabrielle,* I think. *What are you doing?*

But there is no time to dwell on it.

The fact is that this whole time, she was lying to me, she was the one sending the letters.

But why? Why send to me first and then my father?

Why send them at all?

"I don't understand," I say quietly, not wanting to meet his eyes.

"I can see that you don't," he says, his voice dripping with disappointment. "And that should make me feel better, knowing you're not the one behind them. But it also makes me see that you're just too stupid to catch on."

I look up sharply. "Too stupid?"

"You really have no clue, do you?"

I shake my head, my eyes narrowing. "Enlighten me."

"You really don't know who would bother sending me these letters? These immature, laughable, naive little letters?"

I don't want to say it. "Seraphine?" I ask.

"Seraphine knows better than that. And this isn't her style. And before you come up with any other idiotic answers, no, it isn't your brother and it's not Olivier. It's not your mother and it's not Jolie. Who else does that leave?"

Oh, fuck.

He knows.

"Gabrielle," I whisper, staring out the window, watching the rain hit the panes.

"Yes, your little lover girl."

I glare at him, but he laughs in response, showing the palms of his hands. "Easy there. Do you think I'm dumb, son? Do you think it wasn't obvious the way you look at each other, like lovesick teenagers? Did you think it wasn't suspicious that you took her to Mallorca? Do you think I didn't just catch the two of you kissing in the study?"

I gulp.

"The biggest disappointment," he continues, clasping his hands at his front, "is that you didn't even bother to hide it very well. I warned you, Pascal. I told you to stay away from her. I told you we had unfinished business, and you went against my orders anyway. I don't take that lightly."

I ignore that. "Why would she send you letters? What did you do?"

"Nothing," he says. "I also told you she was crazy. Here's the proof." He gestures to the letters. "Who would do such a moronic thing, as

198

if it wasn't obvious it was amateur hour? Oh, she would have gotten caught eventually."

"Caught for what? These letters aren't exactly extortion. They ask for nothing."

"You're right. They are false threats, meant to scare, I suppose. Only speaks of her intellect at the moment. Surely you've noticed that she's not right in the head? Or were you too busy getting your cock sucked for that?"

"Yeah, I probably was," I tell him, sick of this. "Is that a problem? Does it make you feel old and powerless because she's sucking me off and not you?"

Oh, that gets him good. Like I just backhanded him, followed by some spit. The way he sneers makes me realize I've got to be on guard.

"You think you're so smart, Pascal." He seethes quietly. "You think because you're young and rich that you're above it all. I suppose I only have myself to blame for that. I should have treated you like I treated Blaise, hoping you'd grow a pair of balls. But it didn't work for him, and it probably wouldn't have worked for you. You're sheep, son. But you're my sheep. My flock. And I'm going to teach your girlfriend a lesson. Show her that you have to gain the wolf to gain the wool."

Pure, unadulterated heat floods my veins, the anger so sharp and acute that I can scarcely contain it. "You are not to lay a finger on her."

He smiles, so casual, so easy, like this is just a game to him. "I'll try not to, but you never know what you're capable of in self-defense."

Something about that statement makes my subconscious scream, scream that I'm missing something important, that it could be the end of everything.

"You know why I murdered my own brother?" he asks, and the blunt way he admits it makes whatever I was feeling before fly out the window.

He's never said as much to me before.

Now it's just out there.

That can't be good.

"I killed him because he was disloyal," he goes on when I can't form the words to ask. "He was a traitor to his own blood. Sure, I never liked him. My parents always favored him to the point that it was cruel. They would pit us against each other all the time, kind of the same way we pitted Blaise against you. But I was always curious who would be hungrier for our love. The more my mother loved Ludovic, the more I hated her and him. If she hadn't died early, I would have killed her myself and had no remorse. Same goes for my father."

He sighs and gives me a half smile. "I wouldn't have felt a thing if I killed them, Pascal. I didn't feel a thing for Ludovic when I slipped that cyanide into his drink. He deserved to die. Do you know why?"

It hurts to swallow, and I'm barely able to say, "Because he was disloyal."

"Do you know why, though?"

I shake my head.

"Because your uncle, the sacred saint of the Dumont family, slept with my wife. Your mother. They had an affair for years. Thought I didn't know. They thought I was too stupid and vain to pick up on it, too obsessed with my own problems. They didn't realize that it's my job to watch everyone closely, so closely. That's how you get ahead, you know that. Or I thought you did. It doesn't matter, though." He lets out a tired sigh while my mind is now trying to grapple with the fact that my mother and my uncle had an affair. "Ludovic got what was coming to him. He smiled to my face and stabbed me in the back. Took what I had even though it belonged to me. Sounds a lot like you, doesn't it?"

And there's the threat. Laid out for me to pick apart. To know exactly where I stand with him. He killed his own brother over the betrayal. He felt nothing. Now he thinks I've betrayed him.

The blood between us runs very thin.

"What about Mother?" I ask. "It takes two to have an affair."

"You're concerned about her? Never took you for a mama's boy, Pascal. Don't worry about your mother. She has to stay married to me. I think that's enough punishment for now, don't you think?"

He leans forward on the desk, staring right at me. "As for you, you're my son. You're my flesh and blood more than my brother ever was. You have my blood in your veins. You have all the potential to be a great man, but you waste it on women and fast cars and clothes and food and drugs and whatever else you do with yourself when you claim to be running the most important company in France."

Now the blood is pounding in my head, and I know I'm turning red, that there is a vein pulsing on my forehead.

"I'm not going to kill you," he says in a low, guttural voice. "But I know exactly how to make you suffer."

Suddenly there's a knock at the door, making my heart leap from my chest, but my father stays characteristically cool, slowly straightening up.

"Yes?" I call out, voice cracking.

The door opens, and my mother pokes in her head. "Sorry, boys. Gautier, honey, there's a man to see you."

"I'll be right there," he says, flashing her a cheap smile. He waits until she's walked away to turn back to look at me. "I have to go. I have an appointment with an old friend. I hope you enjoyed those sloppy seconds of mine while they lasted. Gabrielle really did have the best pussy I've ever had."

And then he leaves.

All feeling inside my body runs out of me, my blood turning from hot to cold, my stomach filling with dread, the kind of dread that stuns. The kind of dread that drowns you in disbelief, like concrete blocks around the ankles.

*Sloppy seconds?*

He slept with Gabrielle.

When did he sleep with her?

Oh God.

Oh *God*.

I'm going to be sick.

I hunch over, holding my stomach, trying to keep the bile from rising in my throat.

I know I have to move, but everything is happening slowly. Somehow I manage to make it out of the office, and from the upper windows of the hall, I see him getting in a town car and driving off.

I recognize Jones as the driver.

Jones, his number-one hit man.

Shit.

He's not actually going to where Gabrielle's letter says, is he?

*You never know what you're capable of in self-defense.*

My father's words ring in my ear.

He thinks Gabrielle is going to try to kill him.

He's going to be more than ready for her with Jones.

She doesn't stand a chance.

I run down the stairs, yelling, "Gabrielle! Gabrielle!"

I see my mother come out of the kitchen with an apron tied around her waist. "What's wrong with you, Pascal?"

"Where's Gabrielle?" I yell, holding her by the shoulders.

She looks absolutely bewildered. "I don't know. Jolie went for a walk; maybe Gabrielle went with her?"

I let go of my mother and run through the kitchen. I don't think I've ever run so fast, bursting through their back doors and straight to Gabrielle's room.

"Gabrielle!" I yell, almost stumbling into her room.

There's no one here.

I'm too late.

And then I hear someone behind me.

I whirl around to see Gabrielle standing in the doorway.

Aiming a gun at me.

This is the second time this year I've had a gun aimed at me by someone I love.

*Shit.*

There it is.

And it doesn't change anything right now.

"Gabrielle?" I say quietly, trying to catch my breath. "What are you doing?"

Her hand is shaking slightly, and there are tears in her eyes. "I'm sorry, Pascal," she says.

"Sorry for what?"

"Put your hands where I can see them," she says, as if I have another gun on me that I'm going to reach for. She shakes the gun at me, fear coming across her brow. I know that fear can easily cause a gun to misfire, so I raise my hands and stay as still as I can.

"Okay," I tell her. "It's okay. I'm not going to move. I'm not going to hurt you. I just want you to talk to me."

"There's no time," she says. "I have to go. And you're going to let me."

# CHAPTER FIFTEEN

## GABRIELLE

The gun is starting to feel slippery in my grip. My palms are sweaty.

But I refuse to let go.

I just wish I weren't pointing it at Pascal.

"We can talk this through," he says. I want to. I want to so much, but I don't have much time. It's seven, and I'm supposed to get to the meeting point at eight. There's a chance that his father might not show up, but there's also a chance he will, and I need to be ready.

"There's not much to talk about."

"He knows, Gabrielle," Pascal says. "He knows about the letters."

That's a stunning blow. I feel winded from that admission.

"Good," I tell him. "Because the letters were for him."

"I mean he knows you sent them."

I shake my head. "How?"

"He figured it out. I suppose he knew you were out for revenge, though I'm still trying to piece together why. If you just put the gun down, we can talk about it."

For a split second, putting the gun down feels like the easiest thing in the world.

Then I realize what that would mean.

He would hold me down.

I would never, ever get my revenge.

I would get something much worse, and Gautier would walk free again.

"So he told you I sent them?" I ask, my voice warbling a little, unsure of everything.

He nods. "He told me it was you. That you wanted revenge. I figured it out earlier, though, when I saw the pages you tried to print on my printer." Fuck. "Listen, I don't want to judge you, I just want to listen. I can't make heads or tails of this, please just try to explain."

"You're trying to buy yourself time."

"I'm trying to save your fucking life."

"I have to do this, Pascal. I knew you wouldn't understand. That's why I never told you."

"Please, for my sake. You said you love me, Gabrielle. If you truly love me, help me understand what you're doing and why. I want to help."

I almost laugh. I'm beyond fucking help now, and he knows it. This is the proof.

"Why did you send the letters?" he asks.

"I wanted a scapegoat," I admit.

"A scapegoat?" He starts to lower his hands, but I shake the gun, so he raises them again.

"Yeah, a scapegoat. I wanted suspicion to go somewhere else. Everyone would have suspected me, the maid who left suddenly and then just as suddenly came back into his life. I thought the letters would make it look like someone else was after him."

"Why were the first ones not addressed to him?"

"That was a mistake. I left it off."

"Then why didn't you correct it? Why did you go on making me think it was me?"

I shrug. "I guess I wanted to know how bad you were. What you'd confess to. I wanted to know if you had anything to do with Ludovic's murder, if you were exactly like Gautier."

Something hard comes over his eyes. "You know I'm not. You know it."

I swallow, nodding. "I know it now. I do. I know who you are, Pascal, even if you don't. You're a good man. You could be a great man if you just figured out what you stood for."

"Oh, I suppose you're standing for something right now."

"I'm standing up for myself!" I erupt at him, spittle flying from my mouth. "Do you have any idea what I went through with him?"

A heated look comes across his face. "My father said you slept with him. Is that true?"

I want to cry. "Of course that's what he said. Ask yourself this, Pascal—what do you really think happened? Ask yourself why I would be counting down the years until I had all the right means and all the right moves to finally get my revenge. Do you honestly believe that I would have slept with him, if I had a choice?"

Silence falls between us, the only sound my ragged breath and the heartbeat in my ears.

I watch as the understanding slowly dawns on him, his features turning harder by the second until they're sharp enough to cut diamonds.

"He was your monster," he says, his words broken, his voice going so low that it nearly sounds inhuman. "He was the one who raped you."

I can't help the tears that are starting to spill down my cheeks.

I've wanted to tell him so badly.

I wanted to tell someone who would believe me.

"Do you believe me?" I sob. "Please tell me you believe me."

"Of course I believe you," he says. His voice is softer, but the anger hasn't dissipated, not even a little. "I will always believe you. I just . . . I hate myself for not putting it all together. I hate that all this time . . .

And yet I must have known on some level. I must have known and I didn't want to admit it. To admit it is to face it."

"You're facing it now. I've been facing it for a long time. Every single second of every single day."

"You don't have to kill him," he says. "We can do this together. We can take him down."

"No!" I yell. "No! It won't work! You know it won't. You know he deserves to die."

"I know he deserves to die!" Pascal yells back. "But not at your hand! This won't happen the way you're picturing, Gabrielle. He's prepared. He doesn't even care. He's not sweating it, he's reveling in it. It's a game to him, and you walked right into it."

"I set up the game!" My hand is shaking now, and I have to put both hands on the gun, the gun I took from Pascal's desk drawer. "I planned to come here. I wanted you to hire me, Pascal. I pretended I didn't, but I wanted it. I didn't just get back from New York. I've been in Paris for a year, waiting for the right opportunity."

His face pales, jaw goes slack. Stunned.

"You used me," he manages to say.

"This isn't about you right now," I tell him, pleading with my voice, my eyes. "I didn't plan to fall in love with you. That was never on the agenda. I tried my hardest to protect my heart; I thought it would be easy. You were supposed to disgust me! You were supposed to be just like him, but you weren't. You aren't. You're so much better than you think you are, and I fell for you, with every inch of me."

"If you love me," he says, looking pained, "then you'll put the gun down."

"But I can't," I tell him. "Because what he did is still stronger than that. Once he dies, I'm free, don't you see? Don't you understand? Then we can be together."

He shakes his head, his eyes wet and anguished as he breathes in deep. "No. You're free now. We can leave now, we can go to Mallorca.

We can go to California. We can go anywhere in the world, just the two of us, and I will leave all of this behind."

"You can't. You're the Dumont brand."

"It's just a name, Gabrielle. A name I'm willing to discard, a family I'm willing to step away from. I know what I want, and it's you. That's it. Please."

For a moment, I can see it. See us back on the beach, see me back in his bed. The freedom, the lightness, the joy. The safety I felt as I fell asleep in his arms, knowing he'd take care of me. I'd give anything to have that back.

But Gautier would still be out there.

"He would find me. He would find me, and you know what he'd do to me. Pascal, in the days before I left, I discovered I was pregnant."

The words hit him like stones. He flinches. "Wh-what?"

The shame is so great, I can barely see. My arms are getting tired. My heart is getting tired. "I was pregnant. It was your father, of course. I didn't tell anyone. Not even my mother. I went by myself to get an abortion. I couldn't carry the seed of my rapist inside me. I knew enough that I couldn't do that. And it ruined me, it truly did. Until I realized it was the bravest thing I'd ever done. Until I realized that by doing that, I was gaining my freedom, and I had nothing left to lose. So I planned to leave that night, and he . . . he caught me before I could leave. I was so sick, so . . . sore. Abused. In my body and in my soul. He planned something for me that I knew would have been a million times worse than normal, and I had to fight back. I stabbed him with a corkscrew. You ever wonder about that scar on his forearm? That was me. And that was my only way out."

Pascal is speechless from anger. His face is turning dark, a shade of scarlet, his jaw so tense that I'm afraid he might lose some teeth. His eyes are the most frightening of all, just electric coils that burn and burn, seething with rage.

Now he feels it. Now he might know just what it means to get revenge.

I continue. "It was then that I told my mother, and she didn't believe me. She accused me of lying, of attacking Gautier. She took his side. Do you know what that feels like? To have your own mother believe a monster over you? That's when I knew she was gone. She was brainwashed by him. And my first priority when I came back was to get her out of this fucking house. That wasn't a lie."

"Then take her and go," he pleads in a gruff voice. "Leave my father to me."

"She won't leave," I tell him, crying. "What do you think I tried to do today? I sat her down and told her everything, and she didn't care. She got up and walked away the moment I brought up the past. She's too far gone. Your father has a hold on her that's probably a lot more damaging than you think."

"Oh, I think I know exactly how he operates."

"Then you'll see why I have to do this. I have to make him pay. I'm the one who deserves to pull the trigger."

"You're going to lose, baby, please."

He won't let me go, will he? I'll have to shoot him if I want to leave.

I lower the gun. "I won't lose. Even if it all goes wrong, I won't lose. Because I tried. Because I'm going to put this gun in his face and I'm going to let him feel the fear that I felt."

"You won't get close enough," he says. "He has someone with him, a trained hit man. You won't even get in the door."

But I'm not listening to him. I have the gun at my side now, my head down, staring at the floor.

Pascal starts to approach me, slowly, hands out, like I'm some scared and injured animal, and he's right. I am. I'm harmless unless threatened.

"Gabrielle," he whispers to me, and it sounds so pained, so sweet, so sorrowful, it makes a tear fall from my eye. What if this is the last thing I ever hear him say to me?

What if this moment is it?

"I'm sorry," I say to him.

I wait until he's close enough.

"For what?" he asks.

Then I quickly rise up and pistol-whip him across his face, then bring the gun down on the back of his head.

He stares at me, betrayal in his eyes, blood pouring through his nose, before he keels over to the side, crumbling to the floor.

"For that," I tell him, wishing I didn't have to do that but knowing it was my only choice. If I hadn't, he would have followed me, would have hurt himself or gotten himself killed. He'll be out for a while.

By the time he wakes up, I'll have done what I need to do.

I stick the gun in my purse and then quickly walk out of the house.

My mother's on a walk, but Camille is still inside.

I walk through the kitchen where she's making piss-poor sandwiches, keeping my head high.

"Gabrielle," she says to me as I walk past her. "Pascal was looking for you. He seemed rather upset."

"He's in my room taking a nap," I tell her. "I'm going to go find my mom on her walk." I can hear her muttering something behind me as I grab his car keys from the bowl in the foyer and then leave via the front door.

In seconds, I'm in his car, the engine revving and driving down the driveway toward my freedom. Toward Gautier's judgment day.

I honestly never thought this day would come. For a while there, it felt like a far-off goal, a dream—or a nightmare—I once had. When I was in Mallorca those weeks ago, I wanted to call the whole thing off. I wanted to give up my quest for revenge, all because of Pascal. Because I didn't want any secrets between us, because I didn't want to have to kill his father and potentially kill what we had.

Kill our potential.

Very real feelings were getting in the way of a very real goal.

But then this morning, everything changed.

I had tried for a while to talk to my mother. She'd become more elusive to me the longer I'd been here, and sometimes it feels like I'm farther away from her now, living in the same small house, than when I was overseas. If I tried to bring anything up in any way, anything real and raw, she would shut down in front of my eyes. That zombified version of her would come out, the one with the fake smile and the blank eyes and the incessant nodding. I could never get through to her.

Earlier today, I had a plan.

I asked her to have lunch with me, and we started eating on the patio. I played along with her. I talked about boring stuff like fashion and the weather, and I asked her lots of questions.

Then I started talking about my father.

That's something I *never* bring up.

I needed to shock her into reacting. Into getting her head out of that fixed place.

It worked too.

She got defensive, angry. I kept pressing questions about why he was abusive, why we left him, if life with Gautier was truly any better. She was so disgusted by what I was asking that she got up and went inside the house.

I followed her, right into the kitchen.

She always starts putting things away or cleaning the dishes when she's nervous. The tic of a maid, I guess.

I cornered her so she couldn't pass by me without trying to fight me physically, and I kept asking questions, and then I started turning the blame on her, because any time in the past I've said "I feel," it's been met with indifference. But by saying "you did this," I enabled her to be reactive. She wasn't able to shrug and smile and pretend everything was fine.

I told her she was abused by her husband and then abused by Gautier.

I told her she let me be abused by him too.

I told her she's weak and that she's let herself fall in love with him.

I told her that she's dumb and thinks that he loves her too.

I told her she must hate me for letting Gautier do the things to me that he did.

And I told her she must hate herself for letting a man become more important to her than her daughter.

She must hate herself for letting herself be abused for far too long.

These were all horrible things to say, and I was shaking, crying, hating *myself* for saying them to her. She was a monster sometimes, and in that moment, I was the monster too.

Like mother, like daughter.

It almost worked too.

I almost had her.

I saw the cracks in her facade appear; I saw the words sinking in, or trying to. I saw a woman on the verge of the truth that she kept from herself, on the verge of a breakdown.

But then that truth never came. The cracks stopped flowing. The pain in her eyes disappeared.

A blank mask replaced it.

And I knew then that I never had a chance with her, and I never would.

That my mother would be gone forever if I didn't do something.

If I didn't put a bullet in Gautier's head, setting the both of us free.

I swallow hard and knead the steering wheel, peering through the rain, trying to refocus my thoughts. I can't think about my mother anymore. I just have to think about getting this done.

Finally done.

So we're finally free.

The address I chose is an abandoned stone house on the outskirts of the nearest town. I'm sure it used to be quite something back in the day. In a way, it reminds me of the Dumont *maison*, had it succumbed to years of loneliness and neglect. In the right hands, the house could become something beautiful, but no one has loved it in such a long time.

The house reminds me of me. It reminds me of what I once was and what I was reduced to after his abuse. I could have really become something if he hadn't removed my soul, stone by stone, replacing it with something dank and wet and dark.

I also chose the house because there is more than one way into it. I'm not a spy, but I consider myself smart enough. I knew that this would be an uphill battle, that all the cards would be stacked against me. I knew that Gautier might catch on, and either way, he wouldn't come alone.

But I would be ready for him.

I park Pascal's car down a lane a mile from the house, hiding it behind an old barn. Then I get out, leaving my bag behind on the seat, and grab the gun. I hold it low to my side and make my way through the darkened woods of maple and chestnut trees. The clouds have gathered here, spitting with light rain, and thunder rumbles in the distance. It's far darker than it should be for nearly eight p.m.

Near the edge of the woods is another barn, actually a stable meant for three horses. It's all decayed sawdust and spiders now. But this barn has a secret. Back in the 1940s, during the war, whoever lived here prepared for the worst and made a tunnel connecting the barn and the house. If the Nazis ever showed up at their door, they'd be able to sneak everyone out through the tunnel and either hide in the barn or make a run for it through the woods.

The trapdoor in the barn is easy to see. I imagine in the past it was under a bale of hay, but that hay has long since decomposed.

I lift it up and reach down for the first step with my free hand, where I've stored a small flashlight. I was only able to come here twice recently on my days off or if I was sent into town—it's a long walk. But I actually discovered the house when I was a teenager, a place for me to hide and dream about justice.

The light is faint, but it's enough. I slowly go down the six steps until my feet hit the dirt floor. I close the trapdoor above my head and shine the light forward. It's dusty and full of cobwebs, and I hear the squish of gross things beneath my feet, but I don't feel any fear.

I feel nothing at all.

That is, until I approach the end of the tunnel, where in the dim light I see the stairs leading up into the house. The door there is narrow, barely wide enough for one person, and opens up in a closet in the kitchen, what used to be the pantry.

I wait beneath it, trying to listen. I hear footsteps walking on the main floor, slow and methodical. Almost pacing. They probably searched the place already. Gautier knew I was still at the house and he would have beat me here, but he might think I have hired help or an accomplice.

Not Pascal, of course.

My heart sinks at what I had to do to him. It didn't feel good to hit him, but I had no choice. I just hope I didn't do any real damage, though his pretty-boy face can stand to look a smidgen ugly for a little bit.

Okay, here goes nothing.

I'm going to go up these stairs, then I'm going to slowly, quietly open the door in the floor.

I'll wait for the right moment; I'll take all night if I have to.

I'll get up there and wait in the closet. There are wooden slats for me to see through.

I'll stick the gun between the slats, and then I'll wait for Gautier to walk by.

I'll fire the gun.

He's the first target, he's the first shot. As long as he's dead, I don't care what happens next. With any luck, his friend will come running, and I'll shoot him too.

Then I'll leave.

I'll get in Pascal's car and drive back to the house and then try to figure out what's next for me.

I've never really thought about what happens after that last step, after I do it.

Then again, I never anticipated falling in love with anyone, let alone Pascal. I didn't think it was possible to have something, someone, other than revenge to live for.

I take in a deep breath, trying to calm my heart.

I'll worry about it later.

But before I take the first step, I notice the air changing in the tunnel. It happens so fast, I can barely register it. It's like it went from being vast and empty to being . . . not.

There's someone behind me.

I move to turn around and see, but it's too late.

A hand goes over my mouth.

"Gotcha," Gautier says in my ear.

# CHAPTER SIXTEEN

## PASCAL

I wake up on the floor with my face on fire.

It takes me a moment to recall where I am. My cheek is pressed against a rough, unfamiliar rug, and when I open my eyes, I'm looking along a hardwood floor, straight to a chair in the corner, where a flannel shirt has fallen off the stack of clothing on it and crumpled to the ground, just like me.

Gabrielle.

The realization comes at me quickly, and when I move, everything in my head screams in pain.

She had the gun.

I thought I was getting through to her and I approached her, but I should have remembered what she said all those times before. Harmless until threatened.

I was threatening in that moment. I was trying to stop her from doing everything she had waited and planned these last eight years to do.

I got a pistol-whip in the face and a bonk on the head in response.

Jesus.

But I'm not upset with her. There's no time to be upset with her. There's no time to think about the lies she told in order to do what she thought she had to do.

How can I be upset when I now know what happened?

That the monster who abused and raped her was my father.

I should have seen it coming. I know I should have. I should have let myself entertain the thought. Instead, I was lulled by my own delusions, those same delusions that never let me dwell on the fact that I knew he'd murdered Ludovic or that he wanted Seraphine killed or that if I ever stood up to him, if I ever traded in my malice for something good, he would blackmail me. I never let myself think about it because it was safer to operate that way. To think it, to believe it, would mean I would have to change. And I am too much of a lazy, selfish, scared son of a bitch to do that.

Or I was.

Now the change is happening.

I know what I must do.

I struggle to get to my feet and then stumble over to her bathroom to look at myself in the mirror. My cheekbone is bleeding from a gash, my skin a swollen riot of purple and red. I wet a washcloth, press it against my cheek, and try to think.

Gabrielle went to the address.

My father and Jones would already be there.

She has my gun.

She means to kill him.

I know she has every right to. She's earned it. I won't make any moral judgment here because I'm no better than she is.

But I know I have to stop her.

Even if my father and Jones are taken by surprise, I don't want her pulling the trigger.

I don't want that on her conscience.

I love her.

For all it's worth, I love her, and I want to be with her, and I want us to have a chance.

If she kills him, she'll get her revenge. But she's not going to be able to live with herself after.

She's grown up good. She's got a pure soul. She's got a big heart. She's spent her years in pain, hurting and reeling from the turmoil and the trauma. She thinks that revenge will put a stop to her pain, but it will only make that pain worse, and I need to save her from that.

I need to save her.

Period.

I throw the dishcloth in the sink and run out of the guesthouse, heading into the kitchen. My mother is nowhere in sight, thank God, and I don't think Jolie is back from her walk yet.

At the thought of Jolie, anger rolls through me.

Anger that's just waking up again after being knocked unconscious.

How dare she not believe her daughter?

How dare she take my father's side?

Then my thoughts pause, remembering what I know.

How dare my father get away with it?

The anger is now a beast, coming out of slumber, getting to its knees, making me shake inside as all sense of self is being corrupted by this blinding white-hot rage.

My father won't get away with it.

I don't know where there are guns in the house other than mine, which Gabrielle has, so I think I'm shit out of luck in that department, and with the clock ticking, there's no time to ransack the house looking for one.

There's only one weapon I know of.

I run into the study and grab the cane leaning against my father's desk.

Back in the foyer, my keys are nowhere to be found. Of course Gabrielle would steal the car. For a split second, it almost makes me smile, the thought of her ripping out of the driveway in my car, feeling the speed beneath the gas pedal.

But that thought disappears in a flash, replaced by the anger and its new partner, fear.

Fear that if I don't get there in time, I'm going to lose her forever. She'll be taken again at my father's twisted, bloody hands.

I grab the keys to my father's Lamborghini, the one in the garage, the one he never drives, and run out there.

The garage door is already open, so I get right in the car.

I've driven it a few times before but never cared for it. Gaudy cars were more Blaise's thing, not mine.

But this will get me there quicker than my mother's SUV.

I enter the address coordinates into my GPS on my phone, and it brings me to a location not too far away. I roar out of the driveway, swinging the car onto the road with so much power, it nearly takes me into the ditch. I correct, and then I floor it, the car responding faster than my Audi ever could.

There's no doubt that whatever place Gabrielle has chosen had been chosen on purpose and to her advantage, so I'm not surprised when I zoom in on satellite view and see that it's a farmhouse, most likely abandoned.

I slow down, knowing I don't want to get closer than this, and look for a place to ditch the car. I come across a side lane, basically a rutted path along a fallow field, and when I see my Audi parked behind a barn, I know I've come to the right spot.

I park beside it and get out, looking across the field and the woods to where the location must be beyond it. She must have gone through that way, hoping to surprise them from the other side of the house.

It's still raining and getting darker as I start running across the field, cane in one hand, phone in the other. Thunder gives an ominous rumble, and somewhere in the distance there is a flash.

How fitting.

But the wry thought doesn't stay for long. No thoughts do. This isn't a time to think, this is a time to react and hope you've made the right choice.

All I've got is the cane. Gabrielle has a gun, and while I haven't seen her shoot anything yet, she had zero hesitation in hitting me with it, so I don't think she'll have a problem. My father, well, who knows if he has anything at all. He has Jones. That's all he needs.

Someone to grab Gabrielle and hold her down . . .

The thought turns my insides into something molten hot.

He raped her. He hurt her. She had to get an abortion because of him.

All alone, just a teenager, just a girl who was abused and unloved her whole life. She came with her mother to my house, looking for salvation, and instead she was pulled into hell by the devil.

I'm nearly so blind with anger that for a moment I'm afraid my heart might explode, that the rage is too much for it. I grip the cane tighter.

I have no doubt what my father has planned for Gabrielle.

It won't be a quick and easy death.

He means to make her suffer in ways she has never suffered before.

The only hopeful thing about that is there might still be time to stop him, to save her from him and save her life.

Finally, I come to the edge of the woods and find myself gazing at an old stone farmhouse. There's a small stable close to where I'm standing and then a field of weeds and vines between that and the house.

I hide behind a large maple tree and try to assess the situation. The stable makes the obvious choice. Gabrielle would have run in there. But then what? How would she get to the house without anyone seeing her coming?

What if she's still in the stable?

At that thought, I head in through the open doors. It's a small stable, covered in dust and smelling like rotting wood. I search each stall but find nothing until I notice a variation on the ground. In the area that was probably once a tack room, a crack is on the floor. I lean down to inspect it, brushing dirt aside until I realize it's a wooden trapdoor, left askew.

There must be a tunnel between here and the house. That's why she was so confident that she'd be able to do this. She knew the house; she'd be able to take them by surprise, even if she came here after they did.

Before I go down there, I do another quick search of the stable, hoping to find something else that might be a weapon, but there's nothing.

My father's cane will have to do.

I put my phone away and quickly unscrew the brass horse head off the top of the cane, then pull it away from the body.

A long, thin sword is unsheathed. It's remarkably sharp and shiny. My father used to threaten Blaise and me with the cane, though he luckily never revealed what was inside—I found that out later by myself. I always wondered why he needed a cane, since he seemed so able-bodied, but of course, everything my father has is duplicitous.

This time I pray it works in my favor.

I crouch down, carefully open the trapdoor, and make my way downstairs into the darkness. I don't know who or what's down there, so I don't use the flashlight on my phone in case it gives me away. Instead I step off the stairs, my feet hitting the dirt ground, and slowly go forward.

One hand grips the sword, the other hand is out, feeling along the slick dirt walls of the tunnel, heading into total darkness. The faint light from the open door behind me doesn't reach very far, and I have to hope I'm not going to run into something.

Even though I figured out roughly how much distance there was between the stable and the house, it still seems to take forever. Time is running out with each step I take.

Eventually the air in the tunnel feels like it's changing, and I see a faint light up ahead. As I approach, I see the outline of stairs leading up.

Here goes nothing.

I walk up two stairs until my head pokes out of the floor, and I try to look around. I'm in a closet, the door open to the rest of the house.

I immediately duck my head, not knowing if someone is there watching me or not. I tighten my grip on the sword, remembering when Blaise called me a fucking musketeer for pulling this on him in a showdown. I think he'd be proud of this musketeer right now.

Listening hard, I hear nothing but a faint scuffle and murmured voices, somewhere else in the house. I cautiously raise my head again and look.

The house is dim, but there's no one in sight.

Then an anguished cry pierces my ears, and I can feel my soul being torn from my body, ripping me apart.

Gabrielle.

My Gabrielle.

I want to cry. I want to scream. There's no time to quell the rage that I feel.

Instead I let it fuel me.

I'm going to kill my father. I'm going to kill Jones.

And I'm going to save her.

My grip on the handle of the sword is so tight, I think it might have fused into my skin. I don't want to let it go until my job is done.

As quietly and stealthily as I can, I pull myself out of the floor and step into what must have been the kitchen. There's still an old stove in the corner.

The noises, those horrible noises, are coming from the room around the corner. I want to run, but the creaking floorboards will give me away. Instead I walk slowly, so fucking slowly, too slowly, trying to hold it together.

I don't have much of a chance here.

I know that.

A sword and me against a gun or two, against my father, against a trained assassin.

This is a suicide mission.

The only hope I have is that my father might hesitate in having me killed.

That hesitation might save the both of us.

I put my back flat against the wall and look around the corner.

Jones is standing right in front of me, back to me.

He's just outside another room, where I think my father and Gabrielle must be, though I can't see them, keeping watch or perhaps waiting for his turn.

I don't know how these sick fucks operate, but I'm not going to find out either.

Inside the room, I can hear my father whispering something to Gabrielle. I can hear her struggles and muffled cries.

I feel only vengeance.

Now I understand exactly what was driving Gabrielle all those years.

She's passed the torch to me, and I will gladly wield it.

I don't even have to think. I just act.

And I act fast.

Jones is in the middle of turning around, sensing me, when I've reached around him with the blade of the sword at his throat. My hand grabs his jaw for leverage as I slide the blade across his neck.

Slitting someone's throat is harder than it looks. You have to press hard. You have to cut through the windpipe and cartilage.

I fail at that, making only a superficial cut, but it's enough for him to cry out, to try to fight me, for me to lower the sword and for him to play right into it.

I drive the sword deep into his chest.

This time I press hard. I won't make that mistake again.

Jones falls to the ground, crying out and sputtering blood as he holds his chest, the red seeping through his fingers.

"Jones?" I hear my father cry out from the other room. "Jones?"

I step over Jones, who is writhing in a bloody mess on the floor, and head into the room.

My father is on the floor, pinning Gabrielle down, her shirt ripped half off her, breasts exposed. My father looks up at the doorway, and before his eyes turn to the shock of seeing me, I see the lust in them. The malevolence. The pure, oozing evil.

This man must die.

He's not even a man at all.

Not even a father.

He's a monster.

"Pascal," he says, clearing his throat. "I didn't think you had it in you to show up." He glances back down at Gabrielle, who is staring at me with such hope and sorrow and shame in her eyes that it breaks my heart while steeling my resolve to kill him. "I guess you mean more to him than you do to me. A disposable slut. A little treat, a pet who you dump on the streets when you're done kicking them around."

Jesus.

My hand is holding the bloodied sword so hard that it's starting to shake.

"Get. Off. Her," I say through a grinding jaw, rage pulsing in my temple. "Now."

My father smiles and almost rolls his eyes. "Or what? You're going to stab me with your sword?"

"Yes. Just after I cut off your dick and gouge out your eyes."

His brows raise. "My, my. Sometimes you say things that impress me, son. This is one of those times."

"I am not your son," I say, coming forward, trying to see on the other side of him, wondering where the gun is. "I will never be your son."

"It's too late for regrets, Pascal," he says. "You can't change who your parents are. You can't change who you are. It's not even worth trying."

He grins down at Gabrielle and kisses her.

She whimpers, trying to fight back.

I spring into action, running forward, sword extended.

Then he slips over so he's sitting up, one arm wrapped around Gabrielle, hand over her mouth, the other pulling a gun up from the other side of him and holding it against Gabrielle's head.

I freeze.

"You come closer, and I'm blowing her brains out right in front of you," he says. "I did say I had other ways of making you suffer, didn't I? I didn't think I'd have to use them, though. I didn't think you were that stupid, that naive, that . . . in love. In love with her? She's trash. And she used you, Pascal. Just as you used Marine. Karma is a bitch, isn't it?"

"Shut the fuck up."

"Back to juvenile vocabulary, are we?" He gives me a sour smile. "Yes, I suppose you never were as smart as I had hoped. A waste of space, just like your brother, just like my brother. Seems like I'm the only Dumont who got the good genes. The rest of you are insipid. Useless. A total disappointment."

"I'm glad to be a disappointment to you," I sneer. "I wouldn't want it any other way."

That bothers him. His gaze sharpens, like a wolf. "Is that so? Well, then it's your lucky day. You got your wish and I get mine. I get to fuck your lover's brains out before I blow her brains out, and I'm going to make you watch the whole thing. In fact, you're going to beg me to pull the trigger before it's time, just to put her out of her misery."

I can't give him any more of my attention. I won't.

I stare into Gabrielle's eyes, and she stares at me.

I'm trying to tell her I won't lose her.

She's trying to tell me something else.

She gives me the slightest nod, like she's ready for something, and then her eyes dart over my shoulder.

I turn around just in time to see the bloody mess of Jones coming at me in a tackle. I'm thrown to the floor, and everything slows down, frame by frame.

The sword falls from my hands and into Jones's.

My head hits the floor.

I'm staring at Gabrielle.

She opens her mouth and bites down as hard as she can on my father's hand. As he yelps in surprise, she puts her self-defense classes to work by throwing her head back and slamming it against my father's forehead.

The gun drops out of his hands.

Gabrielle picks up the gun just as Jones is about to drive the sword into my heart.

She shoots him in the head.

Jones goes flying back, blood spraying over me.

Now she's trying to shoot my father, but he springs up, knocking the gun out of her hand.

It skitters across the floor, away from them, away from me, just as I'm trying to get to my feet.

I grab the sword.

Gautier grabs the gun before Gabrielle does.

Looks at me first, aims it at me.

Then smiles.

I'm expecting the bullet just as he turns it to the side and aims it at Gabrielle.

Shoots her in the ribs.

I scream and go running toward him.

He swings the gun around to fire at me, but I'm fast.

I throw myself on top of him, the gun flying across the room again.

I hold him down, and I punch him, over and over again.

My fists are merciless.

They are on a mission.

They are looking for salvation. For justice and revenge.

They will not stop until I can feel the bones of my father's face brush against my knuckles.

He starts coughing, choking, sputtering.

And yet he's still smiling at me, white teeth against a face of blood.

"I knew you didn't have the guts to kill me," he tells me, spitting out red, maybe a tooth. "You're such a disappointment, Pascal."

I pause and sit back on him, crushing his stomach.

"Who said I wasn't going to kill you?" I growl.

I take the sword and hold it above my father's heart.

A flash of fear comes over his eyes.

"This is the only time I won't be a disappointment to you," I tell him, my voice coming out so gruff and strained that it barely sounds like me. "And it's going to be at the cost of your life."

Before he can say anything, before I can hesitate, I drive the sword down, down, down, right into his heart. He struggles, and then he stops.

And then he's dead.

He's dead.

I killed him.

My lungs seem to seize in panic and relief, fighting for air, fighting for something to make sense of what I did.

And then I remember why I had to do it.

Gabrielle is lying a few feet away, on her side, bleeding out onto the floor.

I go to her side, beside myself in horror, gently touching her face.

Her eyes flutter as they look up at me.

"Gabrielle," I whisper. Her name comes out choked. "I've got you. You're safe, I've got you."

She barely nods. Her eyes pinch closed, and she struggles for breath.

I quickly rip off my shirt and then sit down beside her, pulling her up onto my lap and holding the shirt against the wound, which is streaming out. I kiss her head, tell her it's going to be okay, even though I have no idea if anything is going to be okay ever again.

Then I pull my phone out of my pocket and call 112.

I talk to the operator, and she tells me what to do for Gabrielle as the ambulance is dispatched. She talks me through it, even when I start crying, even when Gabrielle seems to slip from consciousness.

I hold her, trying to stanch the wound, trying to keep her alive until sirens fill the air.

I'll never forget that sound.

It sounds like hope.

# CHAPTER SEVENTEEN

## GABRIELLE

The world comes back slowly, sound by sound, color by color, feeling by feeling.

First I hear the sound of a machine, a soft whir coupled with a low beep that coincides with my own heartbeat. Then I open my eyes and see white. Nothing but white. So bright that I have to blink a few times.

*Is this heaven?* I think absently.

*Am I dead?*

*How did I die?*

And then I *feel*.

I feel a hand wrapped around mine, squeezing tight. The hand is strong and warm, and it feeds comfort into my veins, just as the IV drip does.

I'm in a hospital.

"Gabrielle."

I'm in a hospital with Pascal by my side.

I move my head slightly and see his face peering down at me, tears in the corners of his eyes.

Those beautiful eyes.

Staring at me with so much sorrow and hope and happiness that I feel it all the way into the depth of my heart, the marrow of my bones.

I try to move my lips to say his name, but I can't, my lips are too dry.

"Shhh," he says to me, reaching over and brushing his fingers over my cheek. "Don't try to talk. You're okay. You're all right. You're safe."

I blink at him slowly. I don't feel safe, especially as I notice the awful bruises and gash on his cheekbone where I hit him with the gun.

Oh fuck. I am so sorry.

I need to say the words, to tell him, but they won't come out.

"It's fine," he says with a soft smile, knowing what I'm looking at. "It's just a bruise. I got some stitches while I was here, so it all worked out in the end. Plus, now I'm going to have a real tough-guy scar. Might fool some people."

*You are a tough guy,* I think. *I think you saved my life.*

"Wh . . ." I try to talk, but my throat is so parched.

"Hold on," he says, reaching over my head to press something. "You need water."

A nurse appears a moment later. "She's awake," she says in surprise. "Let me get the doctor and some ice chips."

She disappears, and Pascal raises my hand to his lips, kissing the top of it. "Just relax," he says. "It will all make sense soon."

My eyes widen as I remember what happened.

I was shot.

I look down at my stomach but can't see anything because of the hospital gown.

"You're going to be fine," Pascal says. "Honestly. You were very lucky. Both of us were very fucking lucky."

It all comes back to me.

Being captured by Gautier in the tunnel.

Him dragging me up into the house.

Being held down.

What he planned to do with me.

The fear.

Oh God, the fear that was so overpowering that I almost went into shock. It was the only way I could have protected myself from what was going to happen.

No doubt, he then meant to kill me in some torturous way.

Then Pascal showed up.

My knight in tarnished armor.

I was saved.

And then I was shot.

I don't remember much after that. It's probably for the best.

"Is . . . ?" I try to say. "Is he . . . ?"

Pascal just nods but with a look that tells me to be quiet.

I press my lips together just as the doctor and nurse come in.

"You're awake, Gabrielle," the doctor says. "How do you feel? Wait, don't answer that yet."

The nurse leans over and gives me a small paper cup filled with chips. I chew them down until I feel stronger, my mouth satisfied.

I then look at the doctor. "I feel like I've been shot."

Everyone laughs, albeit a little nervously. It's true, though—I do feel like I've been shot. The pain in my side is getting more and more intense the longer I'm awake.

"I see," the doctor says, squinting at me. "And I'm afraid we're going to need more morphine." He nods at the nurse, who does something to the drip, and it's not long before I feel strange liquid in my veins, making the pain dull, making the room seem blurry and warm.

"I'm going to leave you two alone," the doctor says. "I'll have to alert the police that she's awake, just so you know."

"Do they have to question her already?" Pascal grumbles.

"I'm sorry, Mr. Dumont, but there are procedures we have to follow in cases like this." He pauses. "Have you told her . . . ?"

Pascal shakes his head.

The doctor nods, giving me a quick glance and a placating smile. "I'll be back to check you out later." Then he and the nurse leave the room, closing the door behind them.

Pascal watches the closed door for a moment before he turns back to me. There's fire in his glacial-blue eyes now.

"I don't want them questioning you," he says in a low voice. "There's nothing to question."

"There isn't?" I ask, my voice cracking. I'm so afraid to get the answer to my question. "Is he . . . ?"

He nods grimly. "He's dead."

And just like that, all the weight I've been carrying on my shoulders, in my heart, the weight that has dragged my soul further and further toward hell, is lifted. It's like it's been filled with air and the strings are cut and it's just floating away.

"He's dead?" I repeat, hoping this isn't the drugs talking.

"I killed him," Pascal says gruffly. "I had to."

"You had no choice."

"I had no choice."

"And . . . what happened to the other man?"

"He's dead."

"Because of me?"

He swallows and doesn't say anything. He reaches for my hand again. "You saved both our lives," he says. "Don't forget that. Don't you ever forget that."

I nod, a tear spilling down my cheek. I'm relieved that they're dead, that we survived, but it does feel different from what I imagined, knowing I took someone's life, even if he had no problem in trying to take mine.

Maybe that means I'm not as broken as I thought.

"So the police are going to question me?" I ask. "Did they question you?"

"They did. I told them the truth. I told them that he found out that you told your mother about what happened to you, and that you told me. He was threatened, so he had Jones and himself abduct you from the house with plans to rape and murder you. Luckily, I knew what they had planned, and after my father knocked me around a bit, I was able to show up at the house and stop them."

"What did your mother say?" She was around. She would have to know it didn't quite go down that way.

"She corroborated the story," he says.

"And my mother?"

"As you can imagine, she's a mess. The police questioned her, but she was crying too much to make any sense. I'm sure they will later, but she was gone on her walk, so she never saw any of this."

I shake my head, and even with the painkillers, I feel the anger in my heart. "She's never going to believe me. No one will. Even in death, your father has all the power. Don't you see? Even in death, he still wins."

All this time, I thought if I could have Gautier killed, then all the pain would be over and I would win. But this isn't the case at all. He's gone, but the world will never know the truth about him. A tattered legacy and death would have been the only fitting punishment.

But Pascal is grinning at me. His smile is crooked and cunning and oh so charming, and my heart turns from anger to lust and love when I see it spread across his face. My Pascal. Whatever he's about to say is going to set my world right-side up.

"You know how I was really paranoid that my father had all those bugs around the house?"

I nod. "Yeah . . ."

"Well, it turns out, I was right to be paranoid. He didn't bug the bedroom, but he did bug the study. And guess what he admitted to me in full in that study before he left?"

I swallow, eyes wide, heart hopeful. "No," I say in breathless disbelief.

"Oh yes. The whole confession. Everything about Ludovic's death, plus a remark about you. It's not going to take long for them to piece it together. The police have the tape now. He'll be convicted posthumously for his brother's murder, and there will be zero doubt of what he did to you."

"Except when it comes to my mother."

"We'll deal with that later. But you can bet I'm taking these tapes to the press. I want them to know exactly what my father did. I want to rip his reputation apart for the whole fucking world to see. I hope he knows it. I hope he feels it as he burns in hell."

The passion and conviction in Pascal's voice, his steely gaze, send a thrill down my spine.

Now I'm safe.

*Now* I'm safe.

I might just burst into tears.

"Of course, that's not the only surprise I have for you," Pascal says. "And it was a surprise to myself. A big one. I'm not even sure how you'll handle it, but just so you know, I'm handling it well. Better than well. I think it's the best thing that could have ever happened to me, happened to us."

I stare at him, having absolutely no idea what he's about to say, but the intense devotion in his gaze is giving me chills.

"What?" I say softly. What else could there be? What could be better than the death of Gautier Dumont?

He takes his hand and places it on my stomach, ever so gently, just below where my body is bandaged up. "The bullet missed all your organs and arteries. It was a clean shot, straight through. You lost blood, but your mother was able to give blood to replace it. So there's that. That's one good thing on her behalf. Just remember all this before I go on. You're going to have a full recovery. You'll have a scar right below your ribs, and that's it. You're fine, and you're going to be greater than great. Okay?"

"Okay?"

He keeps smiling at me, turning sweeter. "You're pregnant."

My eyes go round, brows shooting up to the ceiling.

My heart seems to freeze in my chest.

I can't even speak.

"You're pregnant," he says again. "And perhaps I'm terribly optimistic in thinking it's my baby, but hey, that's a new leaf for me. You're pregnant, Gabrielle. And I know this is all your choice and I'm going to support your choice, no matter what it is. But in case you're afraid of how I feel, just know that I . . . well, I fucking love you, for one thing."

He loves me.

He loves me, and I'm pregnant.

I can't even process this.

I can't even think.

All I can do is feel.

I feel love, love, so much love, so much joy, so much . . . too much.

Pascal is looking teary-eyed again, and I put my hand down over his, over my stomach, grasping it. "I love you," he says again, "and I think I might just be a good father if given the chance. And I know you'd be such a good mother. The baby would have a lot of love, extra love to make up for the love we both never had."

I burst into tears, smiling through them. I cry and I cry, trying to reassure him that I'm happy, but it's all so much, my body isn't equipped to handle this much happiness. I've trained it over the years to carry so much pain, it doesn't know what to do with the opposite.

I feel like I'm drowning in it.

What a beautiful way to go out.

"Please tell me those are happy tears." Pascal sniffs, wiping his nose with his hand.

"They're happy tears," I say between sobs. "They're happy tears. I love you. I love you so much."

All the things I never knew I wanted, never knew I needed, life had a funny way of giving them to me.

And it all started when I first saw Pascal Dumont.

The son of the devil.

My lover, my savior.

The father of my child.

My friend.

# CHAPTER EIGHTEEN

## Pascal

I always knew my father's funeral would be the event of the year. It was something he often talked about, how we would spare no expense in putting on such an extravagant operation that it would draw in mourners from around the world. He wanted every last penny the Dumont label had to be put toward it, because, as he said, the brand would die with him. When he was gone, the label would go down as well. He believed it couldn't possibly survive if he hadn't, as if it hadn't been around through decades and generations of Dumonts, from our great-grandfathers to today.

I think what my father really wanted, though, was to ensure the world didn't forget about him. He wanted everyone to throw themselves on the streets and mourn, scream his name and pound their fists and cry at the loss of such a great man. I know he definitely wanted to go out in a way that would overshadow his brother.

Well, in his death, my father managed to succeed in both those things.

Though he didn't deserve the excessive funeral of his dreams, and we are putting it on with as little pomp as possible, it drew the attention of people all around the world. Except that it wasn't in the way he wanted. People are here because my father is now notorious.

He was a killer.

He was a rapist.

He was an abuser.

And he is dead, slain by his own son.

I guess that makes me just as notorious as he is.

For once, I don't mind the comparison.

He also succeeded in outdoing his brother's funeral, but for the same reasons. While Ludovic's funeral was full of people who actually mourned him for his kindness and generosity and vision, Gautier's is full of those who look upon him with shock and disdain.

I'm going to guess, though, that no one is really all that surprised.

Regardless, it's been a hell of a week. In some ways the best week of my life, in others, the worst week.

When I saw Gabrielle get shot, I swear my whole entire world disintegrated. I thought I had lost her. I thought I'd crawl out of that house with blood on my hands and a missing piece of my heart, never to be whole again. Never to truly live again.

But I kept Gabrielle alive.

Then the medics took over.

It was only when she was in the hospital and the doctor pulled me aside to tell me she was going to make it, that the bullet hadn't hit any arteries or organs, that I finally breathed.

And then the doctor told me the news that would change my life even further.

That Gabrielle was pregnant.

And the baby was safe.

Obviously, I had no idea, and I don't think she had any idea either. We hadn't used a condom that first time, but after that, we were pretty careful. Normally when I sleep with a woman, I am adamant about using a condom, even if they say they're on birth control, because I can't risk it. I don't want the chance of an STD changing my life, and I also don't want a purposeful pregnancy. There are so many women out there who would love to have a bastard son of Pascal Dumont, just to get a foot in the door, to take my money, to mooch off the brand.

But with Gabrielle, the thought hadn't crossed my mind at all.

She isn't like them.

She isn't like anyone I know.

She's going to make me a father, and the feeling . . . it's indescribable. It's something I rarely even thought about, and when I did, I'd dismiss it with a sneer. I wasn't fit to become a father, I didn't want to become a father, there was no woman alive who would ever make me want that.

But with Gabrielle, I knew. When the doctor told me, I knew.

This is what I'm supposed to be.

This is how my life is supposed to go.

I won't give this child the life I had; I'll give it one full of love and devotion and strength. I'll be able to change my legacy into a legacy of good, put light into the darkness in my bloodline, start again.

I glance down at my Gabrielle, the mother of my child, by my side and give her hand a squeeze.

We're standing in the funeral home in Paris, the same one that I was in for my uncle. Despite everything, their graves will be beside each other. I like the idea of Ludovic in heaven smiling down on my father in hell. Two brothers, two different destinies.

Gabrielle looks up at me and gives me a small smile. I didn't want her to come to the funeral at first. She only got out of the hospital two days ago, and now that she's pregnant with my child—my child—I wanted her to take every precaution.

But Gabrielle is still stubborn, even after almost dying. I have a feeling she'll be exponentially more stubborn as a mother. She insisted she come with me. Not just to give me moral support, because we both know people are going to judge the fuck out of me for what I did, no matter the proof, no matter that my father deserved it and it was a matter of our lives or his. But she wanted closure too. This is what she wanted for so long, and to deny her the chance to watch my father's coffin get lowered into the ground would be cruel.

Of course, Gabrielle needs help. She'll get the help. We both know that the revenge and the trauma and the guilt and the pain that she's carried in her heart for so long will only damage her more over time. She needs medication and therapy and a lot of love and support, and I'm prepared to give my whole life to making her better. She wanted to fix me? Well, she has. She has made me become the person I needed to be, the person I was always afraid to be. She made me be okay with being the real Pascal Dumont, not a man in my father's shadow, not a minion following in his footsteps. And now that she's fixed me, I have to fix her.

I have to heal her heart, her soul, help her become the woman she's meant to be without all the pain and horror that molded her into someone else. I want to help her be a mother, a wife, a friend. I want us both to live free from the shackles of the people we used to be.

Those people died with my father.

Now we're starting anew.

"Are you doing okay?" I ask her.

She nods and adjusts the neckline of her black dress. Ironically, it's her maid uniform.

"I'm just worried," she admits.

I bring her hand to my mouth and kiss her knuckles. "Tell me why, and I'll handle it."

She gives me a wry look. "I'm not sure that you can. I'm worried about my mother, for one."

Ah, yes. Her mother has not taken this very well at all. If Gabrielle needs help for her fragile psyche, then Jolie needs ten times that amount. When she arrived at the hospital, even though she saw Gabrielle lying there in bed, IVs and monitors hooked up to her, her first words were about Gautier. Where was he, what happened to him? I guess she had heard the news and refused to believe it.

When I told her the truth—and I mean all the truth—she wouldn't listen. Even when I said I had proof, she waved it away. I was so afraid that she was going to start yelling at Gabrielle and blaming her that I had to remove her from the room before she did any further damage to her daughter's mind.

It's only now, in the last day or two, that she's started to calm down, and her truth is starting to come out. I guess that's what being questioned by the police, psychiatrists, and trauma experts will do to you. Not only was Jolie brainwashed by my father, she suffered his abuse from practically the moment she and Gabrielle arrived at our house.

Again, I feel awful for not having noticed, for never paying the help any attention. I never saw the signs, and I fear that if I had, I would have brushed them off because they didn't concern me. I was such a selfish bastard, *I* was the only thing that mattered in my life.

When Jolie was further examined, they discovered bruises and cigarette burns up and down her arms, covered by the long sleeves she always wore, in the same way that my father almost always wore a long-sleeve shirt, even in the middle of summer, to cover up the jagged scar left by Gabrielle's corkscrew. We all knew it was there, though we didn't know why or care to, but to him it must have been a daily reminder of the one who fought back.

Now Gabrielle doesn't have to fight anymore.

"Your mother will be fine," I tell her. "It's going to take time, but she'll get there. Please don't worry about her." I want to add that she doesn't deserve it, but I know that Gabrielle doesn't see it that way. Ever since she was a child and under the abuse of her father, the two of them became a unit. Even when they split, even when Gabrielle had no choice but to leave to save her own life, Gabrielle's whole focus was to come back and save her mother, even if her mother didn't want to be saved.

And she didn't want to be saved. She made that clear.

Now, though, she might not have the choice.

"So what's the other thing you're worried about?" I ask her. "Is it the press?"

It's just the two of us standing in the room, the wolves at the door. The press has been hungry for the both of us since this happened, and I can't blame them. This is the story and scandal of the century. Two feuding brothers, good and evil, heads of one of the biggest fashion houses in the world, both dying at the hands of their loved ones. One murdered by his brother, the other killed by the prodigal son. We're the stuff legends are made of, if only we weren't legends to begin with.

But as much as I can handle the press—indeed, I think I might even thrive on the attention—I don't want Gabrielle to be exposed to it. It's not fair for her to relive the trauma, especially as she had to recently. The police and our lawyer visited her in the hospital and questioned her about everything, just as they did me. Of course, we left out that Gabrielle intended to kill Gautier. That admission would only fuck up the whole process, and she was smart enough to keep her mouth shut.

She did have to talk about what he did to her in every detail. I wanted to leave the room at some point, the rage that I had toward my father coming back in full force. It didn't matter that he was dead. But I stayed because she needed me there, even though it killed me to relive it with her. Though it couldn't have been nearly as bad as what she went through, over and over again.

I think the police are satisfied. The proof in the recordings is more than enough to ensure neither of us will be convicted, especially as now they have to reopen the case into my uncle's death.

But the press? The media? They're ravenous for Gabrielle, giving her such lovely nicknames as "The Murdering Maid" and "The Scandalous Servant." Little do those papers know I'm about to sue all their asses for defamation, and I'm going to win. Killing Jones in self-defense isn't even close to murder, and they know it, they just want to throw her under the bus and sell copies.

"The press?" she repeats, bringing my thoughts back to the present. "No. I don't care what they say about me. I know what the truth is. And I'm okay with it. I'm worried about your family."

Ah. That.

"Well, if it makes you feel any better, I'm nervous too."

She chuckles. "That does not make me feel any better, Pascal. I know if you, of all people, are nervous, then this is going to be a doozy." She pauses, and this time she squeezes my hand. "It's going to be okay, you know."

I don't know that at all. The funeral starts in thirty minutes, and I haven't seen any of my cousins or my brother. My mother and Jolie are outside, dressed head to toe in black, complete with matching veils. It's almost comical, considering what my father thought of both of them. But my mother seems to thrive on it. The attention she's getting is all she ever wanted, especially now that she gets a chance to be the weeping widow. She's playing it up like a Broadway star.

When my mother first came to see us at the hospital, she was in complete shock. I couldn't get a read on her, what she was really going through. She saw me with my bruised face from where Gabrielle clocked me, she saw Gabrielle in the hospital bed, tubes going into her. She had to ID my father's body. She had to be questioned by the police, and of course her story is the truth.

It wasn't until I was able to leave Gabrielle for a few hours to go home and put on some fresh clothes that I was able to talk to my mother in private.

To my surprise, I found her in her bedroom. When I first entered the house, there was nothing but silence. The air was still, like it was holding its breath. It felt like death, even though my father didn't die there.

Then I heard it. The softest sobs.

I cautiously went up the stairs, not sure what I was going to find.

And there she was, on the couch in her room, crying into the velvet arm.

I stood there in the doorway for a moment, unsure of what to do. I'd never had to comfort my mother before. My family isn't like that.

Finally, she looked up.

And she smiled.

Even with her mascara running down her face and the smudged lipstick and her messy hair, she looked younger than I had ever seen her.

"Can't you feel it?" she said, her eyes glassy from the tears.

I immediately looked around to see if she'd been drinking, but there was nary a bottle of booze in sight.

"Feel what?" I asked her, cautious that perhaps she'd lost her mind in grief, something I hadn't expected.

"The weight." She paused to wipe the tears from under her eyes. "It's gone. The weight is gone."

I couldn't understand what she was talking about. Then she got up from the couch and walked over to me, her back straight, her gait steady. Up close, I could see the intensity in her eyes. It shone like diamonds, buoyed by something like . . . happiness.

She placed her hands on either side of my face and then gently pulled my head down to kiss the top of my forehead.

That affection, so rare, so genuine, combined with everything that had happened, brought tears to my eyes.

"We're free, Pascal," she said to me, grinning as the tears spilled down, her hands still holding my face. "Both of us. We're both free now because he's gone."

And then I understood.

Her tears weren't of grief.

They were of relief.

The weight and power and control my father had held over our lives, whether we knew it or not, had been completely destroyed.

So even though my feelings toward my mother are complicated at best, I'm trying to look at her as another victim of my father's. Maybe all her hate and spitefulness came directly from him, just as mine did. We were both products of our environment, damaged goods.

All of us are. But it doesn't mean we'll stay that way.

When it comes to the rest of my family, though, who knows what they're going to say or think. I can't imagine any of them will be mourning him, especially after the truth came out in a very big, very splashy way. I'll be surprised if they even show, given how my father fucked up all their lives. And I certainly can't imagine their attitudes toward me changing.

Months ago, that wouldn't have bothered me at all.

But now it does.

There's a knock at the door that steals my attention away from my thoughts, and the two of us turn around to see a familiar face poke in. I squeeze Gabrielle's hand tighter.

It's my cousin Renaud, who came in from California, who I haven't seen since my uncle's funeral. Of all my cousins, he's always been rather intimidating. Tall, stocky, and stoic, Renaud is the silent type, and so I've never gotten to know him the way I did everyone else.

"Pascal," he says, stepping inside. "Am I interrupting something?"

I shake my head. "Not at all. How are you, Renaud?"

"Not too bad," he says, coming toward me and holding out his hand.

I shake his and then slap him lightly on the shoulder. "No jet lag?"

He shrugs. "Probably. I have to admit, this doesn't seem quite real." He pauses and studies me. He looks so much like Olivier in some ways, it's disconcerting. "I suppose I should say I'm sorry for your loss."

"And I suppose I should tell you thank you," I say to him. "But I wouldn't mean it. I appreciate the sentiment, but . . ."

He nods, pursing his lips. "Yeah. I know. This can't be easy. Or maybe it can."

"It's easier now that you're here," I say, and then I gesture to Gabrielle. "She makes it easier too. Renaud, meet my girlfriend, Gabrielle."

He gives her a charming smile. "I've heard a lot about you. From the papers, of course. You're even famous in America."

"Don't believe everything you hear," she says, but her voice is light.

"It's hard not to with this family," he says. Then he looks to me. "You know I'm not alone, right?" he says. And then he moves out of the way to show that Olivier and Sadie are standing in the doorway.

Ah shit. I *really* didn't think they'd come.

In fact, I hoped they wouldn't, purely on a selfish level, purely so I wouldn't have to face them again and be reminded what a lying, scheming, extorting piece of shit I was.

"Olivier, Sadie," I say to them, my voice tight with anxiety.

Olivier doesn't move. His eyes lock with mine, and I feel the venom in them. It's enough to make my skin crawl.

Then Sadie pokes him in the side and tells him in fluent French, "Don't be a big baby, go say hello."

I give her a grateful smile. I'm so surprised—not only at what she said but at the fact that she said it in French.

She glares at me in return.

Fair enough.

Olivier heeds her warning and comes forward, with Sadie right behind him. He stops in front of me, and for a very long moment, we continue to stare each other down.

"Wow, this is more awkward than I thought," Gabrielle says from behind me.

Sadie looks to her in surprise with a touch of admiration at that, while Renaud lets out a relieved laugh. "Yes, I thought it would be immediate *fisticuffs*." He says the last word in English.

*"Fisty cuffs?"* I repeat.

Sadie raises her fists. "You know, fighting with your fists. I thought Olivier would be the one to throw the first punch, that's for sure. Followed by me. But I would do more of a *kickintheballs.*"

I laugh, the tension dissipating. I don't think I've laughed in a long time, and maybe it's inappropriate right now, but maybe I'll always be inappropriate in some way. I can't do a complete one-eighty, and I'm not sure I want to.

"Well," I say, throwing my arms out to the sides, "have at me. I more than deserve it."

Olivier narrows his eyes, seeming to think it over, and his jaw goes tense, his *fisticuffs* at his sides. I ruined this man's life for a while, and though it seems he now has everything he's ever wanted, I'm not off the hook. What I did can't be forgotten or forgiven.

But then his features soften, and he cracks a dry smile. "From the looks of it, you've already been through enough." He gestures to my face, which is still bruised from Gabrielle's whacking.

"If it makes you feel better, she did it," I say, gesturing to Gabrielle.

Her mouth drops as she stares up at me. "Thanks for throwing me under the bus."

"Don't worry," Olivier says to her. "That just means you're on our side."

"And you're kind of my hero," Sadie says. Then she comes forward, brushing me to the side and holding her hand out for Gabrielle. "I'm Sadie, by the way. It's so nice to finally meet you."

"Likewise," Gabrielle says, shaking her hand and then pulling her in to kiss her on both cheeks. I swear I see Sadie blush.

"Oh, you French, I'd forgotten all about the *bisous,*" Sadie says, giggling, hand at her cheek.

It's cute. They're cute. If Olivier and Sadie ever moved back to Paris, I think the two of them would be great friends.

While they're occupied, Sadie showing off her engagement ring to Gabrielle, I glance at Renaud, who just shrugs and turns to look out the window, leaving Olivier and me facing each other.

"I don't know if it matters," I tell him, my heart pounding as the words come out, "but I'm really, really sorry for what I did to you. I know it doesn't change anything. I know it sounds like I'm saying this for my own purposes, for my own exaltation, but . . . I just wanted you to know that you've weighed heavily on my mind ever since. I don't ask for forgiveness; I just want you to know that I have a conscience, and it was not let off easy."

He nods, his mouth in a firm line. "Duly noted," he says.

Okay. Maybe it's not the best I hoped for, but it's good enough for now. Olivier is a good man. He'll come around. And if he doesn't, I did my best.

He clears his throat. "I suppose I should tell you I'm sorry. That you lost your father."

"You don't have to. I'm not sorry."

He studies me for a moment, as if to see whether I'm lying.

"He deserved it," I added quietly. "I have no guilt, no qualms over what I did. And that's not because I don't have a heart. I very much have a heart. She's standing right over there. And I did it for her. I did it for me. I did it for you, for Blaise, for Seraphine, I did it for your father and your mother. I did it for everyone, and it was the only thing left to do." I pause, licking my lips. "Even if it wasn't in self-defense, I probably would have done it anyway. Maybe that makes me just like him."

Olivier shakes his head. "No. That doesn't make you like him. That just makes you like yourself."

I can live with that.

"Oh," I hear Gabrielle say from behind me, and when I follow her gaze to the door, I see Blaise and Seraphine slowly walking into the room, as if not to disturb anyone.

"What a bunch of ghouls," Seraphine says with a wry smile. "This looks more like a party than it does a funeral."

She looks good. Dressed in a navy dress instead of black, no doubt one of her own creations from her Seraphine line. It suits her—and the small baby bump she has. Blaise is beside her, his hand at her elbow in a protective manner.

Blaise.

My brother.

I didn't know what I'd feel when I saw him again, but suddenly there's no question. A million buried emotions are rising up out of me, threatening to explode.

Before I can control myself, I'm striding across the room toward him and wrapping my arms around him, pulling him into a tight hug. Tears spill from my eyes as I hold on.

"I'm so sorry, brother," I say into his shoulder, wishing I would stop crying, wishing I could pull it together, but I know that it's too late. I've kept all this inside for too long, and it's like a dam being lifted. No more hiding, no more pretending, no more masks. "I am so sorry."

Blaise is completely still, tense, and it takes him a moment to hug me back.

"It's okay," he says, and I hear the strain in his voice too. "It's over now. It's all over."

"I've been the worst brother," I go on. "I never . . . I didn't realize what that meant. What I lost. I didn't realize who I was until it was almost too late. I hope it's not too late for us. I hope we can start again. This time without his shadow over us. This time without any fear."

Blaise pulls back and holds my face in his hands before kissing me on the forehead in a gesture of brotherly love I've never felt before.

It seems to set everything right in my world.

Our father is gone.

Now we are free.

He then pats me on the back. "I'm proud of you. You did what I never had the guts to do."

"It helps not having a conscience," I say, simultaneously giving him a wicked smile while I wipe away a tear.

"Ah, but you do have one. We've all seen it now. It's too late for you, Pascal, you're going to have to walk the line."

"We'll see," I tell him, patting him on the shoulder right back.

Now that we've broken apart, I can see everyone else staring at us with either interest or shock. I know Olivier still thinks we're cut from the same cloth. I suppose we are: Blaise just reached his own redemption before I did.

"I never thought I'd see the day," Seraphine muses, eyeing us with her hand on her hip.

I give her a winning smile. "Seraphine," I say, holding my arms out for her.

She rolls her eyes, shaking her head. "You and I are not on hugging terms."

"Hear, hear, sister," Sadie pipes up.

I ignore her. With a pleading look from Blaise, Seraphine sighs heavily and then trudges over to me. She puts her arms around me, holding me lightly.

"I still hate you," Seraphine whispers in my ear. "But I do forgive you. Thank you for saying all that to Blaise. He's missed you, if you believe it or not."

She pulls back and gives me a little smile, and in that smile, I know she means it. Maybe not even the hate part, but the forgiveness part.

Then she breaks away and goes back to Blaise's side, holding his hand and kissing him on the cheek. "I threatened him," she tells him, throwing a quick glance at me. "I don't trust him for beans."

I can't help but grin in return.

It's obvious now that Renaud, Olivier, Sadie, Blaise, and Seraphine all arrived at the funeral together, because they're moving along like the well-oiled wheels of a train, circling Gabrielle with interest.

"Blaise, Seraphine," I say, going over to Gabrielle and putting my arm around her waist. "This is Gabrielle. I hope you don't hold the fact that she's with me against her."

"Not at all," Blaise says. "Seems like you're the one who finally turned my brother around."

"I think maybe he's the one who turned me around," she says, shooting me a smile that makes my heart swell.

There's a loud knock at the door, and we all exchange looks, wondering who we're missing here.

But it's just the funeral director, poking in his head.

"The funeral is starting," the director says, giving us all a quick but solemn smile before he disappears.

We start heading for the door.

"All right," Seraphine says, clapping her hands together. "Let's go put this son of a bitch in the ground."

We all stop in our tracks, staring at her with nervous laughter on our lips.

"What?" she says. "We're all thinking it, right? Almost all of us were victims of his in one way or another. Let's not sugarcoat it. Let's call it what it is. Gautier Dumont is dead. And the world is better for it."

Everyone murmurs in response, nobody else being so bold as to say it, but we're definitely all feeling it.

The Dumont brand will go on, in a whole new way, creating a whole new legacy.

The cycle is over.

And it ended with me.

# EPILOGUE

## Pascal

*Mallorca*
*Five years later*

"Pascal. Help."

I put my razor down and open the door to the bedroom, peering out around the corner.

Gabrielle is lying on her back, arms splayed, her bare legs dangling over the edge of the bed. On the floor beneath her feet is a pair of sandals. I can't see her face over the gigantic mound of her pregnant belly.

"What happened?" I ask, coming around the bed to peer at her. I can't help but smile. Even with her blonde hair covering half her face and the anguish in her blue eyes, she looks absolutely gorgeous. This is her third pregnancy, and I swear she gets more and more beautiful every time. It's like she was made for it.

"I can't reach my feet," she cries out softly. "I can't put my shoes on. I'm too fat."

"Not too fat," I remind her, placing my hand on her belly. "Too pregnant."

"I won't survive the next month."

"You say that every time, and every time you do just fine," I tell her, walking around the foot of the bed. "Better than fine. You're a survivor."

"Next time, *you're* getting pregnant."

I grin as I stoop down to pick up her sandals. "You're already thinking of a next time? I thought you were at the *never again* part of the pregnancy."

She just grumbles something as I pick up her feet and gently put her sandals on her. "Want help?" I ask, knowing she's going to have to roll over if she wants to get up.

"Just leave me."

"We have to go down for dinner in a few minutes," I remind her.

"Then shave faster."

I chuckle and head back into the bathroom, quickly shaving my face. Through the bathroom window, the evening light comes in. It's October here, and though the time hasn't changed yet, the days are getting shorter. But it's still warm, and the breeze coming in through the window carries no chill, and I can hear the sounds of our daughters, Adele and Cadence, playing in the sand.

I smile to myself and catch sight of it in the reflection in the mirror. It's been almost five years since Cadence was born and two since Adele. My face hasn't changed all that much—let's say the Dumont antiaging line does fucking wonders for the skin—but what change there is, is in the eyes. They have lines at the corners. They're more prone to crinkling. Maybe from being in the sun but most likely from laughing. Smiling. Enjoying life. Loving my family.

It's not always been easy. There have been ups and downs. Adele has a heart defect and has already had a few operations, and she's just turned two. But she's so strong. She's a survivor, just like her mother. And she's such a happy girl, nothing holds her back. If anything, we're the ones who have to watch for her more carefully.

Being a father has taught me so much. When Cadence was born, I was more terrified than Gabrielle was. I thought I would turn right back into my father. I never had love growing up. I never had support or someone to really watch over me, nurture me, make sure that I would turn out right. All I got were harsh words and hard hands.

I told Gabrielle my fears over and over again as Cadence's birth approached. At the time, I was still struggling with getting the Dumont company under control after my father's death; then this tiny human being was on the way. I figured I would manage to fuck it up somehow. I had never been so scared.

But then Cadence was born, and everything I feared disappeared the moment I saw her face. The love I felt was bigger than me, bigger than us, bigger than the room. I knew I didn't have to be afraid again.

That was a lie, of course. I'm a parent now. I'll always be afraid.

I just don't fear myself. Because I know that I would do absolutely anything for Cadence, Adele, and the little one on the way. I know that I am the opposite of my father in every way that counts and that my girls have grown up feeling nothing but love and support and encouragement.

And so we laugh. We laugh and cry, and we stick through the ups and downs and ebbs and flows of life together. Sometimes it's hard having to be the head of the company, and the work does take me away from the girls more than I'd like. But we make do with it, and I always make it up to them.

Like now.

I've been working like a fiend all summer leading up to Paris Fashion Week, and now that the shows are behind us for now, I arranged for us to come to the family estate in Mallorca for a two-week-long vacation. We haven't been back as often as we've wanted—considering how special this place is to Gabrielle and me—so now we're making up for it.

We're not alone either. Obviously Cadence and Adele are here with us. But so are Seraphine and Blaise and their daughter, who have been here for a few days now. And earlier today, Renaud and his wife, Jen, as well as Olivier, Sadie, and their twin boys, Damon and Ludovic, showed up. I hadn't seen them for a year, so it was a long time coming.

I see Seraphine and Blaise often, though. Seraphine is still the CEO of her own clothing line and works out of Paris now. Blaise is the COO at Dumont. I really didn't think he'd come back, and it took me practically wooing him for a few years until he relented. Okay, so first it was Gabrielle nagging me for months that I needed to swallow my pride and ask Blaise to come back. It might have taken a year for me to finally work up the nerve. But now, everything is fine.

I mean, he still gets on my fucking nerves, and he never lets anything bother him, especially the things that should bother him. But I'm glad I have him by my side.

Most of the time.

From the kitchen downstairs, I hear the dinner bell ring out.

"Time to go," I say to Gabrielle as I quickly smooth on moisturizer, then come out to get her. She's already rolled on her side, so I grab her by the elbows and gently haul her to her feet.

"You okay?" I ask, leaning down quickly to kiss her on the top of the head.

"I'm good," she says, smiling up at me. I smooth the hair away from her face. "I'm glad Seraphine's maternity wear is made for real women." She runs her hands over the sides of her dress. "Unlike the Dumont brand," she adds with a smirk.

"We're working on it," I tell her.

"Yeah. You'll get there once you carry more than small, medium, and large, right?"

"Change comes slowly in the fashion world," I remind her.

"Bullshit," she says. "You have to be the change if you want to see the change. Until you do, I'll be shopping at your cousin's store exclusively."

She sashays out of the room, and I shake my head. She's always teasing me about how archaic we are with the brand. In some ways, we're exactly the way Ludovic always dreamed we would be: stuck in our ways, sticking with the classics, refusing to evolve. But I also know evolution will happen when it's time.

I quickly catch up to her and grab her hand, kissing the soft skin on top of it, and we make our way down the hall and the stairs.

We pass by the kitchen, which has a maid and two cooks running around trying to get everything ready. I smile and nod, trying not to distract them. I used to compliment the head chef, Paula, but she seems to take it as an insult, so I've stopped trying.

This time, she waves a serving spoon at us to keep on walking.

Outside, tables are set up on the beach, one for the adults, one for the kids. They're covered in white linen tablecloths (from our recently opened home collection, one of the few good ideas Blaise has had), with large shells and candles as centerpieces (a craft project started and then quickly abandoned by Cadence and finished by Gabrielle).

Everyone is already sitting down, and it looks like Gabrielle and I are the last to arrive.

"We figured you were having a nap," Seraphine says to us as she pours the kids drinks at the kids' table. "I swear, every day I'm here with you, Gabby, you're getting bigger and bigger."

"Don't remind me," Gabrielle says. "Probably also because the food keeps getting better and better."

We sit down, with me at the head of the table. Blaise is at the other end. Seraphine comes to sit beside him as the housekeeper and chefs come to serve us food.

Much like the time I got Gabrielle paella from the restaurant around the corner, the chef has cooked up the same, in a huge serving dish that takes up half the table.

"Ewww!" Ludovic says from the kids' table. "They still have their heads on. I'm not eating those."

"Me neither," says his twin, Damon.

I smile at Olivier. "Picky eaters," I comment.

Olivier raises his chin. "If I recall correctly, you were the one as a kid who refused to eat anything with eyes or bones."

"Actually, that was Blaise," I correct him. "I'm the one who loved to bite the heads off the shrimp and torture you all with it."

"Of course you did," Gabrielle says under her breath.

"Damon, Luddie," Sadie says, raising her voice as she leans over the back of her chair to look her boys in the eyes. "You don't have to eat them if you don't want to. But if you don't, then you won't get any dessert either."

"That's not fair!" Ludovic cries out before folding his arms into a pout.

I don't see Sadie, Olivier, and the boys that much, because they still live in California, running a whole new batch of Olivier's hotels. They're concentrating on the boutique varieties and guesthouses in amazing locations, like Renaud's various vineyards or up on ocean cliffs, catering to the young and hip crowd versus the opulent and lavishly wealthy side of things. Olivier and I don't often see eye to eye, and I personally think he's cheapened his own name a bit, but I guess he's doing things the American way, and it's really working out for him. After all, it's not about me—this is Olivier's brand and his life, and he's making a killing. Sadie and he seem very, very happy with their little family.

The twins are a handful, however, always running around the place and terrorizing their cousins. I'm not sure how flattered my uncle would be if he knew that his namesake loves to pull my daughter's hair. Then again, perhaps this is his revenge from beyond the grave. Would serve me right, I suppose, since I spent so much of my childhood making Olivier's life a living hell.

But Olivier and Sadie do take a family trip to France once a year, where we all get together at some point. As I said, Olivier and I aren't that close, and I don't think we'll ever be. But the hate and animosity are long gone, and what's there instead is an acceptance. Which sometimes seems harder to swallow. You have to work at it, I think.

When it comes to Renaud and Jen, they both have a lot of Dumont wineries on the go in France and Italy now, so they're often passing through. They don't have children, but they love the girls, and whenever they're in Paris, Jen insists on babysitting so Gabrielle and I can go out and enjoy ourselves on a date. It just doesn't happen as much as I would like.

Still, looking around the table now at my family—brother, cousins, and their wives—I can't help but think it's been far too long since we've all been together like this. This needs to be more of a habit.

It would be even better if my mother were here, but she's off in the Maldives with her boyfriend, Claude. He's this Swiss banking billionaire who has just as much money as she does. There was a period after my father's death that she kept up with her various affairs with young men around the world, affairs she probably had during their marriage. But in the last year or two, my mother has calmed down and found peace within herself. Claude is her age, even a bit older, and enjoys the finer things while keeping a humble and steady head. I think she's finally found someone she can be herself with, and he keeps her grounded at the same time.

I wish I could say the same for Gabrielle's mother, Jolie. After Gautier's death, she was distraught to the point of being catatonic. It took a long time for her to come around, and she's still not 100 percent there. We thought the easiest thing was for her to continue to live at the house with us, but Gabrielle knew that the ties between her mother and my father needed to be broken completely. So we bought her an apartment in Paris, where she still works as a housekeeper in one of Olivier's hotels. She doesn't need to work, but she wants to—it's all she has and knows—and while she hasn't even looked at another man since, Gabrielle believes she'll find her peace soon, whether that means within her or with someone else. At the very least, we take her out for dinner at least once a week, and she's started to take painting classes to express herself.

As the housekeeper comes along and fills our glasses with Dumont champagne, I tap my glass with the side of my fork. I clear my throat. "I just wanted to say a few words . . ."

"Oh God," Seraphine mutters into her drink. "A speech."

"Speech, speech!" Cadence yells from the kids' table with a mouth full of food.

"Not a speech," I tell everyone. "Just a few words, and I'm a man of few words, after all."

Gabrielle snorts at that. I ignore her and press on. "I just wanted to say that it's been too long since we've all been together like this, and I think we need to make sure that times like this happen more often. The days are long but the years are short, as they say, and I know we're all feeling that. We're all here, and we're all living our lives, and as we're living our lives, we're all changing. It's hard sometimes to keep up with that, especially as it's happening. And I think we're all changing for the better. But maybe, as the days and months and years flip past, we can all reach out more to each other. Go through the changes together."

"Look at Pascal, trying to pull at the heartstrings," Blaise says with a smirk.

"No kidding," Olivier says to him. "He's reminding me of the sappy speeches my father loved to give. Talk about change."

"Shut the fuck up," I tell him.

"Daddy said a bad word!" Cadence yells from the kids' table.

Gabrielle giggles, holding her stomach. "I think the baby heard that too. I just got a hell of a kick."

I'm both distracted by Gabrielle and the baby and annoyed at Olivier's words.

I'm *not* turning into Ludovic.

I'm certainly not turning into my father either.

I think I'm just turning into Pascal Dumont. A better version each time.

"Anyway, here's to change, then," I tell them all, raising my glass in the air. "Here's the new and improved Dumont family. May we never stop growing, never stop changing."

"And never stop making money," Seraphine quickly adds.

One by one, everyone raises their glasses, the bubbles sparkling in the setting sun, the smiles clear on everyone's faces.

We all cheer.

# ACKNOWLEDGMENTS

Wow. I can't believe the wild, tumultuous, decadent, and scandalous lives of the Dumonts have come to an end. It has been such a thrill ride to write about this family and their fashion dynasty, their twisted relationships, and their dark family secrets. I was completely inspired by *Dynasty* (old and new) and various soaps, wanting to bring outlandish and edgy drama into the romance genre, and I hope I did just that!

I have many people to thank, but I'll start off with Maria Gomez. You have been the rock of this whole operation. Thank you for believing in me and in this series; I couldn't have done any of this without your support and passion for the work. Same goes for Holly Ingraham, an editing guru like no other, who shaped up *Disavow* and all the books in the Dumonts series into much better versions of themselves.

I would also like to thank the whole Montlake team for making this partnership so damn enjoyable. Your love for the written word and swoony romance was contagious, and your energy could be felt across the board. You made working together such a delight, and I am honored to have been a part of your team.

The usual suspects, Nina Grinstead, Sandra Cortez, Kathleen Tucker, Colleen Hoover, Tarryn Fisher, Hang Le, my Antiheroes group, my readers, my friends, and bookstagrammers: Thank you all for being there when I needed you. This book is for you.

And last but not least, Scott and Bruce. You light up my world. Thank you.

# ABOUT THE AUTHOR

Karina Halle is the *New York Times*, *Wall Street Journal*, and *USA Today* bestselling author of *Disarm* and *Discretion* in The Dumonts series as well as *The Pact*, *The Offer*, *The Play*, and more than fifty other wild and romantic reads. A former travel writer and music journalist, she currently lives in a rain forest on an island off the coast of British Columbia with her husband and their adopted pit bull. There they operate a bed-and-breakfast that's perfect for writers' retreats. In the winter, you can often find them in California or on their beloved island of Kauai, soaking up as much sun—and inspiration—as possible. Visit Karina online at www.authorkarinahalle.com.